TURNABOUT

Vandervelde could do anything he wanted with the girl called Fay.

He could call her crazy for saying she had supernatural gifts, though he had rescued her from a madhouse. He could even use her to satisfy his every sexual desire and sadistic impulse.

But he had better enjoy his power over her while he could.

Because when he died, it was Fay's turn to use his body . . . in the ultimate act of unholy revenge. . . .

IN THE LAND
OF THE DEAD

IN THE
LAND OF
THE DEAD

by
K. W. Jeter

AN ONYX BOOK

NEW AMERICAN LIBRARY

A DIVISION OF PENGUIN BOOKS USA INC., NEW YORK

NAL BOOKS ARE AVAILABLE AT QUANTITY DISCOUNTS
WHEN USED TO PROMOTE PRODUCTS OR SERVICES.
FOR INFORMATION PLEASE WRITE TO PREMIUM MARKETING DIVISION,
NEW AMERICAN LIBRARY, 1633 BROADWAY,
NEW YORK, NEW YORK 10019.

SIGNET, SIGNET CLASSIC, MENTOR, ONYX, PLUME, MERIDIAN
and NAL BOOKS are published by New American Library
a division of Penguin Books USA Inc.,
1633 Broadway, New York, New York 10019

First Printing, April, 1989

1 2 3 4 5 6 7 8 9

PRINTED IN THE UNITED STATES OF AMERICA

For Lee and Jennifer Ballentine

IN THE
LAND OF
THE DEAD

1

Where he walked, the trees had all dried up and died a long time before. Cooper took big strides, the scuffed-up workboots he'd been given crunching through the dusty top layer of leaves. Underneath, the ground had stayed wet, the older leaves rotting into a damp pulp knitted with twigs. He'd been told—and believed—that spiders lived under the leaves, big brown and gray tarantulas come up out of the dry riverbeds. A plank shelf in one of the farm's sheds held a row of rust-lidded mason jars, each one's glass clouded over with silk, a dead thing curled up in the nest of its own legs at the bottom. Old man Vandervelde's son Bonnie had caught them when he was a kid and had left them there, a little collection arranged beside the papery snakeskins nailed to the wood, curling like unspooled flypapers, with little clicking rattles at the ends. The snakes supposedly crawled around under the leaf muck, too. And rats . . . Cooper had spotted the paired sparks of their eyes before, the rats watching as he passed by, then scurrying back to their warrens in the orange trees' roots. This goddamn place . . . Cooper felt his boot slide from beneath him and barely caught himself from falling. Nothing but a bad idea. His luck had been bad enough before coming here. The mud sucked at his heel as he lifted his boot clear.

He walked on, staying among the dead trees, the web of gray branches overhead, the oranges dried to brown leathery fists on the branches. He could have cut over to the rutted dirt path running from the county highway to the cluster of farm buildings, but they'd see him coming then, old Vandervelde and Bonnie, and they'd have time to put their heads together and think of some shitty thing to say. Everybody out here—Vandervelde and all his laughing buddies—all their jokes dealt with shit. As if the smell in the air—the things rotting under the leaves, the animal stink of the honey ditches at the edge of the fruit pickers' camp—which stayed in his nostrils long after he'd left the cardboard shacks and mud-colored tents, as if all that had seeped into the owners' mouths and stained their long horse teeth brown. They spat things into the dust at their feet as if their words had thickened into tobacco phlegm. And smiled. Jesus Christ, who needs that stuff? Cooper had heard enough of it already in just the three months since the sheriff's trustee had brought him out from the county lockup to Vandervelde's place. If coming around to the back of the farmhouse, where he could slip upstairs without being seen, meant tramping through every rat and spider nest in California, he preferred it.

He heard their voices, their laughter, as he got closer to the open space at the orchard's center. One of the sheds by the house had its big rattling doors open, revealing the rusting equipment inside, the squat cylinders of the smudge pots in tottering stacks. Bonnie kept his tools in there; Cooper spotted him around the front of the house, bending over the engine of the Ford, a new one Vandervelde had traded a '36 for, that he'd had less than a year. The old man had a preference for Fords, though he could've bought something classier. The raised hood shaded Bonnie's shoulders, the sweating red muscles of his neck. The job was no hurry, apparently. As Cooper watched, hidden in the trees' dusty shade, Bonnie ducked his head from beneath the hood, took the bottle his father handed him, drank, and wiped his mouth with the back of his hand. The Ford's black grease smeared across Bonnie's cheek. He handed the bottle back, laughing at whatever his father had said, the old man pointing with his thumb in the direction of the workers' camp.

They hadn't seen Cooper or heard his footsteps in the dead leaves. He stood still for a moment, listening. When he looked down, he saw something, a scrap of gray fur and tiny naked hands. A dead mouse, its eyes hollowed. He kicked it away and it landed at the edge of the yard's brown grass. Stupid . . . He held still, looking to see if it had caught their attention.

The two of them went on with their talking and laughing. Cooper circled farther around, still hidden by the tress, then crossed through the waist-high weeds, which had once been the rows of a garden, to the house's back door. He let himself in, catching the door behind him so it didn't bang shut.

In the kitchen, the dishes from that morning's breakfast, and all the meals from the day before, lay piled up in the sink and on the drainboard. Flies, scattered by Cooper's coming in, looped and buzzed before settling back down to the meat scraps clotted in grease. The woman that Vandervelde had hired to stop by the house twice a day—early morning and late evening, after her stretch at the town diner— only scraped out enough skillets and pans to cook with, wiping off a few plates with her balled-up apron so they shone with a layer of fat that you could draw lines in with your finger. She let the mess build up until even old Vandervelde would complain of the stink percolating through the house. The smell made Cooper think of the things that lived and moved in it, like the leaves rotting under the dead trees. The smell of a place where men by themselves had made a nest together, the walls yellowing with tobacco smoke and mingled sweat. He'd smelled it before, in the hallways of rooming houses when he'd had enough money for that, or under bridges, rain making wet cinders out of a little fire, and the men wrapped in sodden coats or blanket scraps huddling closer to one another for warmth. Even though this house had females in it—the old man had a little girl, nine years old or so, and he'd hired a woman to look after her—they made no difference in the way the house smelled. The male stink had won, swallowed everything else up, made it its own. Vandervelde's wife, the sad bride in the oval frame in the front hall, had probably died with the smell in her nostrils, the taste in her mouth.

Cooper stood at the sink rinsing out a glass smeared with fingerprints, then poured the cold water straight down his gullet until his stomach ached. The only water out at the pickers' camp came from a single spigot the Citrus Growers' Association had run out there. The women stood in line for it with their pots and jugs, waiting their turn at the trickling flow. The ground had been churned to mud all around the pipe by the children's bare feet. As the man with all the weight of life and death—money: it was the same thing—in the payout book he carried, he knew he could have gone straight up to the spigot, cupped his hands under it, and slaked his thirst, and all of them would have stood back and waited with a stonelike patience until he was done. That would have been his privilege. He had done it once, the first time Vandervelde had sent him out to the camp. And he had felt the eyes on his back as he'd stooped over, even the children suddenly hushed, silence enough that he could hear the water trickling through his fingers. He'd looked around and seen them, the men and women hollowed around the eye with all the waiting they had learned to do for so long now, just watching him drink, saying nothing . . . at least nothing out loud. *You're the boss's dog.* Their eyes said it. You get fat on his scraps, and the little ones go skinny. After that time, he'd waited until he got back to the house, no matter how much the dust built up in his throat.

Cooper didn't hear anyone else in the house. There should've been someone, a child's voice at least. Iris, Vandervelde's little girl, didn't go to public school down in the town anymore. Her crying and sulking about having to go—"fits," as her older brother Bonnie called it—had led to Vandervelde getting her what he grandly called a nanny. What secondhand notions of gentility had distilled that Britishism into the old man's head, God only knew; maybe something left over from his wife's frail tenure in the household. There was a row of Dickens and Charles Lever breeding dust in one of the back rooms. When Cooper had first come to the house, Bonnie had pointed out the young woman sitting quietly on the back steps as his kid sister's keeper. He'd said something else about her, smiling as he'd looked around at him, about his dad picking her out, that Cooper hadn't understood at the time. Now he knew at least part of what Bonnie's joke had been. He'd lain awake in the upstairs room they'd given him, listening in the night's quiet, long enough to have started figuring these things out.

Right now, nothing, only the buzz and tap of one of the flies against the screen door. He set the empty glass down in the sink's clutter.

The room that Vandervelde's wife had probably called the back parlor still bore signs of her. A claw-footed sofa, the split cushions leaking tufts of cotton batting; on the mantel of the fireplace a milk-glass pitcher and bowl that had become choked with balled-up paper and the chewed-wet stubs of cigars . . . It had become Vandervelde's office, where he met with the other owners, talking the business of oranges, the irrigation ditches, packinghouses, the trucking and shipping, what the railroad was charging for a carload shipped back East, what the market was paying, last year, this year, a quarter-cent sliver up or down, it adds up, it becomes money. Something real you could fill your mouth with.

He'd heard those voices, too, late at night. Downstairs, while he lay in the dark, listening. To the shouting, and the laughter barking louder; sometimes the smash of breaking glass, an empty bottle thrown against the fireplace bricks. The third night Cooper had been at the house, when it had become quiet again, the other growers gone laughing outside to their cars, the engines rasping down the lane through the dead orchard and to the highway, he had slid out of the room and made his way down the hall. He'd found Vandervelde passed out halfway up the stairs, a round mountain of flesh with a little hillock attached, his head, which snored and bubbled spit at the corner of the mouth pressed against the carpet runner. A bigger stain—Cooper had smelled it first, then had seen it, a dark oval in the moonlight slanting through the hallway's end window. The old man had pissed himself, the liquor seeping out of his infirm bladder. Cooper had squeezed past him on the stairs and gone looking for Bonnie, and had found him on the sofa in the office, half on the floor, snoring a tenor version of his father's animal saw. Shit . . . Bonnie hadn't even opened his eyes when Cooper had shaken him awake. Just rolled over and pressed his sweating face against the sofa back. Just leave the old bastard. Forget him, get 'way from me . . . One hand had fumbled out and shoved Cooper away, then flopped back to the floor.

That night he had gone back to his room, squeezing close to the banister to get past the snoring body, leaving Vandervelde there, smelling of booze and urine. The old man was too fat for Cooper to have gotten him up to his bed by himself. The next morning Bonnie showed up at the breakfast table, red-eyed, heavy face even more swollen-looking. His father had made it to his own room sometime during the night; he didn't emerge until lunch the next day, and then with a gray pallor to his stubbled jowls and a look of pure murder in his slit eyes.

The hell with all this shit, Cooper had thought at the time. The old man had started right in on him, yelling about the growers' association account books being out on the desk instead of back up on the shelf where they belonged, although it had been Vandervelde himself and his buddies who had left them there. Cooper was the target simply because there was no dog around the house to kick. This place was going to be, he'd known already, a long row to hoe. He'd almost wished he'd stayed in the jail . . . if he could've stayed there. Done his bit of time, for trying to deal that scam on that grocer—for getting caught at it—ninety days or whatever, buried in the quiet of those cement block walls. But the trustee had sat in his cell and filled him in on that score. So here he was, right in the middle of these loonies and their bad-smelling, bad-tempered house. For just as long as I can take it, he'd decided. The alternatives were worse. Much worse.

He went into the office and laid the payout book on top of the desk, right in the middle where Vandervelde would see it and know that little job was done for another week. In a couple more weeks, the picking season would be at its height, the camp full, and then it would be over. There wouldn't be any call for going out there and doling out the scraps of money to the line of silent, unnervingly patient men (scares you because you don't ever want to get to that point, where all you can do is wait for the scrap, the crumb that'll keep you from starving a little while longer) with the women equally patient, watching you from beside the shoulder-high cardboard shacks and the mud-colored tents, the children silent and watching behind them. Because you're the boss's dog. Aren't you? That was one job he'd had his fill of. With one finger he centered the book on the desk blotter. Outside the office he grabbed the stairway banister and headed up to his room.

He lay down on the bed, careful to keep his muddy boots off the blanket. From a distance he could hear the Vanderveldes, father and son, still talking and laughing, the clink of Bonnie's tools on the automobile's fender. He dug inside his shirt and pulled out the scraps of paper, folded into such tight little squares that he had to smooth them out against the bed. Just to see George Washington's unsmiling face: six one-dollar bills. A treasure, the first cash money he'd held in a long time that wasn't just passing through his hands to somebody else's. Not much ... He picked up the bills and made a fan of them, a crescent of 1's at the edge. Not very much at all. But he was sure as hell going to hang on to it. Money—in a way—had gotten him into this place; it would get him out, too, eventually. Cooper folded the money back into a wad, reached down, and poked it under the bed's mattress. He lay back, his hands behind his head, listening to the voices outside.

Vandervelde had doled out the money—not just the six bucks, but more—from the safe beside the office desk, a big black monster picked up at the auction when the town's second bank had gone belly-up. German-made, shipped from Boston before the turn of the century, with stenciled gold paint decorations around the corners and a dial the size of a child's hand in the center of the square door. The old man kept the top of the safe clear of the room's usual accumulation of old newspapers and other debris, the better to admire the shiny black surfaces, like a cube of frozen ink. (Standing on the bottom step of the stairway, where he couldn't be seen, and watching Vandervelde lovingly dust the safe, with the checked handkerchief pulled from his back pocket, then tucked away again, the private ritual completed . . .) When he opened it, he knelt down, using his wide back to hide his hands turning the dial, even with no one behind him, Cooper making a point of standing in the office doorway, waiting until Vandervelde slammed the safe door shut, spun the dial, and stood back up with a grunt of effort. Still red-faced, breath wheezing from deep within his wattled throat, he'd handed Cooper the money, every cent of it counted out, and the payout book to go with it.

Six bucks over ... So all he had to do was go on out there to the camp and pay the silent, waiting men what was owed them, checking each name off in the book. And pocket the six bucks, and keep his mouth shut. No way to cheat the camp's men, slice a little bit off here and there, and keep it for himself; they all knew, had summed it up over and over, through their own long hungry nights, lying sleepless in the cardboard huts and canvas tents, what was owed to them, how many cents per crate, per orange, up the ladders until the trees were bare, then hurrying to the next. Dreaming about it, when they were able to sleep, their hands curling around the golden taunting fruit; then they'd jerk awake, finding their hands knotted into bloodless fists. And their wives and children around them in the little space, curled up in the blankets salvaged from that long-ago home, the place they'd left, had to leave; or on the scraps of dirty carpet that had taken the place of the blankets when they'd been sold to the rag-and-old-clothes man who made the circuit of all the migrant camps.

It didn't do to think about stuff like that too much. At least Cooper had a nice soft bed to lie on while he studied the brown stain on the ceiling. Just too goddamn bad about those other folks.

The bed in the lockup had been hard, nothing but splintery raw planks nailed together, permanently bowed in the middle. Cooper had made himself more comfortable by pulling the thin blankets onto the cement floor and wrapping himself up in them; he gave up that idea in the middle of his first night, though, when he'd woken with his hand pawing at the cockroaches pattering across his face. For the rest of his stay, he slept curled up in a ball on the planks, waking up in the mornings with his spine stiff and creaking.

This one was all right, though. Cooper cradled the back of his head in his hands, gazing up at a crack running through the ceiling stain. He could still hear old Vandervelde and Bonnie outside the house, their laughing voices drifting up to the window. The bed's cushiony mattress hadn't lost its musty smell—the whole room had been shut up for a couple of years when he'd gotten there, with a fur of dust on the dresser and everywhere else—but he'd gotten used to it by now. He'd put his bare foot through the yellowed lace flounces around the bottom of the bed—more niceties left over, he figured, from Vandervelde's dead wife—and tore the rotting flimsy stuff so that it dragged in a half-circle across the unswept floor. Sheets going gray with his own sweat and dirt: he hadn't changed them since his arrival, easing into the bachelor habits that made Bonnie's room down the hall into a stink of unwashed clothes and rattling empty bottles. Cooper's nose wrinkled at the remembered odor. Pig in its sty—don't care how much money him and his old man have. 'S all they are. He'd at least managed to keep his own resolution to wash every day; Bonnie's neck and shirt collars were black with dirt ground right down into the sweating pores and cloth.

That thought made him itch. He dug his hand under his back, then sat up to reach under the edge of his shoulder blade. His skin scraped up underneath his fingernail; he couldn't feel anything else. In the light angling through the window, he stood with his back to the dresser, pulling his shirttail out of his trousers, exposing the bumps of his spine. Looking over his shoulder, checking to make sure the itch hadn't been a flea, or something worse. The migrant camp crawled with bugs. Nothing, he saw with relief—just his own pale skin, the white lines his nails had made.

He let his shirt back down. From this close to the

window, he could look down into the house's front
yard, the span of brown grass bordered by the trees.
Vandervelde and his son went on talking and laughing; the bottle had been emptied and tossed into the
dry leaves, the shiny glass glittering in the dusty
litter. Neither of them looked up at Cooper. They
can't see me up here . . . He drew back against the
wall, looking down at an angle, just to make sure.

Now he saw why the house had been quiet when
he'd come in. Iris was playing by the corner of the
house that had been hidden from his approach. An
old blanket had been spread out on the grass; she sat
in the center with her dolls in a half-circle around
her.

So where'd her keeper go? Cooper craned his neck,
peering out along the side of the house. The little
girl's father and brother weren't paying any attention to her. She had a habit of wandering off if
nobody kept an eye on her.

He saw the woman then, just barely visible if he
put his side of his head against the wall, making the
window a thin slit to look through. Way over by
the side of the house, yards away from the little
girl, but still within earshot. He even heard Iris calling the woman's name, but she paid the girl no mind,
back turned to her, looking down at something under
the tree's gray branches. Down in the decaying muck
of the leaves.

The little girl's voice became more insistent, whee-
dling. The woman still didn't turn around. She
stepped closer to the edge of the trees. Cooper could
see beyond her, to the trail of his own footsteps
trampled through the dusty litter, where he'd come
back from the camp and circled around to the back
of the house.

As he watched, his cheek against the wall, the
woman knelt down and picked up something from
the leaves. Something small enough to cradle in one
palm. She stood back up, folding her other hand
over the thing and holding it against her stomach,

just underneath her small breasts, like some small discovered treasure.

Iris was screaming the woman's name now. One of the dolls landed in the grass, thrown in a petulant fit. Cooper heard Vandervelde growl at the child to shut up, then shout for the woman to get her ass back over there.

She didn't turn around. Just stood there, hands still folded together around the thing she'd found.

Jesus shit . . . Cooper edged away from the wall and sat back down on the bed. They're all nuts, every single one of 'em. He lay down, shaking his head. Nobody had seen him watching; he found out a lot that way. He'd spotted, dangling from between the woman's clasped hands, the tail of the dead mouse, the little leathery corpse he'd kicked aside when he'd come walking back to the house through the trees. That's what she'd been holding so tenderly.

He closed his eyes, shutting out the cracked ceiling above him. If he could just stay here in the room, he'd be fine, just so he wouldn't have to deal with these lunatics. A little room like this was all he needed. All he wanted.

2

"You never been to the farm." He said it as a simple fact. Not looking at Cooper, but watching the blunt tip of his finger smooth out the tobacco in the little paper trough.

Cooper gripped the edge of the planks, bearing down with both hands. He could feel the coarse blanket sopping the sweat from his palms. Rocking forward, his arms locked straight, shoulders hunched almost to his ears. He didn't want to hear what the trustee was telling him about, and at the same time he couldn't stop from listening. "No."

"Didn't think you had." The fingertip scraped the tobacco back into a heap, a little mound visible between his bunched hands, then began laying it out again, the way he wanted it this time. He bent his head down, the pink scalp showing through the gray strands at top, and licked the edge of the paper. "Want one?" He looked up at Cooper.

"I guess."

The trustee held the cigarette out. "Here you go." He began making another, the slow, caring rituals of drawing the paper out of the little orange pack, the one-handed prying open of the flat can.

The cigarette still had a translucent stripe down the side, the seal of the other man's spit. Cooper

21

rolled it between his fingers so he didn't have to see that. He inhaled and tossed the matches back onto the edge of the bunk across from him.

"Where'd you learn that trick?" The trustee tilted his head as his fingers worked, as if he were talking to the paper and tobacco. "That business with the ten-dollar bill."

Cooper shrugged. "Fellow I met. Out on the road. He showed me."

The trustee nodded. "It's an old joke, ya know. I ain't seen anybody try to pull that one in a while." He pushed the little mound of tobacco back and forth in the paper. "I don't s'pose it occurred to you that if it was such a fine way to make money, that fellow wouldn't have been sitting out on the road, talking to somebody like you. He'd be in town somewhere doing it. Wouldn't he?"

Now he knew that. After getting his head kicked in by a red-faced storekeeper, a couple blocks along this town's main street, and being sat on until the sheriff could arrive, to kick him some more and drag him here to the lockup. The side of his jaw was still sore, with a bruise running up under his ear.

It'd seemed like a good idea—once you got the patter down, and the moves, you walked out of the store with fifteen dollars, when you'd only walked in with ten. And the dumb storekeeper would never know what'd hit him. That was how it was supposed to work, the way the fellow had showed him.

He took another drag on the handmade. The ten-dollar bill he'd used hadn't been come by honestly, either. He'd lifted it off the old boy he'd ridden west with, when they'd been pulled off the side of the road for the night. He wondered vaguely who'd wound up with the money. Probably the storekeeper and the sheriff had split it.

There wasn't any more to say on that subject. You don't wind up in the lockup for doing something smart. He sat and watched the trustee fussing with the tobacco.

"Know how I can tell?" The trustee still didn't look up at him. "That you ain't been to the farm?"

The smoke seeped under his tongue, unable to get past the knot at his throat's hinge. He shook his head. "My hands, I suppose." Doing time on a county farm would have toughened them, he knew, driving the dirt right into the pores until the flesh was stiff and gray, permanently curved to fit the handle of a hoe. That's how they get.

"Nah." The trustee frowned at the half-done cigarette. "There's ways of getting out of work. Even on the farm. There's ways." The black-ridged fingernail pushed the tobacco back and forth. "There's ways . . ." He drew in his breath, a wet hiss between his teeth. Still not looking at Cooper. "Now when you go out there on the farm—'cause that's what the judge'll give you—you get out there with the other fellows doing their pieces—their ninety days, their year, more'n that, some of 'em—there's plenty of work, all right. More than enough. But there's ways of getting out of it. For somebody like you."

A gray cloud hung in the cell's still air. Cooper looked through it at the other man's scalp, the brown dots scattered on the pink flesh, the white flakes glued in place by sweat and grease. He could smell him, their knees almost touching in the narrow space between the bunks. He didn't know the man's real name; everybody here just called him the trustee. Some grizzled old con, rolling from one jail to another, finally landing up here, where he seemed to run the show, doing all the sheriff's work for him. That made him worth listening to; he knew the score.

The trustee finished rolling and held the cigarette dangling in one hand, still leaning forward, forearms just above his knees. He gazed at the cement wall as if it had a window and he could see all the way out to where the men were working, the sun glinting off the rhythmic rise and fall of the hoes, the dry weeds choking the roadside ditches tumbling in yellow and brown sheaves.

"The way I knew . . ." He turned his head, showing his smile to Cooper. "I knew 'cause of the way you walked."

Before he could move, Cooper felt the other's hand snap around his ankle, squeezing tight. The unlit cigarette dropped from the trustee's free hand, tobacco scattering across the cell floor.

The trustee held on, pressing to the bone underneath the thin cotton sock and whitening flesh. He'd leaned farther forward to grab, lowering his head, arching his spine so his shirt stretched tight across his shoulders. The smile grew broader as the gaze turned up toward Cooper.

He couldn't move; the hand had come too fast, taking him by surprise. The trustee looked as if he were about to lay his head in Cooper's lap, still smiling, the gaps behind the stained teeth wide enough to show the wet tongue lolling behind. He felt the other's thumb caressing the hollow behind his anklebone, rubbing a slow circle through the sock. If he'd wanted to, he could've jerked his knee up into the smiling face, smashing the yellow teeth and pulping the thick flesh of the trustee's nose into red. But he knew that wasn't a good idea; the other wouldn't let go no matter what, and might even still be smiling through the blood . . . Then worse shit would happen. The best idea was to just not move, just breathe and stay shut up, carefully holding the burning cigarette over to one side so not even the slightest stray ash drifted onto the face grinning up at him.

"You see . . ." The trustee's tongue protruded when he spoke, with a bubble of spit on its tip. "You see, you walk real good. Just one foot in front of the other, getting where you want to go." The thumb stroked up and down behind the anklebone. "But you wouldn't walk like that if you'd been down to the farm. Not a skinny fellow like you." Grinning. "Know why?"

Just one word, Cooper told himself. You can do that much. "Why?"

"Well, I'll tell you. You see, down there on the farm there's so much work, everybody's gotta do his share. Or if they send you out in a gang, they say, 'This much ditch's gotta be dug' or 'you hoe from here to way over there.' And it's always a full day's work. For everybody. Skinny fellow's gotta do his share, same as the big 'uns. That's fair, isn't it?" The hand, still gripping tight, moved up to bare skin where the thin cotton stopped. "Isn't it?"

Cooper closed his eyes, then nodded slowly.

"You know, I seen skinny fellows like you go out there on the farm—I been there, watching them— and they got ninety days. Ninety days, that's all. And it seems like it's always on the fifth day, it happens. You know?" Ball of thumb against flesh, rubbing back and forth. "If they could just go the six, just get to Sunday, 'cause they don't have to work on Sunday. Not even there on the farm. Then maybe they'd be able to . . . catch their breath. And they'd be a little tougher, maybe, and they could do the next week after that. Get to the next Sunday. And then they could do the next week, and the week after that, and they could just do that ninety days, all the way right to the end. And they could just walk out the way they walked in, just the way you can walk right now. One foot in front of the other." The trustee shook his head, not smiling, sucking in his breath through his teeth. "But it's always that goddamn fifth day. Maybe that's when they realize they got eighty-five more days to go."

Don't move. Don't do anything at all. He wanted to, he wanted to just pull his leg away, his ankle out of the other man's grasp, and just curl up in a ball on the bunk, in the corner where the planks butted up against the wall. Away from the hunched-over figure in front of him and the voice that kept smiling even when the face was trying to tell him it was sorry, sorry about all the things that were going to happen to him, sorry . . .

Just keep still. From the corner of his eye he saw the ash dangling at the end of the cigarette in his hand. If he held still and didn't move, even when the fire got to his knuckle, it would be magic, he wouldn't be here at all. Be someplace far away, the other side of the cement block wall, and just walking. Walking out of this bad-luck territory, hungry as he'd come down the highway into it. That wouldn't even matter as long as he could go on walking . . .

The ash grew a little longer, the paper charring in a ragged black line moving closer to his hand. He watched it, holding his breath to keep from making any movement at all, anything that might break it and let it fall.

"Ever seen somebody spitting up blood?" The trustee kept his grip on Cooper's ankle.

A whisper. "Yeah." The ash trembled, stayed. "When I was a kid." Long time back and far from here; he could remember the narrow box sitting on the table in his mother's kitchen.

"Yeah, but you ever seen a grown man lying on the ground, shaking, and he's got blood all over his face? Enough to make it like red mud all around where he's coughing and puking . . . little skinny fellow like you. That's what happens to a skinny fellow, long about that fifth day. When he's not smart and he tries to pull his share, keep up with the other men. And he just can't." He looked up, smiling. "But you're smart. Aren't you?"

Nothing. Just keep still, don't move . . .

" 'Cause a smart fellow, he'd know what he had to do. When the work's that hard and he can't keep up." The trustee squeezed tight around Cooper's ankle. "A smart fellow would know he had to get a hoe cut, wouldn't he?"

For a moment he thought that the trustee had said hair cut, and he couldn't understand what that meant.

Crazy, just fucking crazy. You could see it in his eyes. Don't move . . .

The trustee squeezed the tendon at the back of Cooper's ankle, thumb and finger rolling the skin over the smooth cord. "Right there—that's the one. Easy to happen, all those fellows working so close, right down there in the ditch. And you can just ask anyone of 'em to do it for you." He squeezed the tendon harder, the smile growing bigger. "And then you're set, aren't you? No more beating your guts out, trying to keep up with the others, doing your share. You're out of that shit."

The black line on the cigarette had almost reached his knuckle. He could feel the orange heat against the little ridges of skin. The ash trembled, bending in a curve . . .

"That's how I knew." The trustee let go, straightened back up. He brushed a few flakes of tobacco from his shirt. "A hoe cut like that, it's for keeps. For the rest of your life, you don't walk so well as you did before. Before you went down to the farm. You see them old fellows, still skinny as ever—like you— and you know they went down there, and they did what they had to do, to get through their ninety days. Sometimes they got one foot that just drags and drags behind 'em, like they're drawing a line in the dirt. Or they'll be like them old jake-legged niggers—just flopping that foot down, the one where they got the cut, just flat down like that." He slapped his hand on his thigh, twice. "Takes 'em a long time to get someplace, walking like that. Plus you always know how those old fellows got that way. Just a dead giveaway."

He felt the burn start, right at the edge of his knuckle. He kept his eyes closed, not moving, not breathing, letting it sting, praying to it. Just don't move . . . far from here . . .

The trustee's voice got softer, kinder. "You're such a smart fellow—aren't you?—I knew you wouldn't have any trouble figuring all this out. 'Course, there's more to it than that. There always is."

He could even smell it now, the cigarette burning the skin.

" 'Cause if you can't work, then the other men gotta make up your share for you. And then they expect you to do something for them, later. When they turn off the lights in the barracks. Yes, sir. Some of those fellows out there, they been there for a long time. And they're gonna be there a lot longer. So they make do, the best way they can." Another draw of breath through his teeth, spit bubbling. "Funny thing is, that's another way you can tell some skinny fellow like you has been down to the farm. You can tell, that's how they got through their ninety days. Look at me." His hand reached out and tapped Cooper's knee.

He opened his eyes and looked at the trustee. No longer smiling.

"Then those skinny fellows, they get out, and you know what? They do something, some stupid damn thing, just to get sent back out there to the farm. And you know why?" Not waiting for an answer. "Because they found out what they are. That's what. And once you know that, you can't be anything else." The smile gone, the voice a whisper. The walls close around them. "That's the worst thing that can ever happen to you. Finding out what you are. You can lie to yourself before that. But once you know—yes, sir—once you know . . ."

The cigarette had just about gone out, the spark squeezed to black by his fingers. The pain had almost died as well, the ache at the end of the prayer.

The trustee nodded. "Yes, sir. You see them old fellows, them old farm birds. They got that walk, flapping and dragging, from the hoe cut. And their faces look all caved in, like a pumpkin you leave out in the field and it rots. Got no teeth, and the jaw-bones go all mushy—they say that's why women don't like to do that stuff, that's why you got to pay 'em extra for it. But that's how it is with them skinny old fellows."

Fire gone, just a tiny ache between his scorched fingers. Cooper looked at the dead cigarette and saw the ash intact, an inch of mottled gray.

"I figured you'd know all this, though. A smart fellow like you." The trustee scratched inside his ear, tilting his head. "Of course, all that doesn't happen until you go up before the judge. And then he sends you out to the farm. So you don't have to fret about it till then." He inspected the wax under his finger-nail. " 'Course, sometimes it's a long while before you see the judge. Long while. And I know some-times a fellow like you doesn't mind doing a little something to . . . earn your keep, sort of. Make yourself useful. Smart fellow like you—all sorts of little jobs you can do for people. All sorts . . ."

Cooper looked around at him. Holding his breath. Far from here . . .

The smile came back on the trustee's face. Almost shy, as if pleased with the cleverness shared between the two men. "Tell you what." He picked up the matches and tucked them into his pocket. "I'll talk to the man." He pointed with his thumb over his shoul-der. Out past the cells, where the county sheriff could be found with his boots propped up on his desk. "He knows some folks that might be able to use a smart fellow like you. For as long as it is—you know—before you go to see the judge." A wink. "You take care now."

As soon as he was alone in the cell again, Cooper let out his breath. He looked at the cigarette—cold now—and saw that the ash had broken, spilling a gray smear across his knuckles. But that was all right, he knew. The prayer had gone up, the little red burn marks facing each other on the insides of his fingers. The magic had worked, one way or another. He'd find out, whichever it was.

Cooper lay on the sagging bed, not sleeping, but

just thinking, remembering. Way deep inside it; he'd been able to feel the splintery edges of the lockup's plank bed against his palms, instead of his broken-down mattress.

He opened his eyes and looked up at the room's water-stained ceiling. There wasn't any point in going over how you'd wound up in a place like this; you were here, and that was all there was to it.

There were other things to think about. If they weren't more pleasant, they were at least more interesting. He rolled the back of his head against the pillow. There was a woman in this house—that was something.

Her name was Fay. He hadn't been told her name when he'd gone out to the house and Bonnie had shown him around—just as if she were a piece of furniture there, a silent thing waiting in the place where it had been put. Bonnie had taken Cooper up to the little room that would be his, told him to pitch his sack of clothes, and the few bits and pieces that had survived getting to this point, onto the bed. The dust had bloomed up from the faded coverlet to his nostrils when he'd done as ordered. Through that he'd smelled Bonnie, sweat and black engine grease on his hands, standing too close, eating up the whole room with his fat-gutted, heavy-muscled bulk, pressing Cooper into some airless corner. He'd turned around and seen the breaking edge of the sly-eyed smile, the grin of the school-yard bully, the jailhouse tough looking over new meat. *That can't get away. We'll see about that,* Cooper had promised himself. The same promise, the same words with no real picture attached to them, that had gotten him down the long highway and to this place. The dust and the other man's sweat had curled in his nose, like the smell of road tar and fruit rotting under the trees. *We'll just see.*

Empty bottles, like brown translucent beetles breeding and multiplying, even under the black-grimed washbasin and bathtub in the room at the end of the hallway. Bonnie had showed him that, part of the tour, the door flung open just long enough for Cooper to catch sight of his own jail-pallid face in the cloudy mirror, with Bonnie's pink, mottled beef looming behind. A greasy shirt, wadded up and shoved into the broken corner of the window. Then he'd pulled the door shut and pushed Cooper ahead of himself, back down the stairs to the kitchen at the rear of the house.

He first saw her there, standing at the sink, filling a glass from the tap and then handing it to the little girl at her side. When the woman turned, he saw her face, the pale oval made severe by the hair pulled straight back into a black knot. No smile; she could've been watering a plant, a chore done for silent things. The girl drank greedily, her round face a miniature version of her father's, looking over the rim of the glass at her older brother and the newcomer in the doorway.

The woman had glanced at them, her face still expressionless. She looked like a child too, in a dress too big for her, made of some stiff black fabric with a high collar fringed with yellow lace—an old woman's dress that had been gathered in and tucked around the slender body inside. The sleeves came right down to her wrists, a half-inch of the aged lace sliding over the back of her hand as she took the empty glass from the girl and set it on the sink counter. She had a child's hands as well, Cooper had seen: no care given to make them look nice, like a lady's, but reddened and chapped, the nails bitten down so that crescents of raw pink showed at the ends of the fingers.

Her eyes had caught his for just a second before she looked back down to her charge, pulling the child along with one hand on her shoulder as she held open the back screen door with the other. Just about a child herself, Cooper had decided even then, without knowing anything about her; all that would come later. But if she'd been out of her teens by more than a couple of years, he'd have been surprised. But the eyes that had met his then looked away, taking their silent gaze with them—the eyes had been old.

Bonnie had leaned into the kitchen, fetching out with two crooked fingers another bottle from a crate under the icebox, where the drip of melted water kept the brown glass shiny-wet and cool. Cooper didn't ask about the young woman as he had let himself be led over to the old man's cluttered office. *You're on their ground*, he'd told himself. *You don't know shit about what goes on around here. Just wait and keep your eyes open, and find out.* Though he'd already had his suspicions.

Later he'd found out her name, just by overhearing it, as he'd lain on the bed upstairs, using his satchel of clothes as a pillow. Bonnie, and then the old man, finally having gotten tired of bending his ears. Stupid fucks, talking and laughing, most of the time to themselves, private jokes—Cooper hadn't gotten much of an idea as to what exactly he was supposed to do out here, though old Vandervelde kept referring to him as an accountant. *His* accountant, as though having gotten him released to his custody from the county lockup made Cooper a piece of property to be bragged over, like the shiny antique German safe in the office. But the old safe didn't watch, and think, and wait; it was just dumb metal. The old fool forgot about that part, the difference between one thing he owned and another. But he'd find out, one way or another; that had also become part of the promise Cooper made to himself. He'd been lying on the bed, waiting and thinking, just the few words going back and forth in his head, and memorizing the brown stain on the room's ceiling, when he'd heard the little girl's voice down in the yard.

In a little, whining singsong, so that it made two syllables out of the name: "Fay-*ay* . . ." Then again, more insistent, the child demanding attention. Cooper had rolled onto his side and raised himself on one elbow so he'd been able to look down in the yard. Vandervelde's little daughter had been tugging at the woman's skirt, a big handful of the loose black cloth balled into the chubby fist. And shouting, though the woman hadn't seemed to even notice the child right at her side. She had just gone on staring out into the deep shade of the orange groves, where the sun barely penetrated to the tangled gray of the dry branches. The woman's neck had looked fragile, a thin stalk emerging from the too-large dress; from up above, Cooper had been able to catch the flash of sun on metal, a safety pin drawing the old-fashioned lace collar together. Something had made him hold his breath, keeping still and silent, though he'd known nobody, especially the woman, could've seen or heard him. He'd been able to see the cords in the woman's neck drawn tight and trembling, a drop of sweat glistening in the stray wisps beneath the black knot . . .

"Fay! *Fay!*" The little girl had screamed the name at last, dropping her grip on the woman's skirt to strike at her with both small fists, with enough force to sway her out of her rigid inattention. The woman had brought her gaze down to the child's furious scowl, one hand stroking a curl of hair away from the wrinkled brow. She'd murmured something to the girl—too soft for Cooper to have heard—and the child had run back into the house to fetch some favorite toy or other.

The woman's hand had stayed where it was, touching nothing; she hadn't lowered it, but had suddenly glanced up to the window before Cooper had been able to drop back out of sight. For a moment her eyes had locked onto his eyes, her unsmiling gaze burning into the rush of blood across his face. His embarrassment, caught peeping and watching like that, had hung him there, pinned by the two dark points in the white face, unable to move. Until she had looked away, turning back to the unlit spaces under the trees, looking for whatever she saw in there.

Cooper had rolled onto his back then, the bed creaking with the shift of weight. Looking up at the discolored ceiling and thinking—thinking nothing. Not because she'd been so goddamn beautiful or something—Fay, he'd repeated to himself, hands behind his head; that's what the little girl had called her—because she wasn't. That had been the first good long look he'd had of her, the glimpse in the kitchen having been shortened by Bonnie's pushing him on to the office. He hadn't wanted to be seen taking a long look at her. (In a house like this, that smelled like men, where everything in it had the sweat odor of that father and son rubbed off on it . . . and a woman in it, who made no difference to how it smelled; no more than did the beat-up old sofa or the wicker chairs on the front porch . . . You don't have to be a genius to figure it out, to catch the sharper, harder scent under the old ingrained sweat . . .) So, finally having gotten to take a good look at her—longer than he'd even wanted to, after she'd hooked him on her sudden gaze—he knew she wasn't pretty. Not really. Passable enough; skinny inside the old-lady dress. A fat man like Vandervelde, and like his son Bonnie would be someday, *would* go for them like that, on the scrawny side. And young, not much more than a kid herself, with maybe just a little swell of tit above the fan of ribs . . . Cooper had closed his eyes and imagined them, underneath the stiff black cloth of the dress, the safety pin unlatched to pull the lace collar down over the hard ridge of her shoulder and the white skin in the hollow underneath it . . .

He'd opened his eyes, looking up again at the stain on the ceiling. The picture behind his eyelids, the old black dress parting and the skin beneath it: the hand that gathered up the cloth into its fist, squeezing tight, that had been his own hand he'd been imagining. And right there beside him on the bed, his hand had clenched and pulled the worn-thin coverlet into a crease in his palm. He had let go, smoothing the coverlet back down. And had made another promise to himself . . .

A little bit of tramp wisdom, the advice the old men—old because the road had made them that way, mile by mile—what they told the young ones, all the raggedy figures huddled around the fire under the railway bridge: *You can't get very far hooking yourself up with a woman.* Nodding, some old 'bo whispering through the three yellow teeth left in his jaw. *Nothing but trouble. Better to do without. Make do with whatever else you can* . . . And then a smile that was just a string of spit between the gums, and the sidelong glance, stupid and clever all at the same time, winking at the new one, crepe paper over the cobweb of blood in the corner of that old, wise eye . . . "Make do . . ."

When the fire had died down to red embers, Cooper had slipped out from under the bridge with his bundle and headed down the tracks in the dark, the moon behind clouds picking out just enough of the straight rails from him to go by. Not waiting around for the rest, the initiation into what else the old ones knew—and what you'd have to be a fool not to know, no matter how young you were and how short a time you'd been heading down the road. Right off the bat, you know . . . Like the trustee had said later: *skinny guy like you* . . . Just telling him what he already knew: that you get born knowing. He'd walked all night, losing his footing in the railway gravel just once, so that he'd fallen and caught himself on the thin strip of iron, cold and hard in his bruised palm. And had picked himself up and kept walking, putting the distance between himself and that mouth with its three yellow teeth, the smile that crinkled up the ancient skin around the eye with its web of blood in the corners.

Which all goes to show, thought Cooper, that you can learn something from anybody. Even the goddamnedest disgusting old fucks you meet up with on the road. He gazed up at the ceiling, seeing the face of the old tramp in the brown water stain, the exact dirty color of that creature that time had chewed up and corroded from both inside and outside its skull. But even a stupid old 'bo like that knew what he was talking about; he didn't know much except how to get a little farther down the road and how to get a few scraps into your belly along the way, but that subject he knew like a book whose every soiled page he'd memorized. And he'd been right about women, thought Cooper. You couldn't get very far dragging one along with you. Or worse, you wouldn't get anywhere at all; you'd stay nailed down to one spot, never get out no matter how bad it got. Until you goddamn well starved to death. Like those poor bastards on the long highways, in their beat-up old cars with every little scrap of stuff they had left to them, the farms' remnants of skillets and shovels, all piled in around their snot-nosed kids. And their wives, up front beside them, the anchors that had kept them locked down tight to a few acres of dust, where nothing had grown except the debt to the bank. Until they'd had to leave, like running out of a house on fire, getting out with just the clothes on their backs.

The men behind the wheels of those cars all had that half-crazy look, part of it their brains having started to shrink down from simple starvation so that they knocked on their brows like a fist inside the skull. And the other part of that look, like a scared animal in a trap, but smarter than that, just smart enough to know it's in a trap, and the bit that was still a man, but just barely, even more scared because it's wondering if it's possible to stop being a man, to just . . . leave. Like the animal chewing off the foot that's caught in the trap and hobbling away leaving little bloody stump-prints on the ground. But still alive, still hungry, still with sharp little teeth to get something into its empty belly. And a man goes

crazy, wondering if it's possible he could do that—
just chew off the foot that kept him there, starving
while he put food, what there was of it, in her mouth,
in the children's mouths that always gaped wider
and wider, like baby birds, with an unending, unfillable
hunger that went on screaming at you while you
spread yourself wider and wider, every nerve and
muscle skinned into a net to keep the land in place
but the wind kept blowing the dust away anyhow.
And all the while the poor sonuvabitch knows what
the tramps on the road know, what all the hungry
men know, that a man can travel a lot farther on his
own, he can get someplace where the land stays put
and the fruit on the tree, even if it's another man's
tree, you can bite into it and fill your mouth with its
juice. He could get there if he didn't have other
mouths to feed, to drag along behind himself. He
could just leave the foot in the trap, he could get
along without it . . . he could *make do.* The way the
tramps under the bridges do. And if that meant
you'd be something different than what you were
before, the way a three-legged animal's different from
what it used to be, and maybe it would mean you
wouldn't be a man anymore at all, but something
else without a wife or children, just huddling with
the others like you around a fire under a bridge, but
still alive . . . hungry, always hungry, but alive . . .

That was how those old boys went crazy, Cooper
knew, with their thoughts going all scramble inside
their heads as they kept driving their loaded-up rattling cars down the highways, their eyes all red and
itchy from staring at the lines in the road, trying to
get someplace where they wouldn't have to think
those crazy thoughts anymore. Watering down the
milk for the children, until it was blue and so thin
you could see through it, and resenting the nickel
out of your dwindling poke of money that it'd cost, a
shameful resentment that made you even crazier
because you were ashamed of feeling it all . . .

To hell with that old crap. Cooper shifted on top

of the bed, easing his shoulders into a different position in the sweat-warmed hollow. He was going to make goddamn sure he wouldn't wind up like that; he'd seen too many of those poor bastards out there on the long highways, even that sucker he'd ridden most of the way out here with. The same crazy look, the eyes bugging out as if the pressure from all those swirling thoughts inside was about to crack their skulls like boiled eggs. Those suckers had gotten themselves into that trap, stuck their foot right in it; nobody but themselves to blame. Even if the trap had been hidden so goddamn well—more fools them, for not knowing it was there, for not knowing that there was always a trap somewhere.

That was what Cooper promised himself: not to be that particular kind of a fool. Every trap had its bait in it, and he wasn't going to fall for this one. This deal isn't so rough, he told the empty room, no one else here for him to speak his thoughts out loud to. For now, it'll do, till I get to the next place down the line. Got a roof over my head, another man's food in my gut, fed as well as his dog would be. You'd be an idiot to screw all that up—and for what? Some skinny-ass broad—(white as milk)—that belonged, like everything here belonged, like Cooper himself, for now, belonged—(the gleam of the safety pin inside the lace collar, where the white skin lay hidden)—to the boss, the owner, to the old man Vandervelde. You get what you pay for. And then you keep it: fat old sonuvabitch like Vandervelde didn't get so fat by letting some other dog snatch away even the skinniest meatless bone. So there wasn't even a question of Cooper getting his foot stuck in the big trap, the slow one that took years of work and having children and all the rest for it to spring on you, and slowly drove you crazy as you watched the teeth come meshing together around your ankle . . . No, he knew he wouldn't be in for that one if he were so stupid as to sidle closer to the house's trapped woman, the old man's other pet. A whole other shitload of trouble would fall on his head, the only virtue being that it would happen a lot faster. And be over quicker.

And if all that was part of Vandervelde's pleasure—getting a big laugh, him and Bonnie, out of holding the bone just within reach of the hungry dog, letting him look but not touch, the dog being smart enough to be afraid of the consequences, yet still wanting the bone, to clamp his teeth onto it, so bad that he could taste it (the safety pin warmed) in his watering mouth (by the white skin under the lace)—then that was fine, too. You're the boss, you fat sonuvabitch. And if the two of them were just waiting for the day when the dog snapped and went for the bone, so they could have the pleasure of beating it into the ground until it puked up blood and died, all right. Cooper closed his eyes and nodded, chin touching his breast-bone. *I can outwait 'em. I've been smart a long time already. I can keep it up a lot longer.*

Something else the trustee had told him, in the sheriff's car on the way out here: *Hard times will make a rat eat a raw onion.* You just wanted to make sure you had an onion to eat; that's all. Then you could start thinking about anything else.

He could even let himself think about her, about Fay, the slender body inside the stiff black dress. There were other ways to *make do*, the way a fellow on his own could manage without having to mess with old grizzled 'boes and work-farm birds. The way he'd managed just about all his life, except for the few times he'd paid the cheapest price he'd been able to negotiate, and had felt like a fool afterward, the little need changed into a furious disgust, enough for himself and all the sweat-smelling, slack-breasted women in those tiny, thin-walled rooms . . .

With his eyes still closed, Cooper tried to bring a picture of her around, how she looked inside the black dress, the way his fingers would slot into the span of her ribs, the angle of his thumbs and fore-fingers below her small breasts. But he had to give up after a couple of minutes. He'd been thinking about bad things, the way people were in hard times, and now he couldn't get all that out of his mind, until whenever sleep would come.

What he couldn't stop thinking about . . . something he'd been told, something some other traveler out on the road had told all the men. By the side of the highway, where a few, maybe half a dozen, of those old loaded-down cars had pulled over for the night, people seeking a little shared warmth and security, talk about where they'd come from and rumors about where they were going. Late at night, when the fire had died down and the men were dark shapes hunkered around the embers, the children swaddled in old quilts inside the cars, and the women had gone off to their own little circle, with their own things to talk about . . . This one fellow, whom none of them had seen before, either on the highway or elsewhere, and who'd pulled into the makeshift camp later than anyone else, after the sun had already died red under the horizon, with his silent wife and silent, whey-faced kids; he'd squatted around the fire with the rest of the men and broke the silence with a soft voice, with no feeling in it, just the dead words in a string, one after another. The fellow told of something he'd heard about, something that'd happened maybe a few days ago, maybe a couple of weeks, on some other of the long highways heading west, or maybe somewhere behind or ahead of them all on this one. Some family, wife and two little kids, and some other poor bastard trying to get them all to someplace where their luck would be better. Only it was hard getting there: the car broke down, blown gasket or one of the million other things that are a catastrophe when you've only got twenty dollars to get the rest of the way to where you're going. All the men listening around the fire had nodded, a couple scratching in the dust with kindling splinters, making no calculations, just little nervous marks. A warm night, the new fellow said, and the family slept out on the ground by the highway, grass softer than the cramped inside of the broken car. Only the man hadn't slept, he had just gone on staring up at the night, his eyes pushed open wide by all the stuff churning around in his brain. Until he'd gotten up, quiet so as not to wake his wife or children, and had gone over to the car and untied the old square-bladed shovel from the side of it. Then he'd gone over to each of the children, his own flesh sleeping there, and the way you'd take care of a sick pup or a barn rat caught in a barrel, the man had put the blade of the shovel on one child's neck, done it, all his weight sinking into the ground beneath. And then the other one, without hardly making any sound at all; children so fragile, like snapping the stalks of flowers. And then he'd gone over to his wife, but she must've woken up, she would've known—wouldn't she have?—the way a mother would. Only she hadn't moved; she'd reached that point, too, maybe she hadn't even been asleep at all, but had also been staring up at the dark sky, waiting. And she must've looked up at him, not saying a thing, accepting the thin weight of the shovel blade at her throat, trusting him to do what was best . . .

And that, said the fellow beside the dying fire, was the way they'd been found the next day, each of them in two pieces, a little one and a big one, and the dirt all soaked red around them. Except for the man, who was leaning up against a wheel of the car, his wrists dug open with the point of his jackknife.

Must've been crazy to do something like that . . . must've been. All of them listening agreed on that, without any of them saying a word. Just a poor crazy bastard.

The fellow who'd told the story had been gone the next morning, cleared out with his own wife and children before the sun had come up. Cooper had stood around with the other men by the fire built in the ashes of the night before, waiting for the coffee to bubble up in the pot. One of them had spoken for all, spitting in the flames and saying, "That fellow was

a damn liar. Ain't nothing like that ever happened."
They'd all nodded, all of them unable to think about
anything else except things on the ground, like two
little parcels that'd come undone and spilled their
contents all over. "Some folks just like to make up
crap like that. Just to put you off your feed. They
think that's damn funny." That was true, they'd all
agreed. The fellow was just a liar. Or maybe ...
somebody who just thought about bad things too
much. Wondering what might be possible, what some
poor crazy might wind up doing someday ...

Hard times. The onions don't come any rawer.
For people to talk about crazy things like that. They'd
all packed up, got their families and cooking gear
loaded back into the old groaning cars, and one by
one gotten back on the road, heading wherever they
were going.

Crazy bastard. Cooper rolled over on his side,
hearing the springs creak underneath him. You get
something like that in your head and it's impossible
to get it out again. It just stays there, going round
and round. He could try to think about women all
he wanted—about the one in this house, about Fay's
white skin underneath the lace collar—and still it'd
be there. A little warning, a reminder about the
promise he'd made himself. Not to get into that kind
of deal, where you could wind up doing something
like that.

When sleep finally came, he dreamed about an old
square-bladed shovel. When he saw its edge resting
on a collar of dingy lace, he woke up and didn't
sleep again, watching the gray trees outside until
morning.

3

You can promise yourself everything in the world; you start out with a pile of things you know you'll never do, not even with a gun pointed to your head. But then, Cooper knew like everybody else, you get what happens. The pile of *won't ever do* becomes a stack of *sorry I did*. That's how it goes.

He couldn't avoid her, not squeezed together in that house the way they were, short of running down the hallway every time he caught sight of her and hiding himself under the bed. Even if he didn't see her, to be lying on his bed and hear her, beyond the thin panels of the room's door, coming up the stairs, responding to the little girl's whining questions and pleas with her own quiet, patient murmur; or later, when he'd be awake and looking out at the night sky, all the rest of the house asleep, old Vandervelde and his son passed out senseless somewhere, not even bothering to negotiate the steps up to their own beds, he'd know one other person was awake, the way a burglar can stick his nose inside a window and sniff out what might be waiting for him. Not even a sound, but you can tell somebody's awake, the same as you. Sometimes he'd hear her bare feet, going from her door to the washroom at the end of the hall. He always knew she was there in the house.

And she'd spoken to him. The first night he'd been there, after the trustee had brought him out from the lockup ... She hadn't spoken a word all during supper, with old Vandervelde and Bonnie stuffing themselves with what the woman from the town diner had brought out, the two of them talking and laughing around big gobbets of white bread soaked in gravy. The little girl didn't understand what the men's jokes were all about, but she'd laughed and shrieked along with her father and brother just for the sake of making noise, banging the butt ends of her knife and fork against the tabletop. Cooper had kept his silence, watching and waiting, and glancing over at her, the woman whose name nobody had told him but he'd learned anyway. She'd kept her eyes on her plate the whole time, pushing a cold piece of chicken around with her fork. At what Cooper guessed was some appointed hour, she'd pushed her chair back and taken the protesting little girl up to bed. Cooper hadn't even turned his head as they'd left the dining room, but had just kept his eyes around front of himself, going on with his progress through the pile of food on his own plate, good even if cold—and plenty of it, a big improvement over the lockup. It satisfied his body enough that he didn't think about the woman at all, even after he was done eating.

He'd cadged a sack of Bugler, still a third full, and some papers from Bonnie, tossed to him like a toothmarked bone to a dog, Bonnie's smile showing how pleased he was with himself. That'd been fine with Cooper, sitting on the dark back porch of the house, digesting his pleasant gutful and rolling a cigarette. Let the big fool grin all he wants to if it keeps him happy. Plus Cooper had gotten the tobacco out of the deal. He'd been smoking and watching the dark trees around the house when he'd heard the screen door open behind him. The person had stood there, not stepping out. He'd known who it was without turning around to see.

The first words she spoke to him, not something he'd eavesdropped on, in her quiet, flat voice: "You're going to be here awhile." A statement, not a question.

The cigarette glowed red on his knuckles. "Seems likely."

Inside the house, Bonnie shouted at his father about something, the words hot and incomprehensible, the old man growling something in reply. Outside, all was silent. "It's not so bad," said Fay. "There's worse places to be."

That made him laugh, coughing out the smoke. He nodded, his eyes watering. "Yeah—you could say that." Something they could agree on; he and this girl were right in tune on that one.

"You'll get used to it."

The way she said it ended what remained of his laughter, leaving him with just the smoke rasp in the hinge of his throat. He heard the screen door swing shut, her steps across the kitchen floor, then gone. A moment later, a square of light fell on the weed-choked back garden; he looked up and saw her drawing the curtain across her bedroom window.

You'll get used to it . . . Cooper pinched the cigarette stub between his nails to get the last hard draws out of it. Sweet Jesus . . . He shook his head, wondering. If that was how you got, staying out here in this godforsaken hole . . . Her voice had sounded like something made out of paper, the way a drawing looks like a human being. You can tell that's what it's supposed to be, but it's really just a flat, dry thing, white with black ink scrawled on it. But not old—that wasn't it, what made the red spark at his fingertips tremble as he held it. Still young, younger than him, but changed . . . words and sound stripped of something, the way the dead mouse he'd seen her pick up from the gray twigs, that little scrap of fur and leather, had been squeezed of whatever had made it run around and twitch its nose before. How long had she been here to get like that? Or maybe she was that way before? You could never tell.

"Shit." He dropped the butt to the dirt and ground it out with his heel. Spooked yourself, you big fool. You don't like a girl's voice, you think there's something wrong with her. There's something wrong, all right, but it's not with her; it's with you. She's not yours, is the fact of it. So be smart and hands off. Crazy bitch anyway, the kind that, even somebody with as little experience as him would know, spelled nothing but trouble, and not of any sort that would be fun.

After a couple of minutes, the square of light disappeared, the garden with its dragging vines of rotted tomatoes going back into darkness. She'd gone to bed, most likely. That was something to think about, but not too much.

A week or so later, he was working in the office, at the desk next to Vandervelde's pet safe. Going over the old payout books, or trying to; the older ones were a complete mess, slips of paper with dollar amounts scrawled in pencil, ringed with the marks left by the bottoms of glasses and bottles. Undated, crammed into the pages of the ledger books. Papers that had nothing to do with the running of an orange grove, just lists of names, in Vandervelde's looping childish handwriting, some marked with an X, some crossed off with a black pencil line heavy enough to have torn the paper. Old bills for irrigating equipment, invoices from the Citrus Growers Association packinghouse. In the back of one ledger, Cooper found a crumpled wad of photographs, dog-eared and sweat-stained, of some hick-looking family, cheap studio poses in stiff Sunday collars and hand-sewn dresses, people who didn't look even remotely related to the Vanderveldes. Plus papers, a carefully folded army discharge, a page torn out of a Bible with the Twenty-Third Psalm on it, a letter on lined paper in a woman's handwriting—the stuff some poor cracker would carry around with him, the little treasured scraps Cooper imagined the men out in the workers' camp had tucked away somewhere. He could just about smell the fellow these belonged to, the pictures bent by the warmth of the man's body. Somehow they'd wound up here, in the boss's litter. He debated throwing them away before finally tucking them back where he'd found them. Maybe they meant something to the old man, even if he couldn't guess what.

He went back to farting around with the old bills and invoices. Not even knowing what he was supposed to be doing with them; he could've set a match to the whole pile of papers on the desk without it having much of an effect on how the place was run. Or how Vandervelde made his money, his acres of orange trees being more a cemetery of gray things planted in neat rows than a place where the sweet golden fruit could be grown. The rest of the valley, for miles and miles up and down the highway, looked like it was carpeted in dark-green leather if you looked at it from up in the surrounding hills. Rich and green, the paradise every preacher had promised for another life, and the labor-recruiting flyers had promised for this one. And just Vandervelde's patch marring the sight, a dead spot stretching off both sides of the highway, gray in the middle of the green.

And you had to be real shit-for-brains to screw up growing oranges. In a place like this, where the sun came buttering down in waves and all the irrigation ditches had already been put in, some of the trenches going all the way back to the Indian slave labor the missions had hired out to the old rancheros. Just a natural, like plunging your hand down into the leaf muck around the trees' roots and pulling out fistfuls of sawbucks, like God had put the money there just for you to have. Plus the Citrus Growers Association did all the hard work, anything that called for actual brains; the association negotiated the prices for the fruit, ran the packinghouse at the edge of the town, set up the shipping with the railroad; did about everything except wipe the owners' asses for them. Which left plenty of time for people like old Vandervelde and Bonnie to lie around and cultivate their beer bellies and hand out shit to other people like Cooper. (*Soon enough*: a little promise, renewed every day.) All going to show, as if it hadn't been shown to him enough times already, that the difference between the person kicking butts and the persons getting their butts kicked was who owned the boot.

No way he could've learned all about the growing of oranges, and the growing of money, which was everybody's real business, from the mess of paper and shit on Vandervelde's desk. Cooper had figured out the deal just from keeping his eyes and ears open, listening to people, both what was said straight to him and what he picked up from being a fly on the wall, Vandervelde's dumb flunky to be ordered to fetch more beer from the kitchen for the growers laughing and playing poker around the big table in the office. You could learn a lot that way, just by shutting up and listening; pretty soon, they forget you're even there, and the door into their little private jokes and sniggers gets opened a little wider, just enough for you to peek in. Learn a lot, and they don't even know you know.

He'd also been sent into town a few times already, with the old Ford that Bonnie had chopped the rear half of the body from, jury-rigging a bed of planks on it to make a sort of truck. With a full tank of gas and money to pick up stuff—odds and ends, cases of beer like nobody's business—he could have hit the highway and just kept on going, not even bothering to swing through the town. Leave it all behind him—except they all knew how short a leash he was on. As the trustee had told him; *People like that got friends. Here and in the next county, and the one beyond that. And they get awful mad, somebody fucks with 'em*. He knew, the Vanderveldes knew, even the smiling-ass people in the town. All in on the joke, of giving a fellow a truck with gas and a handful of money, and knowing he'd come back with the receipts and the exact change, like a well-whipped dog. Beat to the point where he wouldn't even run away from the stick. Cooper knew what the smiles meant, what the joke was; Vandervelde sent him with the list and cash right into the same store where he'd tried the con with the ten-dollar bill. And had gotten a big grin from the same old sonuvabitch behind the cash register, who'd then made him wait until he was done shooting the breeze with a couple other jerkwater notables. Cooper had just kept his mouth shut, not even blinking at the joke everybody's smirking gaze spread around on his face. Mouth shut, ears open, working on his education.

That was how he'd found out the Citrus Growers Association didn't do everything for Vandervelde. Vandervelde did something for them in return, something for which they were happy to let him be even fatter and lazier than the average orange nabob, giving him a cut of the association's profits based on the acreage of his groves, never mind that he'd let the ditches on his land go all to ruin, silted up with rotting twigs and leaves. Never mind that his few live trees, which caught the water runoff from his neighbor's carefully tended rows, yielded hard little knots of burnt leather that weren't even worth picking. All that didn't matter; Vandervelde still got his cut for doing what he did, for taking care of those little things the other growers in the Association didn't want to dirty their hands with.

Learn a lot, keep your mouth shut, just listen. Cooper scooped the loose papers together, made ragged stacks of them on the desk.

Things the other growers didn't want to do. For all their poker games together, the braying laughter along with Vandervelde and Bonnie, some of the growers still thought of themselves as country gentlemen, the golden fruit giving them a sense of aristocracy beyond grubbing dirt farmers. They made movies about orange growers, for Christ's sake. You didn't see movies about goddamn turnip farmers. There were tons of crap about the romance of the haciendas, old Spanish land grants, just as if these bastards had married into that old haughty blood instead of just having been lucky enough to have been the first ones here with the money in their fists, the proceeds from selling off some fat Indiana insurance bussiness. Gonna be a citrus baron, Martha, out where the sun shines all the time and your ass doesn't turn blue from the snow. Shit—Cooper straightened the edges of the stacks—still nothing but a bunch of corn-fed, smalltown Rotary moguls, puffed up in love with themselves. Some of them handled their own payouts during the picking season, just so in love with their own money they'd go right out to the camps at the end of the week and dispute every nickel with the lean-faced, rough-handed men, the wives breaking their watching silence to join in the squabble over the differences between the crew bosses' tallies and their own accounts of what was owed them, carefully scrawled on little scraps of paper and dug out of the pockets of their ragged overalls. Other growers didn't want to bother with the lice and the stink from the camps' honey ditches—and maybe even a twinge from their own consciences—so they let the association take care of it, same as they'd let the association take care of recruiting the migrants into the area, sending out the PICKERS WANTED flyers up and down the highway. A lot of the growers, the ones with their land closest to Vandervelde's place, let him take care of it; just easier that way, to let Vandervelde send out his flunky to dole out the dribbles of cash. You didn't have to worry about some nerve of feeling for one's fellow man leading to an extra nickel being handed out—the flunky, as Cooper had learned, couldn't afford the luxury of conscience. If he didn't get the dirty stick poked right in his eye, it was only because he was the stick.

But for all the growers in the area—the whole Citrus Growers Association—there was something else

Vandervelde took care of for all of them. Cooper had started to catch on, first from just the look in the men's eyes out in the camps—a narrow-eyed look of pure, ineffectual hate. They hated his guts, just because he was closer to the bosses, the owners of the land they labored on; the nickels, the bare crumpled dollars had to pass through his hands to get to them. Cooper knew the men would've loved to have thrown him in the shallow, foul-smelling ditch at the edge of the camp, just to pay him back for being Vandervelde's dog. The same look in the women's eyes, despising him. And behind that hard glint, another look that he could see, of fear, pure and simple. Hated him, hated Vandervelde, hated all the rich fat orange growers ... and couldn't do a damn thing about it, except eat their own guts out, that hate as corrosive as bleach poured down their throats. It chewed them up so bad, from the inside out, that they wound up hating themselves more than anybody, for being afraid to toss the bosses' trained dog into the shit creek.

Learn a lot. Keep your mouth shut. You'd have to be a goddamn idiot not to be able to read what those eyes glaring at you had to tell you.

The little business Vandervelde took care of for the other growers: that's what the people in the town, the ones in the store when Cooper had come in with Vandervelde's order, had smirked and laughed about. The big joke: Cooper had asked for a couple cans of roofing tar—there'd been a spat of rain and Bonnie had announced that he was finally going to take care of the leak that made a sopping rag of the hallway rug—and some galvanized nails, a few other things, then had folded the piece of paper and put it back in his pocket. There'd been a big cage fan bolted up in the store's corner, rattling a couple of grease-furred strips tied to the wires. An idiot sound. The storekeeper and his buddies had looked at Cooper and smiled, their eyes just about disappearing in crinkled fat. "You sure that's all that's on your list?" The storekeeper had folded his arms across his gut and smiled even wider. "Sure your boss doesn't need maybe a couple dozen new ax handles?" Keep your mouth shut; he'd just gazed back at the smiling men, not saying a word himself. "You can go through a lot of ax handles, you know."

One of the other men had pushed himself away from the counter. "Ball bats," he'd said, cocking his fists up by his ear and taking a swing at an imaginary pitch. "Maybe ol' Vander would like to start himself a team."

They'd all laughed at that. All in on the joke. Cooper had just watched and listened. The one fellow had taken another swing with his invisible bat, his eyes closed with pleasure as he'd connected with whatever he'd aimed at. Fuckers are all crazy, Cooper had thought when he'd finally gotten out of the store with the tar and the rest of the stuff he'd gone in for. Laugh like hyenas—Jesus jumpin' Christ, when I leave here, I'm leaving for good.

There'd been no rain since that time, and the tar cans had sat unopened in a corner of one of the sheds. Bonnie's resolution about the leaking roof had melted away in the sunshine.

Those smiling faces, the big joke they savored leaking out of the corners of their mouths . . . Cooper pushed the old ledgers and the jumbled sacks of paper away from himself, leaving a clear space on the desk for his elbows. He cupped his jaw in his hands, easing the kink in his spine. He hadn't accomplished a damn thing with all of this stuff, just rooted around in it like one of the rats that lived in the dry leaves under the trees. Not that it mattered; he knew by now that the old man didn't have an idea what a bookkeeper was supposed to do with the so-called books. Just another grand idea on Vandervelde's part, like the nanny for his kid, when the slow brat would be just as well off roped to a stake in the yard to keep her from wandering off. He must've gotten these notions, if not from the late Mrs. Vandervelde, then from one of the other orange growers, one of the really rich ones, with more class than to come out and get sloppy drunk at the weekly poker parties. There were a couple of them in the valley; Cooper had spotted one, dressed all in crisp white like something out of the movies, pulling up a cloud of highway dust in a big coffin-nosed Cord roadster. Wearing a pith helmet, for Christ's sake, just as if he were a big-game hunter in darkest Africa. Which just went to show that they all had their funny notions of living their lives like one big costume party. And if they tried hard enough, they might even be able to forget there was dirty work to be done, that those sweet golden fruit didn't climb off the trees by themselves, jump into boxes, and catch a ride east on the train; forget that somebody like Vandervelde was necessary, even if you had no more to do with him than just letting him have his cut of the pie. They just had to look the other way while he did those little jobs they paid him for. You could pretend to be anything that way.

And if Vandervelde wanted to join the costume party and have a nanny for his daughter—or at least tell people that's what she was there for—and have some other trained dog *do his books* without a goddamn clue as to what that was supposed to involve . . . Cooper was happy to oblige. The old fool had a superstitious reverence for pieces of paper with numbers on them; maybe he thought they were all mystically related to those genuinely magical bits with the pictures of famous dead people in the center and the numbers in the corners. That giveth life. That made lean-faced men and their silent, hollow-eyed wives come scrambling all the way across the country with their snot-nosed kids in tow, just for the chance to go swarming up ladders and pick those oranges. That you could almost hear breathing away in their rubber-banded stacks inside the safe beside the desk, the few crumpled bills tucked in Cooper's pocket sighing in time with them . . .

That's how you go crazy. Thinking about things

like that. He could still hear that bastard hunkered around the fire with the rest of the men, talking a load of crap about a family sleeping on the ground and a poor crazy sonuvabitch with a shovel.

The air had gone still, soaking its warmth into the sticky patches of sweat under Cooper's arms. Smell of dust in his nostrils; he felt like folding his arms and laying his head upon them, letting a drowsy half-sleep pull him under. Not giving a shit if old Vandervelde came in and found him snoozing away in his precious office. As long as Cooper jumped when he was told to and dragged his ass out on every stupid errand the old fuck came up with, he figured that was all that really mattered. He was staying out of the county lockup by being Vandervelde's dog out where people could see that's what he was. What people didn't see made no difference.

Cooper rubbed at the grit that had collected in the corner of his eye; a thin film of dust had drifted across the desk, made a soft scraping noise as he pushed the paper stacks back to the wall. Windless, yet the dust seeped in anyway, as though things were slowly breaking into the tiny dry bits. When the air moved again, everything would blow away, right down to the skeleton of rocks beneath.

He could hear voices outside the house. Bonnie shouting something at his kid sister. That meant Fay was probably out there, too, watching in that silent way she had. There, but not really, her gaze drifting off to whatever she watched for under the dead trees. The old man himself wouldn't be around, though; he'd made a big flap around lunchtime about going into town for a meeting of the Citrus Growers Association. Some bigwig from the railroad was making the circuit, something to do with new carriage rates. Vandervelde had put on a reasonably clean suit for the occasion, the double-breasted jacket straining across his gut like a ship's sail caught in a storm. He'd ordered Fay to do his necktie for him, stretching his bullfrog throat in front of her as she sat at the table. She didn't know how to knot a man's tie because she'd never done it—or least that's what she'd told him. Vandervelde had gone all mottled red, his disappointment at not getting this small female service right there on his face for anyone to see; his own fat fingers had tried to make a knot until he'd wound up cursing and jerking the whole tie and celluloid collar off his neck. He'd shouted something about not being back until after dark as he'd tromped out to the Ford in front of the house.

Just as well. Bonnie was always freer about offering Cooper a beer from the crate below the icebox whenever his old man wasn't around, the way kids delighted in sneaking scraps to the dog under the table, not because they loved the dog so much as they enjoyed sneaking. In this thick heat, one would be enough to go upstairs on, lie down in his little room, and forget this whole damn place. Worth hanging around at the desk for, waiting until Bonnie came inside.

Cooper's head snapped up from his cupped palms when the voices outside all went up a notch. He could hear the little girl scream in pain, then burst into a tearful wail. Bonnie was shouting, louder and in anger; under that, Cooper could just make out Fay's voice, calling for someone, something to stop it.

The chair toppled over backward as he stood up. He ran outside, the back porch door slamming behind him.

Out front, Cooper saw what had happened. The little girl was blubbering, her face all red and sopping, clutching one forearm with her other hand. Three red stripes ran down the white soft flesh, from the inside of her wrist to the elbow. A trickle of blood oozed out from one of the scratches. Bonnie, grumbling his profanities now, had a cat trapped in the corner of the front porch and the house: a big gray tom, big with hunting muscle, not just fat and fur. It hissed and spat at Bonnie, its face straining back from its bared teeth. Cooper had seen the animal before, prowling around in the dead leaves for mice and other prey. Maybe it had been somebody's house pet once, let go out here when they couldn't feed it any longer, and now gone feral and hungry. The stupid little girl had probably tried to play with it, yanked its tail, and gotten its claws right down her arm. When they went wild like that, they wouldn't abide the fooling around a tame cat would.

And now big brave Bonnie had the cat trapped in the corner. Working not out of anger about his little sister crying, but for his own slow amusement. Cooper saw him grin, mimicking the cat's snarl. He stepped closer; the cat arched its back against the angle of the porch.

Cooper saw Fay then, a couple yards away. Her face was flushed, and a couple strands of her dark hair had come loose from the knot at back, dangling now across her cheek. Her eyes were wide, staring into Bonnie's shoulders. That's who she'd been shouting at, Cooper knew, shouting to stop it. And Bonnie had pushed her aside, with an easy sweep of his big arm, and had cornered the animal. To do what he wanted with it.

She glanced at him, and he felt his own face fill with blood. Her face was taut, looking at him the same as she had at Bonnie.

Cooper turned toward him, his hand lifting as if he could reach across the distance and touch the other's shoulder. "Hey . . . hey, Bonnie—"

"Shut up." Bonnie didn't look away from the cat. Nothing was going to interfere with his fun. His sister sobbed and gulped for breath, still clutching her arm.

The cat's hissing stopped. It broke away from the corner, its arched body snapping down close to the ground as it tried to streak past its captor's legs.

Bonnie was as quick. His boot caught the animal in its ribs, spinning it around. The cat yowled in fright, then in pain as the boot struck again, straight down, pinning the cat's haunches against the brown grass.

The little girl's sobbing became a snuffling whimper as she watched, the scratches down her arm forgotten. Her eyes went even wider when Fay grabbed her brother's arm and he pushed her away, sprawling on the ground.

"For Christ's sake, Bonnie—let the damn thing go." Cooper stood watching, impotent. Fay's eyes had locked back onto Bonnie.

The other didn't bother replying. The cat twisted around, its claws scrabbling at the thick leather of the boot. Cooper saw Bonnie's smile and glittering eyes as he lifted his other boot and brought it down hard upon the cat's middle.

Fay's hands flew up to her ears, to shut out the cat's scream.

Bonnie stood back from it, laughing. The cat writhed into a knot, then straightened out, its front claws tearing at the grass and the dirt beneath. It screamed, in quick panting bursts now, as it dragged its broken spine and twisted hindquarters behind itself.

The little girl, transfixed, wiped snot and muddy tears across the red streaks on her arm.

Fay drew herself up on her knees. The cat crawled toward her, its face wild with fear and pain, knowing who had tried to help, had tried to stop its tormentor. Its scream choked as a red sop bubbled over the points of its teeth. Fay's hair, pulled loose, tangled across the hands clutching at the sides of her head.

"Aww, shit . . ." Cooper felt his disgust well up in his throat. He turned and strode to the shed at the house's corner. He came back with a shovel.

The cat had crawled close enough to Fay that she could've reached down and touched it. She rocked back and forth, hands still to her ears against the sound, her eyes shut tight. Cooper grabbed her under one arm and lifted her to her feet, pulling her out of the way. She opened her eyes and watched him set the blade of the shovel against the cat's neck.

The cat's idiot, pain-dazzled gaze rolled up at him, its muzzle dark with its own blood.

In the shed, pushing aside rakes and coils of rope to get to the shovel, he had seen things come flashing up out of memory, the animal scream tearing away any means he had of keeping them down in the darkness where they belonged. Even as his hand had closed around the sweat-polished handle of the shovel, he remembered a farm boy about ten years old, his own age when the woman who called herself his aunt had brought him with a little suitcase and a ten-dollar bill out to the family who'd agreed to board him. He'd known they weren't his kin, any more than the woman was. And he'd still been in his good city clothes when the family's real son had led him out to a muddy stream bank behind the house; the boy had quickly, expertly caught a frog in the reeds. And then, with a knowing smile, he had slit open its pale belly with a jackknife dug from his pocket. Smiling with delight over his godlike knowledge, which could make the creature wriggle in his fist, its guts squeezing up in a red bubble while the dumb city kid stared in sick fascination . . .

Only going back out into the yard's sunlight had made that memory fade and fall away. Cooper brought his foot up and jammed it down on the top of the shovel blade, up by the handle, all his weight driving it down into the earth below the cat's neck . . .

Another memory, a voice whispering in the circle of men around a roadside campfire, about a woman and children sleeping on the ground, and a man who took a shovel and . . .

He felt the small bones snap, like twigs. The shovel blade scraped an inch into the gravelly dirt. No place for an echo to come from, but he heard it nevertheless, in the silence when the screaming had suddenly ended.

Cooper let the handle drop away from his hand. He looked up and saw Bonnie, still smiling, watching him. Waiting for him to say something.

Go fuck yourself. He said it inside his head, looking straight into Bonnie's eyes so Bonnie would know what he was thinking. You want me to say it out loud, call you a big dumb bastard, so you could have a fight, and I'd wind up back in the lockup, with my face all pounded out of shape. That was what the fellow wanted, Cooper knew. But he wasn't going to get it.

He turned and watched Fay, her face set, go around to the back porch. He heard the door into the kitchen slam, then creak open again. She reappeared with a dish towel, the one the woman from the town's diner covered the food in the icebox with. Kneeling down by Cooper's legs, she wrapped the two objects, the larger and the smaller one, in the cloth. The cat's blood seeped through.

"Give me the shovel." She cradled the dead animal against herself, holding out her other hand.

Cooper reached down, picked up the shovel, and gave it to her. She turned and walked toward the gray trees.

He heard Bonnie give a snort of disgust. The little girl, mouth gaping open as she watched, scurried away when Cooper looked at her.

To hell with all this. He went into the house and helped himself to one of the beers from under the icebox. Up in his room, he set the cold, wet bottle on his stomach as he stared up at the ceiling.

4

He kept his nose clean after that. After what happened with the cat out in the yard, Cooper didn't know what Fay thought about him. Which could be important, he knew, given the way things were set up in the Vandervelde household. Just my luck, he thought, trudging back from the workers' camp. The old fool will think she's got the hots for me, just because of putting some damn cat out of its misery. Vandervelde had been told all about it the next day by his still-excited daughter. When she'd finished recounting the whole drama over the lunch table, her father had glanced up from sopping his bread in the gravy on his plate and had given Cooper a long look, nodding as he chewed. He hadn't said anything —what was so important about one cat, when the orchards were full of them?—but when he returned his attention to his plate, Cooper could almost see the wheels slowly turning under the liver-spotted skull.

And it'd be a pisser if the old man was thinking that there was something going on between him and Fay. The look she'd shot at him when Bonnie had cornered the animal by the side of the porch—two little slits and below them a mouth set in a bloodless line. As if she hadn't been able to decide, in her fury, whether she hated him more for being the same sort of sweaty male creature as Bonnie, or for being too chicken-shit to stop Bonnie from tormenting the cat. Cooper kicked aside a knot of twigs as he walked, exposing the dry earth underneath. Either way, he thought, she could do without me as easily as she could the rest of these sonsabitches around here. That made it easier for him to keep up his promise to himself, to have nothing to do with her. Though a fat lot of good that was going to do him if old Vandervelde had a bug up his ass that there was something going on between the two of them.

Cooper halted in the middle of the dead orchard, sucking his breath in through his teeth. Too angry to walk; pissed at himself, pissed at all the rest of them. That's what I get. He should have just let the cat go on screaming, dragging its broken spine toward the petrified Fay, howling and bubbling its guts up at her face. He'd had to be a fool, though, and get the shovel. Now all it'd take would be for Vandervelde to get drunk enough—the kind of drunk who got meaner the more he put away, the little pig eyes turning into raw red dots—and Cooper would be on his way to the county lockup and the farm beyond that. He could just imagine how sad that'd make the trustee, shaking his head over a fool who hadn't been able to make use of all those good words of advice.

If he made it back to the lockup at all . . . Shit, I'd be lucky to. Any place that had that many jokes going around about ax handles and ball bats . . . Bonnie would just love to take care of this little matter for his old man. Cooper closed his eyes and saw Bonnie grinning away. The cat would be the lucky one by comparison.

He wished he'd never seen the damn animal. He should've minded his own business, which these days, in this place, consisted of keeping his skin in one piece.

The leaves rustled near his foot. He kicked at them, and some small creature, a mouse, scurried away unseen.

And something as small, a single thought, that made him shake his head in wonderment at what a fool he was; it uncoiled and flexed, like a moth tickling at his ear . . .

No sense in getting your head bashed in for something you didn't do.

"Jesus Kuh-rist," he said aloud. The buzzing of flies in the still air answered him. What was the point of having brains if your nuts could come up with ideas like that? An absolute, surefire route to complete disaster.

Forget it—one part of himself talking to another. That's how you knew you were going crazy. He started walking again, heading for the house. With the back of his hand holding the payout book, he smeared a trickle of sweat away from his eyes. No way, he promised himself fiercely; no fucking way. He wasn't that crazy yet.

She was waiting for him, sitting on the top step of the porch, the folds of the heavy black dress gathered up into her lap. Must be broiling inside that thing, thought Cooper. Day like this. The stiff black cloth would scratch someone raw; that also didn't bear thinking about. He nodded at her and started around the side of the house to the back door.

"I have to go into town," she called to him, her voice cutting through the heat-laden air. "You're supposed to drive me there."

He stopped and looked at her. She had her chin set almost defiant, her pale neck stretched above the lace collar. Ready for whatever argument she'd get back from him.

"Oh?" He used the payout book to scratch the back of his own neck. "I don't know if that's the sort of thing I'm supposed to do. Might not be allowed

—me just being out here from . . . you know." She knew the score about that, he'd figured, even if nobody had told her. Easy to piece together how things worked around here.

Fay shrugged. "You don't have nothing to worry about. Whatever he wants you to do, it'll be okay."

He being Vandervelde. And true enough: if he got let off his leash for a little while, even at the wheel of a car, nobody in the county would give a damn. They just grinned when he came into town with Vandervelde's lists of stuff. The leash was invisible but just as real. And if it snapped and the dog lit out for the hills, they'd enjoy that, too, savoring the inevitable consequences. When he was caught again.

Which might be what the old man was grinning about, too, wherever he was. Maybe watching from the house, unseen behind the screen door. Setting a little trap, cornering him the way Bonnie had stepped in toward the cat, with the same smile of anticipated fun. Every time Vandervelde had sent him into town with the car . . . A certain childish delight, the kind that children had with helpless animals, when Cooper had come back to the tug of the invisible leash. There'd be even more fun if he didn't come back, if he pointed the car out on the highway away from the town, away from the whole fuckin' mess here. Trying to put enough miles between himself and the hand reaching for the scruff of his neck.

And sending Fay along with him, out on the road where anything might happen or where you could say something had happened . . . He could come right back and still find himself in a world of trouble. Maybe Vandervelde had gotten tired of this smart dog sliding by without giving him an excuse to take a stick to its hide; for a pig-eyed sonuvabitch like Vandervelde, suspicion would be as good as proof. That was the fun in having the whip hand: you could work yourself up into a nice satisfying rage without having to wait for a real reason.

Sometimes, thought Cooper, I think I should've let 'em ship me out to the farm. Just to have gotten it over with sooner. He could feel the blood ticking at his brow, from the pressure of the considerations scrambling around inside.

"Well?" The edge of Fay's voice broke into his thoughts. "You going to stand there all day or you going to drive me into town?"

He looked up at her. "What do you have to get there?" If he could just go into town by himself and pick it up, whatever it was, he'd be off the hook.

Her exasperation showed in the set of her mouth. "It's personal, all right? You're not supposed to ask every damn thing." She gazed at him, waiting.

"Where's Iris?"

Fay sighed, tired of questions. "Bonnie took her with him. He went over to fool around with some of his buddies, and she wanted to go with him. That okay with you?"

Couldn't even refuse to take her; that would look just as bad, as if he already had enough to hide that he couldn't risk anything more. "All right. Let me get rid of this"—holding up the payout book—"and then we'll go."

She nodded, letting her gaze drift away from him and back to the trees. Loony bitch. Cooper stomped to the office and threw the book down hard enough to flutter the papers on the desk.

All the way into town, she said nothing. They passed the rows of orange groves, butting up against the ditches at the side of the road. Thick and alive here, away from Vandervelde's place, the leaves forming a green trough with the car churning up dust at its asphalt bottom. He drove, glancing over at her every once in a while; she paid him no attention.

When they got into town, Fay pointed out a space close to the drugstore. She got out and came around to his side as he killed the engine. "I'll be right back."

"I'm not going anywhere." The radiator hissed a

little steam; he could hear the spatter of water into the street's gutter. "Take your time." He slouched down, closed his eyes, and tilted his head back against the seat. Through his eyelashes he watched her go into the store.

Ten minutes later she came back out. She opened the passenger door and tucked a white paper bag, the kind pharmacists always give people, under the seat.

"That it?" Cooper looked at her without lifting his head from the top of the seat. "Got what you needed?"

She nodded as he started the engine. "Do you got any money?"

The question took him by surprise. He pulled himself up in the seat. She hadn't climbed into the car; she stood against the running board, looking at him.

"Maybe." The six bucks that had fallen miraculously into his possession were folded and tucked in his pocket; he could feel them through the cloth of his trousers.

Fay tilted her head, the gaze unchanging. "If you did, maybe we could go get a cup of coffee or something."

Now, what the hell . . . He shrugged. "What'd you pay for that with?" He pointed with his thumb to the paper bag under the seat.

"Are you kidding? That all goes on Vandervelde's tab. Half the stuff's something for his heart, anyway." She stood waiting, framed in the car's door.

Six bucks in his pocket, and coffee a dime. You could sit in a diner booth, just like the people who knew they belonged there, and not have that smell in your nose, of Vandervelde and Bonnie's sweat soaked into the house's age-browned wallpaper. That'd be worth it right there. And to have a woman, batty or not, sitting across from you, folding her small hands around the cup of coffee that you had paid for,

unfolded the green bill and got the shiny change in
return . . . That was worth even more. The things
you dreamed about if you'd had to sleep for even a
little while under one of the railway bridges, in the
smoky camp with the men who knew they'd never sit
in a diner booth again, drinking a cup of coffee with
a woman across from them doing the same. That's
what you dreamed about, head nodding toward the
dying fire, a circle of men like roosting pigeons. Not
harems and golden plates, but something as simple
as that.

And another treacherous thought, which he wouldn't
even allow himself to think, but just knew was there,
like a spot on a lung that you only felt when you
drew your breath in deep: *no sense in getting your head
bashed in for something you didn't do.*

"All right." Cooper pushed the door open on his
side. The folded money felt like a square thumb-
print pushing into his skin. "Come on, then."

They sat at one of the booths up by the front
windows. He could look out along the street, all the
way to the last of the small stores, and the association's packinghouse beyond. For a moment, he
thought he spotted the trustee crossing the main
street on one of the sheriff's errands. None of the
passersby on the sidewalk glanced in through the
window, but he kept his own face carefully turned
away, watching from the corner of his eye.

What's to be so jumpy about? He knew he'd already done it for himself, just by coming into the
diner with Fay. The woman who brought the covered meals out to the Vandervelde place had spotted
him through the little window behind the counter,
where the dishes were handed through from the
kitchen. Her eyes had latched on to his for a moment, then dropped back to whatever her hands
were doing at the sink. She wouldn't tell Vandervelde:
her sniffy disdain for him was such that the meals
she brought out were paid for with cash always sit-

ting inside the cupboard, and never a word ex-
changed. But she'd say something—*know who that
was?*—to the fellow grooming his teeth with a matchstick
behind the cash register, and he'd say something to
some customer, one of Vandervelde's old buddies.

Or maybe he wouldn't. A lot of the townspeople,
those who weren't in on the money that could be
shaken out of the orange groves, hated all the growers. Vandervelde and his coarse, flaunting ways would
be the most irksome to them. You always hate the
guts of anybody whose butt you have to kiss. They
might think it a pretty funny joke to see Cooper
sitting right here in the open, having a cup of coffee
with Vandervelde's kept piece. And just keep it to
themselves, letting their imaginations work it up to a
whole steamy rendezvous.

He'd be really screwed then, Cooper knew. He
scraped the sugar at the cup's bottom with his spoon.
When they got it blown up that big, they'd let it loose
in Vandervelde's face. If he hadn't been building up
to some head-thumping before, he'd be ready for it
then.

Shit. He'd forgotten that he'd sugared the coffee
already, and now it lay like syrup in his mouth. The
things you have to worry about.

Fay hadn't spoken since they'd left the car. She
stared at the black inside her cup, the reflection of
her face shimmering from the constant tremor of
her hands. Only a couple of slow sips down from the
restaurant china's thick rim.

She looked up suddenly, her gaze direct on Cooper. He could see a thin line of white above and
below the pupil. "Bonnie's got it in for you, you
know." She raised her cup and sipped again, still
looking at him.

Cooper snorted. "Bonnie's got it in for everyone. I
think he's the kind that likes to get mad. Starts out
that way, and stays that way." He shrugged. "Nothing I can do about it." The spoon's tip grated through

the undissolved crystals at the bottom of his own cup.

"He got all ticked off about—about that cat." She bit her lip, drawing it even more bloodless for a moment. "He was laughing about it all, when you did that. When you killed it. But he would've liked to have killed you, right there. That's what he's like, even when he's laughing."

Cooper rolled the sweet coffee on his tongue, wondering why she was telling him all this. Stuff you'd have to be an idiot not to have latched on to already. Just worried about his skin? She'd be risking her own if she got caught on the wrong side of the fence. If she were smart, she'd keep her mouth shut and let whatever little arrangement she had with the old bastard and his son just go rolling along.

He came back from mulling this new thing over and saw that she was no longer looking straight at him. Her eyes were still open wide, but looking past him now, a shot by the side of his head; he knew if he turned and looked behind him, he'd see nothing, just empty air running to the corner of the diner. Her eyes had locked on to something private, her own thoughts almost visible in the dark centers of her pupils.

"You did the right thing, though." Her voice had gone quieter; he had to lean and turn his head slightly to make out what she said. "When you did that. With the cat."

"Maybe." Cooper shrugged. "Maybe all I did was get myself in dutch, just for the sake of some animal that was about dead anyway."

"No . . ." She shook her head, hard enough to make the coffee slop over the rim of the cup she held. Her eyes came back to him, even wider. "It wasn't anywhere near dead. That's why it kept trying . . ." A whisper again, as she looked away from him, down to the cup and her trembling hands, as though she were embarrassed. "Trying to get to me."

He tapped the side of his cup with a fingernail, trying to think of something to say. "Maybe it thought you could help it. Animals, you know, they can tell who's . . . kind." He had no idea if that was true or not.

"I couldn't help it." Her gaze moved away again, seeing the cat crawling, its hind legs twisted behind it, the red trail from its jaws dark on the brown grass. "Not when it was like that. It was like it was stuck." She looked at him, trying to see if he understood. "It wasn't alive anymore, not really, and it wasn't dead yet. That's why it kept yowling. 'Cause it couldn't be one way or the other. It was just stuck there between them." She turned her face toward the window, not seeing the bright sunlight outside. "That's the worst way something can be, stuck between like that."

He looked at her sidelong, wondering what had brought all this on. She had connived to get him into town and to have coffee together so she could talk about stuff like that? A goddamn broken-backed cat, puking blood, no less. A joke, complete with an attempted smile: "Oh, I don't know. I'd imagine being dead's about the worst. You never hear anybody say they like it, do you?"

She didn't smile back. She had found a fly on the windowsill, behind the napkin holder and the salt and pepper shakers; it lay on its wings, the bristly legs bent into a knot above its tiny belly. He watched uneasily as she poked at it with her finger, the nail chewed down to the pink rim beneath.

"Have you ever wondered—" Voice even quieter now, a whisper. "What it'd be like . . . to be dead?"

Sweet. Fucking. Christ. Cooper looked around to see if anyone else in the diner had heard her talking. They were the only ones there. The fellow behind the cash register had finished with his matchstick and now leaned back against the wall behind the counter, the back of his head pushing askew the

chalkboard with the daily specials on it. GRAVY AND
MEATLOAF, read Cooper. No; they'd spelled it LAOF.
The stupid hicks in these kinds of towns . . .

It took him a moment to look at her again. He
couldn't believe it; she really was loony. Not just the
way she looked—any underfed little tail would've
looked strange in that oversize funeral dress Vandervelde had stuck on her. But now he couldn't have
been sicker at heart if she'd leaned forward, lifted
the top of her head like the lid of a lunch pail, and
had showed him a rat running around inside her
skull, its little red eyes glittering up at him with their
own hunger and crazy intelligence.

He shook his head, for his own benefit. He was
risking getting his own skull broken, to hear stuff
like this? "No," he said finally. "I don't think I've
ever really thought about it." He pushed away the
cup with the last tepid coffee at the bottom.

Fay held her hand out, looking at her own upraised palm. He saw that when he hadn't been watching, she had picked up the dead fly. It lay there in
the little valley her hand made. Her fingers came up
around it, hiding it inside her fist.

She looked up at him. Almost smiling, for the first
time since they'd come into the diner and sat down.

He heard a buzzing sound, faint, just at the edge
of his hearing. When he looked down, breaking away
from her gaze, he saw the fly crawling on her hand,
its wings a blur above its ridged back.

The hairlike legs scrabbled the insect up toward
her thumb; the sun caught it and a piece glistened
with metal colors. It flew up from her hand and
batted against the window a couple of times before
blundering a zigzag path into the center of the
diner.

Cooper looked at her again. He found his own
smile coming up on his face, like an idiot's grin. "It
wasn't dead." He knew that. "It must've been just
stuck there. Somebody must've spilled something and
they didn't wipe it up."

She turned and gazed out the window as if he'd ceased to be there.

"Come on." He slid out from the booth, the point of his anger moving up in his gut again. He'd already paid, and he wasn't going to leave a tip, not for two cups of coffee. "Let's get out of here. I got things to do." He headed for the door without looking behind him. The rustle of the black dress let him know she was following.

5

It turned out that he got out of it scot-free. Wound up not even getting a hair mussed out of place for his little public dalliance with Fay. That tempted him to think there was some sort of justice in the universe, after all. It'd griped his ass to think he might get his head broken *and* be tossed out to the work farm, just for having a cup of coffee with someone. Even worse, someone whose loony talk—dead cats and what it felt like to be dead—had convinced him to renew his self-made promise to have nothing to do with her. He had troubles enough without someone like that added on.

What happened—if old Vandervelde had been going to make a fuss over that, if the brain behind the little pig eyes and grinning yellow teeth had been planning on using the unchaperoned trip into town as an excuse to kick Cooper's head in . . . if that'd been the plan, to have some fun by getting mad and raising a little heat at someone else's expense, it got swallowed up by a ruckus Vandervelde hadn't planned on. Bonnie was the one who, without meaning to, got Cooper off the hook.

Cooper had come driving back from town, with Fay beside him, not saying a thing, still just staring out at the trees, lost in her spooky thoughts. He had been able to hear the voices shouting inside the house even before he switched the Ford's clattering engine off. The loudest he'd ever heard the old man; the windows trembled with his voice and his stomping around; a couple of thumps sounded like his fist hitting a wall. And another voice, a woman's, shouting loud enough to match Vandervelde's.

"We'd better wait out here," Fay had said. Cooper had asked her what was going on and had only gotten a shrug and a disgusted expression in return. A couple minutes later, the front door had banged open, and a woman—built like a barrel, with the female version of Vandervelde's toady features—had come storming out, leading the little girl by the hand. The child had spotted Cooper and Fay sitting in her father's car and had waved to them with her free hand, smiling with idiotic delight at the furor that had somehow centered around her. The woman had scowled at them before tossing the little girl like a rag doll into an old Packard and driving away, churning up a dust cloud all the way out to the highway. Vandervelde appeared on the porch, red-faced from all his shouting, his eyes slitted down to razor nicks. He tossed a bottle after the car, foam spewing across the dirt. His glare swept across Fay and Cooper without even seeing them as he turned around and stomped back into the house.

Cooper got the full scoop from Bonnie that evening as they sat down to eat. They were the only ones at the table; neither Vandervelde nor Fay had come downstairs. Bonnie was just the kind of dumb hick to brag about whatever trouble he got himself into. He and his pals had gone out to shoot quail up in the hills, dragging his little sister along; only there hadn't been any quail, at least none stupid enough not to scatter at the elephant-foot approach of this gang of drunken farm boys. So they'd gotten drunker, draining every bottle they'd brought along and finally passing out in the heavy afternoon heat. One of the

ladies from town—"stupid nosy bitch," Bonnie had
called her—had come driving along the highway and
had spotted the little girl trudging along, crying big
muddy tears down her dusty face. She had been
heading home, more or less, dragging one of the
boys' loaded .22 potshot rifles behind as though it
were her favorite doll. The town lady, properly hor-
rified, had snatched the kid up from the road and
had taken her to her aunt's place on the other side
of the valley. That was the first Cooper had heard of
there being any more of the Vandervelde clan. That
had been the old sonuvabitch's spinster sister yank-
ing the little girl out of the house and into the
Packard.

He would have been able to figure out the rest for
himself without listening to Bonnie's grumbling account. The aunt had come out to return her niece
and to take the opportunity to give her brother a
good piece of her mind—according to Bonnie, they'd
always hated each other—and had taken one look at
the condition the place had gotten into—filthy, filled
with rolling empties under every piece of furniture,
—and had jerked the kid right back out with her.
That's what all the shouting had been about. Not
that either of them wanted the pasty-faced little brat;
mostly just an opportunity for the stuck-up old biddy
to score points on her loathed brother. And to de-
prive him of something, anything; he'd get riled just
at the notion of somebody taking something away
from him.

A lot of the yelling, which Cooper could recall
from his listening post outside the house, had been
the aunt going on about raising the little girl in "a
decent home." There had been a couple of other
words attached to that argument: *whore* and *floozy*. So
nobody else was being fooled by Vandervelde's cozy
little arrangements, even if that was putting the harsh-
est possible labels on it. That accounted for the particular venom in the glance the little girl's aunt had

leveled at Fay sitting in the Ford—outraged morality, revved up to its highest pitch.

All that cleared the decks for some kind of change, Cooper figured. He thought about it, lying on his bed and studying the ceiling stain. His own problems would be solved—at least a little bit—if Vandervelde sent Fay packing back to wherever he'd gotten her from. After all, without his little daughter around, he didn't have much pretext for keeping a so-called nanny at the place. And if he wanted to get his daughter back, just to salve whatever pride his own sister had gored, he'd have to get rid of Fay. Seemed to be pretty common knowledge in the area, what he really had her there in the house for. The way things worked around these little hick towns, Vandervelde's getting his daughter back would be less a legal process than a matter of him convincing his neighbors that he'd gone on the straight and narrow and that the gossip spread around by the little girl's aunt was just a lot of slanderous bullshit. Or at least making some concession to outraged public feeling by getting rid of his live-in piece of tail. He could dispense with Fay and still be as big a boozer as ever and have every working girl from the town's little shanty district behind the packinghouse out to the place every night, and nobody would care. Plus the occasional woman from the camps, during the picking season: sometimes you'd come across one who wasn't too skinned down, still enough meat on the bones to pass as pretty, though you knew she'd be all leather gristle and straggly hair this time next year. Nobody was fooled around here, least of all Cooper; he bet that plenty of these fat orange growers, and the store-owners in town, piously going along with their families to church, were also taking care of that other business, men's true and genuine business, later on at their lodge smokers and all-night poker sessions. That was the great thing about hard times, at least for some people; that rat eating that raw onion might be some Okie woman on her knees, who knew that a quarter from each of the ten men standing in a circle around her came to $2.50 and you could feed three starving children for a week or longer on that. Nobody was fooled, especially not the wives of the growers and the store-owners; arrangements like these allowed them to be ladies twenty-four hours a day, even at home, in private. Let some other woman put up with the old man's grunting and puffing and sweaty, cigar-smelling flesh; they'd all be just as happy to be shut of that part of being married, thank you.

Nobody was fooled—but Vandervelde had really been rubbing everybody's noses into it, actually keeping Fay there all the time. Plus making himself obnoxious with that crap about her being a nanny for the kid; that kind of pretension always rubbed people the wrong way.

The way Cooper figured it, as he lay there pleased with the cleverness of his own brain, old Vandervelde would have to choose between the little girl and Fay. And he could get his ashes hauled any number of ways, by any number of women who'd mastered the trick of closing their eyes—and noses, ears, and every other sense, if possible—long enough to get the money in his hand. Whereas the kid—whining little monster that she was—that was his own flesh and blood. That always meant more.

There'll be some changes made, Cooper sang to himself. He cradled the back of his head in his interlaced fingers. And with that loon Fay out of here, that would give him a while longer before old Vandervelde came up with some other excuse for kicking his butt. And who knew what could happen even in that little bit of time? He might just find some way of getting his ass out and down the highway.

And besides, he'd had enough of this look-but-don't-touch stuff. Bad enough being stuck out here with no chance of getting any; he sure wasn't going to spend any of what was left of that precious six dollars on any private arrangements of his own, town whore or one of the women from the camp. Bad enough, without having it rubbed in his face like this. Loony or not, still a woman, no matter what.

It'd be a relief. Cooper closed his eyes and let himself ease down into sleep. He'd heard Fay go down the hallway, barefoot, to Vandervelde's room, and the old man growling and laughing about something. Probably just knocking off a last little piece before giving her the boot in the morning.

He pictured himself loading whatever little bag of stuff she had into the car and driving her, sullen and silent as always, to the train station. Or maybe the trustee would come out and get her, take her back to some lockup for women. Too bad for her but he had his own skin to look out for.

Flat wrong, of course. He should have known, should've been able to see the signs. So much for being a smart sonuvabitch, for having brains between his ears. He had it completely ass-backward.

The very next day, Cooper realized there weren't going to be changes made. Instead, the way things really were, the way they had been all along, only he'd been too stupid to see it, would be made clear enough so that even an idiot like him would be able to tell. The way things were arranged in the house smelling of men's sweat and spilled beer, in the middle of all those gray trees and rotting dusty leaves.

He spent the whole day out in the pickers' camps, marking off the previous week's tallies and counting heads. Not much of a payout to be made; the early crop that had come in was almost entirely scoured off the trees. A couple of groves right at the edge of the foothills took up half the men; the rest were debating whether to push up north to be in time for cotton, or hold out where they were for another couple of payless weeks until the late Valencias turned gold and ready for picking.

Came back to a house apparently empty except for Bonnie sprawled on one of the sofas, still puffy-faced and snoring off the remnants of his spree the day before. The absence of the little girl's constant singsong whine made the house unusually silent. Maybe Vandervelde had taken Fay to town, handing her over himself to whatever disposition was in store for her. Cooper went up to his own room and managed to fall asleep, sweat drying on his skin in the still heat.

When he came down to eat, hours later, he saw how wrong he'd been. As soon as he rounded the bottom post of the staircase, he saw them there, both Vandervelde and Fay sitting at the table, the food from the diner lady in front of them. Before, the little girl had always sat next to Fay, so some pretense of a nanny's proper duties could be performed, getting the kid fed and supposedly teaching her table manners—as if those had ever been needed here. But now that chair had been dispensed with, pushed back to the side of the dining room; the cloths that had covered the dishes were draped across the seat. Fay sat right next to Vandervelde now; in the doorway Cooper could see the wisps of black at the nape of her neck, the strays from the tight knot of her hair. Beside her, Vandervelde's spotted bald patch bent low over his plate as he shoveled the food in. Fay, as she'd always done before, prodded a cold chicken leg around on her plate.

Cooper circled around the table to where he sat. No one spoke; they never did. Bonnie smiled around the broad fingernail prying a bit of gristle from between his teeth, and gave him a slow, conspiratorial wink. With a tilt of his head, Bonnie indicated the subject of his humor, his father and Fay at the other side of the table. The smile grew broader and uglier as he sucked at his nail.

Pulling his own chair back, Cooper saw what Bonnie meant, why he thought it was so funny. Not funny to him—Cooper ran a finger around the edge of the plate, looking at the old man and the young woman across from him. So much for all of his daydreaming about things getting a little easier around here for him, with Fay booted out. Wasn't about to happen; he could see that now.

Fay looked up from her plate, gazing straight into Cooper's eyes. Beside her, Vandervelde didn't even seem to have noticed his coming into the dining room. His fat-swaddled eyes were locked sidelong onto Fay, looking at her as he went on eating. Looking at her with a gleam of triumphant possession, even—the thought filled Cooper with amazement— a sort of love.

He dished himself some potatoes from the bowl in the center of the table. So that was how things were; he ate and worked it out in his head. The aunt coming and taking the little girl away—that had cleared the decks, all right. The changes were already made. He'd just have to live with this new, clearer situation and figure out what to do next. *Loonier than I thought. Not Fay, but him, Vandervelde.*

The old boy had made his choice between blood and desire. Whatever she meant to him, whatever hook she had into his pants, it meant more to him than his own child, more than the sharp bit of his own sister stealing something away from, telling him he couldn't have it whether he wanted it or not.

Fine with me, thought Cooper as he helped himself to another go-around. What these people did with one another was no business of his. And he was going to keep it that way. No matter what. He chewed and swallowed and promised himself.

When he went up to his room, he saw the door to Fay's standing ajar. Through the narrow opening he could see her lying on her bed, still dressed, asleep. He stood for a moment, listening to Vandervelde's and Bonnie's raucous noises downstairs. They were yelling about something, as usual. He reached out and touched the cold metal of the doorknob, then pushed the door wider open and slipped inside.

She didn't wake up. Holding his breath, he looked around the room.

You could learn a lot that way, usually—taking a peek at a woman's room. Like going inside her head, seeing the things inside there. Just fluff, most of the time: sad, worn bits of it if she were poor, nice and fine if there was money. Some other things, too, sometimes. Bibles, or an embroidered sampler up on the wall; his mother had had one of those—Flee from the Wrath to Come—that she'd done when she'd been a little girl. Stuff like that was what you usually found.

There wasn't anything in Fay's room. Bare and empty. Cooper felt his stomach crawl uneasily as he looked around. It wasn't right.

An old dresser with an oval mirror on top—other than the bed, that was the room's only furnishing. There was a cloth-wrapped bundle sitting on it, round, about the size of a large apple.

He glanced over his shoulder at Fay, still sleeping. Then, with his forefinger, he poked the folds of the rag open.

First, he thought it was a doll's head; in the dim light from the hallway, he saw the eyes. Then he saw they were filmed over with gray. There was patchy gray fur, starting to rub away on the cloth around the object. He prodded the rag farther back and saw the sharp-pointed teeth, frozen in a snarl.

Now he knew what it was. The head of the cat he'd killed out in the yard. A crust of dried blood stiffened the fur behind its ears. The blind eyes stared up at him, the pain and terror still locked inside. He jerked his hand back and wiped it on his trousers.

She'd kept it. When she'd taken it away—to bury

it, he thought—she'd kept this grisly little reminder. *Jesus Christ*—his stomach felt as if it were trying to crawl up into his throat.

Gingerly, he picked up the corners of the rag between his thumb and forefinger and folded them back over the thing. He glanced at her again, over on the bed, then slipped out of the room.

That did it. He shook his head when he was safely out in the hallway. If he hadn't known before, that had told him everything he needed to know. The sweat chilled on his neck as he headed downstairs, to go out for a breath of fresh air. It'd be real easy to keep his promises to himself now.

He knew it was her standing behind him. He'd heard the screen door swing open as he sat on the front-porch steps, then silence. But he knew, without even looking around, that it was her.

She didn't come any closer, just stood with her back to the door. "I saw you," she said quietly. "Up in my room. I wasn't asleep."

He didn't move, sitting forward with his elbows on his knees, propping up his chin. If he said nothing maybe she'd go away without doing some loony thing.

"I saw you looking around." Her voice went on, soft and level, as if she weren't nuts at all. "I know what you saw."

A shrug, his shoulders twitching nervously. He went on gazing across the yard to the dark trees.

"You remember what I was talking about, before, when we were in town? About wondering what'd it be like to be dead? Well . . . I don't have to wonder. I know. I know what it's like."

Sweet Jesus. He closed his eyes, gritting his teeth. He felt like just picking up and running, anywhere. Just to get away from her.

She wouldn't stop. "I know, 'cause I can go in there, inside them, when they're dead. I can feel what it's like. It's not so bad. When they're dead, they're not hurting anymore. That was why I was so glad you ... took care of that cat. When Bonnie hurt it. It was in pain, real bad. It wanted to be dead, I know. And then when it was dead, I could feel it, I could go inside it and feel what it was like. Not to be hurting anymore. That's what it's like. It just doesn't hurt anymore."

Cooper held still, waiting. Eventually it'd end and she'd go away. He just had to keep the soft words from drilling too far into his skull, making him crazy as she was.

"There's more I can do." A trace of excitement entered her voice, a small ecstasy. "I can make them move. When they're dead, and I'm inside them—I can give them a little bit of me being alive. That fly, when we were down in the diner—even something like that. And bigger things. I tried to do it with that cat, with its head—that's why I had it up there in my room. And I could, I made it move, it could open its mouth a little bit and move its eyes, but that was all."

Good for you. He could have turned and shouted it at her, but didn't. The skin on his arms crawled, all this crazy talk tightening his shoulders.

"When I was real small and my granddaddy died—that's when I found out I could do it. Go inside them like that. 'Cause I remember staring at him in his coffin, when everybody else had gone out of the room and they'd forgot about me, forgot I was there. I was just staring at him, I guess I must've dragged over a stool or something so I could look down in the coffin. And then I was inside him, I could feel it. And when I was outside of him, looking at him, part of me was still in there with him. And he spoke to me, he did, I heard him. He called me Princess, he always called me that. His mouth opened, and he said it. Just that. I wasn't scared."

She fell silent for a moment. Her voice was different, hollow, when she spoke again. "When they buried him, I had to try not to think about him. 'Cause I could feel it, the wood of the lid they nailed on, pressing against his hands; that scared me. But it got easier after that. That was just the first time. But it got easier, every time I did it. Till I could do it with anything. Anything dead."

Her hand touched his shoulder and he flinched. He steeled himself from bolting upright, away from her.

"You don't believe me." A whisper. "But I told you for a reason."

She was gone. The screen door opened and shut, and he was by himself again.

6

Maybe Vandervelde was playing a slow and mean game with him. Cooper couldn't decide if the old bastard, with his red face looking as if it were ready to explode, had the patience for something really wicked. When someone wheezes just going up the stairs, dragging himself up by his grip on the rail, after stuffing his big frog mouth full of biscuits and gravy so fast that he starts to gasp for air, as if each wad of flour and brown grease might be the last he'd ever have a chance at, then you just naturally figure he doesn't have time for jokes where the payoffs are months down the line. All you had to do was stay out of the way of the quick, satisfying—to him, the old man—punch in the mouth, most likely delivered by the fist of his junior version Bonnie. And I'm smart enough to do that, Cooper promised himself except for a couple of lapses, like that stupid cat, for which he was still berating himself. Stupid bastard; what's a goddamn cat matter to you? But it's not the cat, it's her. Shut up and don't be stupid. Don't be stupid. As long as you can see the quick ones heading for your jaw in time to duck and there aren't any slow ones sneaking up on you, then you'll be all right . . . for a while.

Cooper thought about all that, slow seconds ticking off inside his head, as he looked down at the two hundred bucks old Vandervelde had just slapped in his hand. The morning of a day already setting out to be a scorcher, the dull heat parching the leaves under the orange trees like a dust-filled oven. Only dry things, papery brown grasshoppers and other small creatures, moving; Cooper could almost hear the scratching rustle of their barbed legs. Everything had gotten so quiet, he was thinking so hard, staring down at the money, the green, sweaty—the old man's sweat, seeped through his trousers pocket—little bundle in his hand.

"Hey, are you listenin' to me? Jesus Christ."

He looked up and saw Vandervelde shaking his head, face even more disgusted-looking than usual. As if Cooper were the dog shit on the bottom of his shoe. Cooper nodded, folding his hand around the money. Out through the trees, when he looked away from the old man, he could see the cloud from a passing auto out on the highway, the dust just hanging there, nothing in the still air to knock it back down to the road.

"Yeah, sure." He tried to remember Vandervelde's exact words that had come with the two hundred dollars. "What is it you want me to pick up for you?"

"That's none of your business, is it?" Vandervelde wedged his thumbs under his gut, hooking them over his belt. "You just head along out there and get it, then bring it back here. Understand? They know you're coming and you got the money with you. That's all you need to know."

Cooper shrugged, running his thumb over the edges of the folded bills. If Vandervelde hadn't told him it was two hundred bucks—*ee*-zactly—how much would he have guessed it came to? A lot—a couple twenties wrapped around the rest in tens, a nice little traveling bundle. Not enough to choke the usual horse; he could've eaten it himself, like lettuce leaves pulled out of the weedy garden out in back of the house, crumbled up in his hand like Vandervelde's sopping biscuits and stuffed into his mouth the same way ... Cooper gritted his teeth; he could fuckin' taste 'em—the way money smelled, the salt of other men's sweat staining it even darker green; that's how it would taste, he knew, as he bit and chewed. The way starving men get, dreaming of cheese, hoarding every little scrap—the money that'd been hidden in his pocket so long it's molded to the shape of his thigh—dreaming until their mouths filled with sour spit.

The old man's voice went needling on at him. "You sure you know how to get out there? I'll draw you a goddamn map if you need it."

Goddamn map, goddamn this, goddamn that and everything else ... The old bastard couldn't open his yellow-toothed mouth without taking a shit in your ear. To the point where Cooper was glad of any chance to get away from him, away from the house that smelled like him and his son. He'd been heading out across the brown baked lawn, to make his way through the orange trees and out to the pickers' camps, when Vandervelde had stopped him, plucking the black payout book out of his hands and tossing it over onto one of the chairs on the front porch.

"I can find it all right." There was a slip of paper on top of the wad of cash, an address scrawled on it in Vandervelde's big looping handwriting. In his hand, Cooper could see the edge of the white paper peeking out from the surrounding bills. Damned if he was going to ask Vandervelde to draw him a map, wherever this place was. The Ford had a cardboard box underneath the seat, stuffed with gas-station maps; he could figure it out from those.

Vandervelde peeled a couple more bills from the roll he took out of his pocket. "Get it filled up when you go by Ed's." Like the other growers, he ran a tab at the two-pump station where the highway split away from the town. He handed the money, a couple of ones, to Cooper. "That's for when you get there. You'll need to get yourself something to eat. I don't want you tear-assing out there and back, trying to make it in time for dinner. You got me?"

He nodded again, sliding the money, the thin singles and the thicker wad together, into his own pocket. Keeping his mouth shut while his mind went racing.

What did the old bastard want? Giving him a car in good running condition—clever Bonnie saw to that—with a tank of gas—soon as he filled it at the station—and two hundred dollars. Holy shit . . . He almost said it out loud as Vandervelde turned and waddled away from him, heading back to the shade of the porch. That's serious traveling money. You could go a long way with that much cash. Jesus Christ, there were poor bastards with their whole families loaded up in dismally worse autos, crossing the entire country with a tenth of that, greasy fives and ones, wadded up in an old tobacco can. He could feel the money Vandervelde had handed him, folded up in his pocket, warming up to the pump of his blood as though it were new skin grown over an old wound. A lot of money . . . You could go a long ways on that.

You bet, a long ways and picking up speed on the straightest highway away from here . . . you'd be going so fast that when you reached the end of the long, long rope with its noose around your neck you'd go all stretched out like some rubber cartoon character, hands still gripping the steering wheel as your arms went *boinng*, your tongue waving like a flag in the breeze, your eyes bugged out from the sockets of your skull from the sheer interrupted momentum of your flight. And then, another funny *boinng*, you'd be snapped right back here where Vandervelde's fist would be clamped around the other end of your leash. Then the fun would really start.

Cooper looked around, his neck smearing sweat inside the collar of his shirt, and saw Bonnie standing in the doorway of the shed. Just standing there, leaning against the unpainted wooden frame, watching him and smiling. With a screwdriver in his hands, rust-specked metal and cracked black handle, that he lazily slid through the ring of two fingers, flipped it around, and slid it back the other way. Smile all lazy, as though the morning's heat had already made it too much of an effort, and eyes half-lidded, watching him . . .

Screw this old shit. Cooper turned away and mounted the front-porch steps, heading up to his room to get his coat. Take a piss, do anything else to get ready to run Vandervelde's little errand. And then he'd be away from here, away from the father-and-son goat stink and all their sly-eyed scheming; away at least for a little while, with the road wind coming in through the Ford's rolled-down windows strong enough to blow out all the cobwebs that'd come from these weeks of sitting around both bored and antsy, waiting for the steel toe of a Vandervelde boot to arrive between his eyes. Away, so he could think; Cooper could almost taste what that'd be like, too, as though his brain were a squeezed-out honeycomb with one last golden drop hidden inside, rolling out onto his waiting tongue. He ran up the staircase inside and splashed cold water on his face until he gasped for breath. Shook his face like a dog and looked at himself in the clouded mirror. Be smart, he told the wet face. Just run out there and get whatever it is and bring it back here. A rope that's two hundred dollars long is still a rope. Nobody else loved him enough to tell him these things. Don't be a fool.

The words kept rolling in his head—*a fool, a fool, don't be*—as the Ford bucketed over the ruts in the dirt lane leading from the Vandervelde house out to the county highway. Cooper kept the gas floored, just to feel the leaf springs bottom out, knowing it would've gotten Bonnie's goat if he'd seen the carefully tended machine treated that way. But the thick gray and brown mesh of the dying orchard screened the Ford's jerking progress from the view of anyone back at the house.

He was about ready to start singing just as he lifted his foot from the gas, letting the Ford slow down for making the turn off the dirt lane. Happy, even: he'd decided that this was the absolute best way to tweak old Vandervelde's nose. The old bastard had probably already alerted all his farmer and cop buddies in every little jerkwater village up and down the line, in every possible direction that Cooper might point the Ford. Telling them to watch out for the fugitive with the two hundred bucks melting like an ice cube in his trouser pocket, flying with the wheels just touching the high spots of the road. *When I come joggling back, this little piggy home from market, that'll piss the sonuvabitch off,* all right, because he won't be able to say anything about it. Cooper smiled, just thinking about that golden moment. Worth coming back and putting up with more of his shit, right there. He could imagine Vandervelde's face going all angry and sour, the heavy jowls like sacks of gray oatmeal, as he sat glowering over his poker hand, enduring the other growers' jokes about his little plan, which was supposed to have been so much fun for them all, coming a dud instead.

Sometimes, when somebody got so mad, somebody who already had that huffing, sweating look about them, with the veins standing out on the brow, sharper with each clocklike throb—sometimes a person like that would get so mad that the pressure inside would just blow the top of his head off like a steam cooker blowing its seal. *Now there was a plan.* Cooper hadn't worked it all out yet, but he could see it approaching, like a long-waited-for train that you could hear singing through the tracks, yet at the same time you were riding on it. As the Ford slowed to the highway, he could close his eyes for just a second and see the old man sprawled out in the dirt in front of the house, lips skinned back to show the yellow teeth clamped against the swollen tongue, the eyes staring so hard they'd soon start to leak blood at the corners . . . just lying there, the long anger finally ebbing away as everybody stood around and shaded him with their watching. For some reason, he didn't picture Bonnie kneeling down, loosening his father's collar or anything like that; instead, the son and heir prodded the body's ribs with the toe of his boot, the way you would an animal you found out in the fields, with the crows clustered around the wet, broken eyes.

How the rest of it would work out . . . Cooper let himself dream. Anytime somebody died, especially the big cheese the way Vandervelde was, there'd always be a little span of confusion, a couple of days when things got sorted out and back to business again. That'd be the time to go, to walk straight through the rows of trees until you came to a highway you'd never seen before, right under the brow of the hills; then turn left and head north, riding shank's mare, as he remembered his grandmother calling it. That was how everybody of his blood seemed to wind up, beating their thin shoe leather against the stones in the road. You didn't get to drive a car like this for long, at least not in this world.

Though he could almost imagine it being different. The Ford came to a stop and he took it out of gear, then leaned his arms across the top of the wheel and rested his chin on them. Gazing down the county highway . . . Now, if Vandervelde were to blow his cork while he was squatting down to open his big old safe, his sweating face reflected in the shiny black depth behind the gold leaf Teutonic lettering, squatting down to swing the heavy, square door open and breathe in the smell of the money stacked inside, that smell sharper and more potent than the layers of rotting leaves underneath the orange trees, the smell of other men's sweat soaked right into the paper . . . If Vandervelde felt himself dying, the thin walls in his brain splitting open with a red tide that couldn't be stopped, that's where he'd go, wouldn't he? Like some old dog crawling to its kennel, to thrust its nose into the musty wrap of its own warm stink. Cooper could just picture the old man taking one whiff of the safe's insides, the way those mackerel-snappers put one of their gory Jesus crosses on the wall across from the deathbed so it'd be the last thing seen before passing over to the other side: just one drag into the straining lungs, and then Vandervelde would pitch over on his back, if not happy, at least fulfilled in some way.

Cooper had caught that smell himself, sitting at the desk rummaging through the papers the way Vandervelde expected him to do, or standing right outside the room's doorway. That was even better, where he couldn't be seen, but could see the old man down on his knees, with his head practically thrust all the way into the safe, like a pig at a trough. If there'd been some way Vandervelde could've actually eaten the money and still had it piled there on the safe's shelves, Christ, the old bastard would've come to the dinner table with green bits still stuck all over his fat jowls.

Out of the tree shade that had covered the dirt lane, Cooper let the dream run on, eyes closed in the buttery sunshine coming in through the Ford's windshield. The pretty picture of the safe door still open, and maybe having to give Bonnie a hand to drag that dead or dying mountain of old lard up to his bed—that's what you were supposed to do with them, so other people, the doctor or the county coroner when they came, would know you were civilized. Then tiptoe back down the stairs while all the fuss is still going on, back to the office and the open safe, then reach in, like a jam jar up to the elbow, and pull out—what a smart boy am I!—a handful, close your fist around them, squeeze 'em till the other men's sweat ran down your wrist. Who'd ever know if any was missing? Vandervelde being just the sort of cagey old bastard who'd never tell anyone, not even his own son, just how much money he had stashed away. And then just mosey on out the back door, slowly across the yard, your hands deep in your pockets, feeling that wad of bills picking up your pulse like a new heart grown out of your thigh; maybe kick a pebble out of your way, looking up over your shoulder toward the window of the bedroom where the dead man lay. So that anybody watching you would think that you were at the most grieving about this cushy job coming to an end. Then you'd be at the edge of the trees, then in their shade, then hidden behind their scratchy skeleton branches . . . and then you'd be gone. Just running, every stride crackling harder through the dry leaves and into the wet rotting things beneath, the wet smell sucking into your nostrils along with the dust, but that was still better than the stink of that house, the stink of the father and son, the dead and the living . . .

The rim of the steering wheel was cooler than the morning air. Cooper slid his hands down around the wheel and laid his forehead against the black ring; he felt feverish with all this dreaming. Couldn't even stop, not yet, but squeezed his eyes closed tighter and watched himself on some other highway, some other compass direction, walking with head held high, the way money in the pocket pops your chin up in the air, happy with the knowledge sure in his heart that the sheriff had asked Bonnie, *Where's that Cooper fella, the one we sent out here from the lockup?* And Bonnie, busy counting the windows and doors of the house that was all his now, had said, *Aww, he must of skittered away, forget about him. That was my father's dog. Who needs 'im?* The trustee, with all his good advice, cocks his head and gives a low whistle, just to himself. *The little sonuvagun made it, he got away.* And that dream figure on the dream road behind Cooper's brow just goes on walking, starting to whistle in the bright sunshine . . .

Yeah, that'd be lovely, all right, money in your pocket and a road in front of you, with nobody gaining on your ass—a fool could sit at the wheel all day, engine turning and going nowhere, and just dreaming of how nice that'd be. He rubbed his forehead on the wheel and smiled at the stupid picture he made now for anybody who cared to look at him. Dreaming away . . . He turned his cheek to the wheel's curve, to look back down the dirt lane to the Vandervelde house. That was when he saw the arms folded across the top of the seat, the face above them, and the grave eyes silently watching him.

"Shit." In one quick burst that left his heart pounding in his chest, Cooper had fumbled open the door and scooted out of the car, almost tripping on the running board and sprawling headfirst on the roadside gravel. Anger at being surprised, at being made a fool, surged up to replace the fright. Jaw clamped tight, he yanked the rear door open, and glared at Fay sitting in the back seat.

She had her hands folded in her lap, the skin of her wrists white against the black dress. She bit her lip but couldn't stop from smiling. "I thought I'd have to wake you up." Voice soft; she knew she'd scared him. "You had your head down so long like that I thought you were asleep."

"God *damn*." Cooper's breath finally started to slow; he lowered his head bull-like as he stood gripping the edge of the car door. The blood that had come surging up ebbed back into his limbs. He raised his head to look at Fay. "Just what the hell are you doing here?"

She drew back, offended by the mean tone in his words. "I'm coming with you. I decided to."

Simple as that. It figures . . . Cooper shook his head, looking down at the road, dust the same color on the toes of his shoes. It fucking well figures. He'd been doing a good job not thinking about her, doing his best to avoid her, inside and out of Vandervelde's house. Since the night she'd come out and talked to him. About all that crazy stuff: dead things, and stuff like that. All of which he'd decided he didn't need, not now or ever.

He'd about convinced himself that it hadn't happened, that he'd fallen asleep sitting on the porch steps and he'd dreamed her coming out and saying all those loony things. But one look at her and he knew, he remembered. There was a severed cat's head sitting on her bedroom dresser.

For a moment he had the urge to slam the door right in her face, loud enough to scare the crows, and just start walking now. But he didn't; just took another breath—*don't be a fool*—and held on to the door.

"What the hell do you think you're doing?" He looked up at her after he'd spoken.

Her hands had balled into fists, white-knuckled against the dress. "What do you mean? I told you—I'm going with you."

"No, you're not." Cooper grabbed hold of the roof edge with his other hand and leaned down toward her. He heard his own voice going hard. "I don't know what you're playing at, but I sure don't intend to get my butt kicked to find out. If the idea is to get me in dutch with the old man, you'll just have to cook up some other way." He shut up, but the words kept rolling inside his head: damned if I'm fool enough to drive into shit like this.

Fay lifted her chin, her lips pursed tight for a moment. "You don't have to worry. I can take care of him."

"Sure you can." Stupid little bitch. "That's fine for you. Then when you're done taking care of him"—he made it sound dirty, exactly what it was—"then the old boy comes rolling out and takes care of me. Oh, no." Cooper reached into the car and grabbed one of Fay's thin wrists. He stepped back, pulling her up from the seat. "Come on, get out. You've got a walk back to the house ahead of you."

She braced herself against the door, resisting him

with a surprising force, shaking her head like a child. "No—I'm going."

He could jerk her out of the car and snap her across his knee like a bundle of twigs. Cooper knew that from the way his hand went all the way around her skinny wrist, his thumb lapping against the nails of his fingers; inside his grip, her pulse sped and trembled. She knew it, too. The things women know; as much as they pulled back and fought against the big hand, the bunched shoulders, right to the edge of their strength and going all hysterical, they knew. Even for somebody like me . . . Cooper squeezed the wandlike bones, the white skin, tighter. His own heart sped up, the blood pumping in two directions, up into his head, surging behind his brow and down below his belly. That's what touching a woman did, holding her so she couldn't pull away: the blood gets thick and heavy down there.

"That hurts."

He saw her when she spoke, the two soft words sluicing away a red curtain behind his eyes. She wasn't even pulling against him any longer, but just letting her forearm dangle in front of her like a rope. He was holding on to her, and she let him. She watched him, her child's eyes large and waiting.

Don't be—

Cooper let go of her. She let her wrist lie in the open curve of his palm. Red marks the width of his fingers, they faded as he watched, the blue of the veins beneath the skin rising once more.

—a fool.

He wasn't even excited any longer, at least not that way. The blood ebbed away; he could feel it, a slack hollow scooped out of his gut. But not the way it was before he'd grabbed her and squeezed the bones and flesh and her blood all together in his fist.

In the Ford's dusty side mirror, he saw his face, his head swung down low in his shoulders, like some brooding animal. Eyes narrowed, as though the wash of blood across his brain had left a heavy sediment in his eyelids, weighing them down. He turned his head and spat a salt wad onto the gravel.

He could hear Fay talking, her thin, high voice clattering inside the car, with a mean tone of its own, the pitch women could work themselves into. They always sounded like children then, spiteful over some long-held, childish grievance.

"I'm not going back, I'm going with you. If you don't take me with you, I'll tell him you made me go with you and then you got chicken and dumped me out on the road. That's what I'll tell him. Then you'll really be in trouble."

She didn't need to say anything like that, or anything at all. Mind's made up—what there was left of it. If only he hadn't grabbed her wrist, felt that little tremble of pulse under the white skin . . . He'd been all right until that happened.

"Well? What're you gonna do?"

Cooper looked around at her. Beyond her, on the other side of the Ford, the bright sunlight filled the window. He could smell the dust on the leaves beneath the gray branches. Something rustling under there, a mouse or a snake moving in the cool, damp spaces . . . but still quiet enough.

If he closed his eyes, he could see a hand, his own, sliding the black dress up across other skin, even paler, the secret parts, the tip of his thumb grazing the seat cover where the curved flesh pressed against it . . .

Not that much of a fool. Not yet. Cooper opened his eyes and looked straight into her wide-open, waiting gaze.

"I guess I'm gonna get back in," he said. "And just drive."

7

He made her crouch back down on the floor in back, hiding out of sight, while he filled the Ford up at the gas station. The old fellow leaning his chair back against the front of the square little building, with its black loops of fan belts dangling over yellowing girlie calendars, was lazy enough to let Cooper handle the pump himself, letting the tall glass cylinder on top fill up and then gurgle its contents into the car's tank. He didn't even have to sign a chit or anything for the gas—the old man just waved him on, having recognized the Ford.

When they got past the town and onto the main highway, Cooper pulled over and let Fay come up front. He glanced over at her as he let out the brake and pulled back onto the asphalt. Settled back against the seat, she was undoing the hard knot of her hair. After a moment, she took away her hands, one with a black pin in its grasp, and the hair fell across her shoulders. A few strands lifted in the breeze from the window.

"I just had to get out of there." Fay gazed at the highway ahead as she began braiding her hair, her hands working up by her collarbone. With her flat, usual voice, a dead calmness in it—the screeching from back at the edge of the Vandervelde place had all drained away. "Drives me crazy, sometimes. Enough of it does."

"Mm." He watched her from the corner of his eye, glancing over from the straight-cut highway. "I can believe that."

Her hair—more of it than he could've guessed had been squeezed into that little fist at the back of her head—twined into a rope dangling between her breasts. She caught him looking at her as her fingertips slid between the buttons of the dress and pulled out a bit of ribbon, something she must have had tucked inside her brassiere. She smiled at him, and he felt his face coloring as he looked back toward the road.

"There, that's better." She turned her head, swinging the braid, with the knotted ribbon making a little brush tip at the end. In the confines of the Ford's front seat, he felt it graze his arm. She meant something by that, he knew. The simple acts of moving the car down the road, smelling the raw odor of the gas as he'd pumped it into the tank and then slapped the lid down on it, then just driving, the road traveling up through the steering wheel and into his arms and shoulders—that had been enough to draw away the last of overheated blood that had surged up into his head. His brain had been heavy with it then, like one of those giant snakes they had in India or some other faraway place that he'd seen the picture of in the big cracked-leather dictionary that had sat on its own little podium in the corner of the schoolhouse. The kind of snake that could eat a whole goat, or a small boy looking at a yellowing page with eyes wide, swallow 'em down whole and then lie on the ground with its great swollen snake's belly for a week digesting the skin and bones and the wide staring eyes. Lie awake for nights on end, back then, squeezed in between his brother and his littlest sister, thinking about that, his own eyes wide open in the dark. Now, it felt more like a red racer inside his skull, one of those little whips that could scoot across the ground faster than a man could run, looking for the tall grass or a hole to dive in.

That's the problem: you make your big decision, then you have to live with it. Keeps you hopping. Out here in the sunlight beating down on the highway, falling through the windshield straight onto his face so he had to squint against the glare as he drove, in that bright world there was time to think.

When he looked around at Fay again, sitting beside him, her elbow resting on the windowsill, he saw that her face had become smoother and more relaxed, prettier now, as if loosening her hair from that hard little knot had also let the blood back into the drum-taut skin over her cheekbones. Not so pale now; the wind from the Ford's barreling down the highway had brought up the color in her face. Maybe this was how she'd looked when she'd first gone out to the Vandervelde place. Cooper wondered how long ago that had been, before he'd gotten out there. No wonder the old sonuvabitch had gone for her in his greedy, slobbering way. Cooper could picture Vandervelde getting fatter and greasier around the jowls, as though he was stuffing fried chops into his thick-lipped mouth, while Fay went on getting skinnier and paler, her watery blood being the gravy the old man sopped his biscuits in. The bastard's just about eaten me up; what chance would a little stringy girl have?

"Know where you going?"

It struck him suddenly that he didn't. He had just pulled out of the gas station, stopping a little ways on and out of sight to let Fay come up front, and had headed north on the state highway without thinking. He fumbled at his shirt pocket for the folded scrap of paper there. "I got the address here. And there's some road maps under the seat—"

"You don't need 'em." A wisp of her dark hair had escaped being braided; the wind tangled it across her face and she pulled it away with the tip of her finger. "I've been there. Vandervelde took me once."

"Yeah?" That would solve one problem at least.

Fay nodded, rolling the strand of hair between her fingers. "Sure. I can tell you how to get there; you don't need no maps. But it's a ways to go; you got some driving ahead of you."

"That suits me fine." He smiled at her. You're not the only one who was going nuts back there. "What is this place, anyway?"

She'd caught the message. She made a little brush out of the strand of hair and stroked her throat with it. "Some people he knows." A shrug. "That he gets stuff from. I think they all work down at the docks, where the ships come in. So they got . . . you know . . . ways of getting stuff. Then they sell it to people. You know what I mean?"

Cooper's smile grew wider, knowing just what she meant. "Sure, they steal stuff. They sell it to people hot." Now there was a deal to get in on, if you could. Everybody knew dockhands spent more time stealing than working. And made good money, twice over. They were making out all right—maybe not all of them, but most of them, he bet—even in times like these. "We're picking up something stolen, for Mr. Vandervelde."

"Oh, you don't need to be worried about it . . ." She clutched his arm as if he were about to swing the car right around in the middle of the road and head back. "You won't get in any trouble for it."

"Huh." He leaned back, squinting down the glare-white highway. "I don't give a damn about it. What old Vandervelde buys is his business."

She pulled her hand away from his arm. But she was still closer to him on the seat than she'd been before. "I didn't think you'd care." Her voice soft and conspiratorial, that was even better than the touch of her hand. "I knew you didn't."

The way she said it—low like that—brought a pump of blood inside, like an echo from back at the edge of Vandervelde's dead orchard. Cooper one-handed the steering wheel, arm straight out, resting the other one on his windowsill. They could sure whip you around, with just some small thing like that. A couple of words was all it took. He'd have to go on thinking, working out what he was going to do. What was going to happen later on, when it was nighttime. Have to be ready for it. For anything.

Amazing, in its way—he was having a normal sort of conversation with her, the way you would with somebody who wasn't crazy. Maybe that proved she really was crazy. Not acting, just to spook him. If she'd been acting, when she'd been saying all that loony stuff before, she'd have been careful now to keep the act up. That she was okay now, maybe that meant she really believed that other stuff: it was all just normal to her, nothing to get worked up about. The thought ran a finger of ice along his spine.

"So we're heading the right way?" He pointed out the windshield. "To get where we're going?"

Fay nodded. "I'll tell you when you gotta turn off. It's not for a ways." She'd twisted the strand of hair into a rattail, wet and shiny where she'd chewed on the ends.

Cooper glanced at her. She was staring straight ahead, eyes looking at something not out on the road. Could just about see her falling into that deep silence, the way she walked around back at the Vandervelde place, as though she weren't really there.

"So what'd you get from these people?" He couldn't think of anything else to ask her, to cut into that silence. "When Vandervelde took you with him?"

She looked around at him, eyes wide, as if she'd already forgotten he was there, in the world at all. Gone back down there, wherever she went. Some dark place . . . In the sunlight, hot as it was coming in the car, he felt the skin contract across his arms, the sweat chilling.

Fay shrugged, looking back to the windshield. "It was a radio that we went and got. It was a nice one too, all made outta wood, and it stood 'bout so high." She held her hand out in front of her breasts, as though patting a child's head. "We had to go out there with the pickup truck to get it, it was so big. I think he took me along so I'd see him peel the money off the roll in his pocket, and see how smart he was, the way he could get things like that. Only when we got back and he and Bonnie carried it inside the house, they plugged it in and the big round dial in the middle lit up and everything, but there wasn't any sound come out of it." She smiled, remembering. "They fiddled with it for hours, and not a thing. Till he got so mad that he busted it up with an ax, just cursing away the whole time. Then he went back out the next day, with the dial stuck in the middle of a piece of wood; I don't think he got his money back from 'em, though. He wouldn't talk for two or three days after."

Cooper snorted. Sounded like a typical Vandervelde story. With what him and his dumb son knew about radios, no way of telling if there'd been anything wrong with it at all.

"That the only time? That you went out there for something?"

She shook her head. "No. I went with him a while back. He was grinning and laughing the whole time. I knew he was up to something. When we got out there—it's like a house, you know, where a bunch of these dock fellas live—there was a couple of women there, too, their wives or their girlfriends or something. And the women took me to a back bedroom, and there were all these big steamer trunks there, real old ones with these big leather straps." Her voice brightened, a child talking about Christmas. "And they were just stuffed with things, pretty things, dresses and stuff." Then dreamy: "Made outta silk and stuff."

"He bought you silk dresses?" That was hard to believe. The black get-up was all he'd ever seen her in.

A moment passed before she said anything more. Cooper glanced over at her and saw her face turned sullen and brooding.

"There was other stuff." The child's voice gone now. "That was what we went out there for. The women made me put it on, and then they brought him back to the bedroom to show him, and they were all standing there looking at me." She threw her head back, sticking out her chin. Her voice went louder. "They said it all came from France, but I think they just told him that. So he'd pay more."

The dirty old bastard . . . Cooper could just see the little pig eyes squinting down into even tighter slits and the heart wrapped up in the blubbery body thumping and straining away. A wonder the old boy hadn't keeled over right then and there.

Something else to picture, which blotted out the highway rolling under the Ford's wheels. That skinny body, with its little-girl tits, wrapped up in whatever cheap finery had come floating in across the ocean, or from wherever; the white skin crawling under the see-through silky stuff, the stuff of dreams and expensive whores, and watched by the little pig eyes and the laughing dockworkers' women . . .

Cruel to think about something like that. It made you excited and sick at the same time. Sick at yourself, your own piggy little eyes becoming like his. Cooper shook his head and stared hard at the glaring road.

"It didn't last very long. Those things . . ." She went on, though he wanted to tell her to stop. Maybe she knew. "They were real flimsy, and they kinda fell apart after a while. 'Cause of him." A giggle, which made him feel sicker. "Then they weren't so nice anymore, and he took them out to the yard and burned 'em all."

That's what I get for asking. Every little peep inside her head was like looking down a rat hole: all dark, and sometimes you saw two beady little red dots looking right back at you. Completely loony.

And yet he was driving on; he wasn't turning back or pulling over to dump her on the side of the highway. Which, either one, if not the smartest thing to do, would still be smarter than what he was doing, what the blood still simmering away in his brain was making him do.

He thought of something that he hadn't before. Maybe old Vandervelde knew she was out here with him; maybe Vandervelde had sent her, told her to hide in the car, get him to take her along. Maybe the calculating old sonuvabitch was that smart, that far ahead of him. And the girl was in on it with the old man, all of them busting up inside themselves, trying to keep the laughing inside . . . not to give away the game . . . at least not before the big payoff, the really big laugh at the end.

Jesus jumping Christ; now *there* was something to think about, to while away the long hours driving away. He could feel his hands sweating on the steering wheel.

Sweating, and doing nothing else but keeping the Ford right on the road, heading straight on for wherever they were going. However you worked it, he knew he was a fool.

8

It turned out to be a house like other houses, if a bit more run-down and shabby-looking. In that, the place reminded Cooper of Vandervelde's, with the identical smell of spilled beer and men's sweat and unwashed laundry seeped right into the walls. You could find places like that anywhere.

He was tired from driving most of the day, the ache from the steering wheel settled in his shoulders. Late afternoon by the time Fay directed him off the highway and onto a grid of narrow streets. A region of flat brown earth, scraped of trees or anything else green, with only the shapes of oil pumps, like rocking mechanical grasshoppers, breaking the barren vista. Even the air smelled like oil and gasoline. They drove past a skinny pipe stuck in the ground; at the top of it a flame shimmered, barely visible in the afternoon sunlight, trailing a black plume of smoke.

The road crawled up into low hills, with houses and the usual signs of people. The trees had been left standing, though even here you'd see a pump rocking away in somebody's back yard, with scrawny chickens pecking at the grass grown high around its base. A woman in a print dress threw a bucket of soapy water out into the street as they drove by, and she stood watching them as they went on, one hand shading her eyes. In the Ford's mirror, Cooper saw her turn back toward the white frame house.

With Fay pointing which way to turn, they got around to the dockworkers' place. She told him to drive right on up close to the porch, the way Vandervelde had done before. Behind the house's screen door, somebody watched them for a moment, then disappeared into the darkness behind. The Ford's engine rattled and coughed for a few seconds after Cooper switched it off. A dog, mottled and lopeared, barked as they walked up to the porch. The animal didn't get to its feet, chained as it was to the side of the house, but just lay on its side, raising only its head, making noise with no threat.

The screen door rattled and banged on its hinges as Cooper knocked. A longshoreman's hook, a curved piece of iron with a wooden cross handle, hung embedded by its point in the doorframe. The wood was pockmarked, like a tree with woodpeckers, and the white paint was flaking away to show the grain beneath.

Fay waited down at the bottom of the porch steps. Cooper figured she probably had something against going inside. Understandably; the same women were probably waiting inside somewhere. He knocked again, standing at the door and inhaling the musty smell from within.

"Whatta ya want?" A man had appeared on the other side of the screen. He looked like he'd just gotten up.

A side-of-beef, just like Bonnie. Cooper felt like telling this one to go screw himself. He could smell the man's heavy breath right through the screen.

"Mr. Vandervelde sent me." He reached into his trouser pocket and fetched out the two hundred bucks, holding up the little wad so the man could see. To tell you to shove this up your ass.

The man rubbed his stubbly jaw, massaging his red face right up against his eyelids. "Oh, yeah— right." He'd managed to work himself awake. "Hold on a moment, will ya?" He turned and walked back away from the door. Cooper saw now that the man was bare-legged; under the barrel torso, the legs were matted with black hair and surprisingly skinny. They bowed out, as though the weight of the gut and muscles above was too much for the slender bones.

A couple minutes later, the man reappeared, pulling the end of a broad leather belt through the buckle under his gut. He pushed open the screen door, and Cooper had a brief glimpse inside the house. There didn't seem to be anyone else around; a floor lamp had been knocked over on its side, the painted shade askew, next to a stack of half-empty coffeecups and grease-speckled plates. In a nest of newspapers spread out in the middle of the floor, a stalk of bananas lay, bigger than he'd expected from the picture in the schoolhouse dictionary, the overlapping fruit dark green, like the scales of a tropical snake. He was still staring at it when the dockworker let the screen door slam back against the frame.

"Come on." The man clumped down the porch stairs.

Fay drew back against the car to make way for him.

He led Cooper to a shed behind the house. Wooden crates of varying sizes were stacked inside. The dockworker drew a tarp off one pile and motioned Cooper to go around. "Give me a hand with this."

Cooper slipped his fingers under the bottom edge and lifted. The crate was lighter than it looked, but awkward in its bulk. Between the two of them, they carried it out into the sunlight and over to the Ford.

Too big for the car's trunk—they finally managed to wedge it into the rear-seat space, Cooper pulling from inside as the dockworker pushed.

"There ya go." The dockworker slapped the crate with the flat of his hand.

Cooper picked a wood splinter from his own soft palm. A red dot welled up in the tiny wound. He

dug into his trouser pocket and handed over Vandervelde's money.

The dockworker didn't even bother to count it. He
took a flat red tobacco can from his back pocket and
tucked the money inside. "Nice doing business with
ya." He headed back toward the house. "Tell your
boss to have a good time with it."

"What all do you think is in there?" As they drove
away from the house, Fay knelt on the front seat and
looked at the crate.

Cooper glanced over at her rear end under the
heavy black fabric. "Beats me." He dropped the Ford
into first gear and pulled out onto the road. In the
rearview mirror he could just see the top of the
crate, sitting in the middle of the back seat. When
he'd helped carry it out of the dockworker's shed,
he'd smelled something familiar through the wood
slats, something that he couldn't place at the time.
Something sharp, which made the inside of his nose
itch.

"Booze?"

He laughed. "Naw, it's not heavy enough for that.
Besides, you don't think he'd send me all this way
out here for liquor, do you? Got all he wants already." He steered the Ford past the small houses
and the nodding oil pumps.

Fay twisted about, her hands gripping the top of
the seat, looking at the crate from another angle.
"It's got writing painted on it. But I can't make it
out. Some other language, or something." She turned
around and flopped back down beside him. "Wonder what it is."

"Me, I don't care." Cooper downshifted to take a
hill. "The old boy could be buying himself diamonds
and emeralds a pound at a time, and it's no concern
of mine. It's not mine, so I don't sweat it."

Fay stared ahead through the windshield. "Maybe
it is something real valuable." She rubbed her lip as
she mused. "Real, real valuable."

"Yeah, and we should steal it, I suppose, and just

take it somewhere and sell it, and set ourselves up for life." He shook his head. "Forget it. If it's so valuable, why'd Joe Blow back there let it go for two hundred bucks? Come on—it's probably just some old crap they palmed off on him, like that dud radio you told me about." Or that French women's stuff, he could have said, but didn't. French, via Tijuana.

"Yeah, you're right." She sounded bitter in her disappointment. "Forget it."

Cooper leaned over the steering wheel and squinted at the sky. A red tinge had just started to trace over the hills. "We made pretty good time getting out here." He leaned back. "We could probably head on back, if we wanted to. Get there before too late." He looked over at Fay. "That what you want to do?"

"You kiddin'? I don't even want to go back at all." Her voice brightened; she actually bounced on the seat as she turned toward him. "Hey, I know what. Why don't we go someplace and have some fun? Enjoy ourselves. Then we can go back." She laid her hand on his arm. "You were planning on going back tomorrow, anyway. Weren't you?"

Jesus Christ—he kept himself from slamming on the brakes, but only barely. God knows what she meant by fun. He gripped the wheel tighter, his brain revving up again, the way it had back at the edge of Vandervelde's gray orchard. He'd managed to keep himself from thinking all the way out here, at least about things like this. Things like what it might be that she actually wanted, and—in some ways scarier—what he wanted.

It had been a relief to get rid of the two hundred dollars, to pull the wad of the old man's money out of his pocket and hand it over to the dockworker. While he still had it, and Fay knew he had it, he'd been worried that she might make some suggestion about a more suitable disposition of the cash. The scary part being that he didn't know whether he might not just agree and do whatever she said. (Underneath the black dress . . .) All those carefully maintained resolutions going right out the Ford's window, falling into the dusty road behind, along with that useless thing pretending to be his brain. (. . . white skin, pale enough to trace the veins beneath with your fingertip. Fool.) Anything she suggested . . .

He managed to find his voice. "I suppose so." He nodded. "That's what I was figuring on, going back tomorrow."

"Well, and you got some money, don't you? I know you do."

Without turning toward her, he could feel the weight of her gaze upon him. The little bit of cash that he'd been hiding for so long it had almost become a second skin, plastered through his pocket to his thigh—did she know about that? She must've seen Vandervelde give me that extra two bucks, he decided. When she was hanging around some corner, eavesdropping to what he was telling me.

"I got some." He shrugged. "Not much."

"Well, I guess it all depends on what you want to do. Doesn't it?"

What I want to do is just paste you one right in the mouth. Pull over and just spread you all over the seat, this one right here, with the top of your head knocking against the door handle and your skirt in your face—that's what I want to do. His head ached, worn out from having to deal with her. And her little mystery talk, and her eyes staring off past the side of his head, like she was always spotting a truck barreling down the road onto his back, only he was too stupid to have heard it coming.

Of course, if he was going to do that, he should've done it right at the start. He felt like getting out of the car and kicking himself. Right back there at the edge of Vandervelde's place, he should've first given her the fist, then the other. Then booted her can right back to the house. They'd both have been happier for it—maybe Vandervelde, too. Maybe that's what the game had been, if there'd ever been one. Maybe he had the old fart figured all wrong: it was actually *her* tail the old man wanted kicked, and that little extra on top of it just to slap her back into her place, let her know what she really was. That'd be just the sort of thing to please a sick old bastard like Vandervelde; when they got old and wheezy like that, half the time they couldn't get it up, and the only way they could enjoy it anymore was through somebody else doing the dirty work. And if Vandervelde got at least part of his pleasure from rubbing the girl's nose in it, what better way than letting the hired help have a crack at it? Like taking a bucket of beer out to the field on a hot day and passing it around. The workman's worthy of his hire. The old man could probably puff himself up into feeling like some sort of biblical patriarch, the stern Old Testament kind.

Cooper doubted if all that was true, but it was something pleasant to think about. If that had really been what Vandervelde was scheming at, and he himself hadn't been such a clever jerk, always bedeviling his mind with trying to figure out what other people were up to. If I'd just done what I'd wanted, when I wanted to, Christ sake, all that blood would've ebbed back where it came from, and I'd be driving around with some seven bucks cash money in my pocket, smiling like a well-fed dog.

"I suppose so." He had to say something, after spending a couple minutes in his dark, silent thoughts.

"I know someplace where we could go. And have a good time."

Christ only knew what she meant. Anymore, Cooper didn't care. "Sure." The Ford had gotten to the top of the hill; he could take it out of gear and let it coast all the way down to whatever was on the other side. "Why don't we do that?" He glanced over at her and got one of those strange, half-shy smiles in return.

He hadn't ever seen an ocean before. He could have stayed looking at that, leaning over the wooden rail along the edge of the pier, watching the slow waves surge into milky foam around the pilings. It smelled different than what he'd expected; he didn't know what he'd thought it would be like. But if you leaned far enough over the rail, you could see the pier's wet, mossy underside, with creatures living and rotting under there. That was a big part of the smell, along with the ocean's salt. Cooper could imagine eyes, crabs or something, peering back at him from the dangling weedy growths.

The planks of the pier shook with the tramping of a crowd of people. Over their talking and laughter, he heard Fay's voice.

"Whatta ya see down there? Anything interesting?"

She was laughing at him, he supposed, inside herself. At him being such a dirt-farm hick, mesmerized by the big water. When they'd come driving down out of the oilfield hills and he'd spotted it for the first time, with its rolling zinc-colored skin in the distance and flat ruler edge across the horizon, she must've caught something, some widening of his eye, a little tremor against the gas pedal. She'd kept on smiling, a little one, smug and superior, all the rest of the way to the pier. As if she'd been born out here, seen things like this all her life, and wasn't just some windblown ragtag like himself.

He straightened up, pushing himself back from the wooden rail. Farther along the pier, one old geezer with a bamboo pole trolled a line in the deeper water. He ignored the foot traffic brushing past his ass, heading out to the lights and carny noise at the end of the pier. The ocean had turned a smoky red as the sun lowered into it; the man fishing, stub cigarette clamped in his mouth, was a silhouette against the curlicue lettering of the light bulbs in the distance.

Fay took his arm, drawing him toward the tidal flow of the crowd. Once you were in it, there'd be no stopping, you'd be pulled along by the crush of other people's bodies, their shuffling feet sliding up against the heels of your shoes. Cooper felt somebody's breath, a man's, right up against the back of his neck; he could smell exhaled beer, flat and sour, reminding him of Vandervelde and Bonnie, miles away, surrounded by the dead trees growing dark underneath with the same night as here. But Fay's arm was still linked with his, the slight weight tucked in the curve of his elbow. The crowd pressed her up close to his side. That was nice; he didn't mind letting them push him along over the splintery, salt-eaten boards, until he could look up and see the strings of glittering lights overhead.

The crowd thinned out once they were past the narrow neck of the pier and into the wider space beyond. Where the amusements were. Cooper found himself standing there, Fay still holding on to his arm, like one of the pilings when the wave rolls back out to the ocean. The crowd had gone bumping up against the backs of the ones who'd gotten there earlier, shuffling along against the fronts of the gaudy-painted stalls.

He craned his neck, looking around. Up close, right here in the middle of the attraction, the shabbiness showed through. A good third of the bulbs in the strings of lights were burned out or busted, a flower of sharp-edged thin glass around a twist of wire. Dark enough now that you could see where the neon, above the door of some kind of fish-and-clam place, had whole letters gone dead, so you had to work at it to figure out what it said: the name of the owner, or whoever had bought out the owner and now was barely making it himself, with no money left over for fixing up the sign. Cooper could hear the neon sizzling, like flies caught in a bottle, with little sparks of electricity snapping blue where the wires went into a little box on the diner's roof. There were maybe all of two people inside, eating and feeding little bits to the child between them, while the counterman watched them, leaning back against the menu painted on the wall behind the cash register, with its crabs and mermaids dancing in seaweed garlands.

A man and a woman bumped into him; for a moment, Cooper thought the woman was laughing, maybe drunk. The man turned a sullen, angry face toward him, his eyes just begging Cooper to say something so he could drop the woman he was half-carrying, half-shoving along on her wobbly legs, and let fly. The woman's face was wet, with a bright-red dribble at the corner of her mouth. She kept making that sound in her throat. Cooper watched them push through the crowd, heading off the pier.

"It used to be better. Than it is now." Fay had looked up at Cooper and guessed that he was disappointed somehow.

He shrugged. "It's all right." He wondered why she'd had him bring her here. Hard to figure out why any of these people were here. None of them seemed to be having a particularly good time, except for some of the youngest kids, darting between people's legs and running to gawk at a palm reader's booth or a bottle big as one of them, with something skinned pink and glass-eyed floating in a cloudy liquid. The barker wouldn't even waste his spiel on small fry like that; he knew they didn't have any more money than their parents shuffling somewhere along behind.

That was the problem: nobody here had any money. The kind of people who had money—there was always that kind, somewhere—that kind wouldn't ever come to a place like this. You had to go search 'em out if you wanted to get your hand in their pockets. Even Cooper knew that. Which put him one up on the lean-faced carny types leaning on the sills of their stalls, watching with their glittering gypsy eyes as the marks shuffled by or stood long enough to gape at the shelves of dolls and cheap ornamented crockery. Long enough to see the prizes, but not long enough to lay down a dime and pick up the little toy rifle on the sill and plink away at the tattered card ducks and tin bull's-eyes, or scoop up the pyramid of four baseballs and chuck them at the stacked lead milk bottles. When that dime had only a couple of brothers nestling in the lint in your pocket, you weren't going to risk it on the off chance that the toy gun and its sight didn't look in two different directions, or that the milk bottles didn't have a poker that came up from the bottom so that you couldn't have knocked them over with a two-by-four. Or if you did, if the carny took pity on you and stood on the treadle that drew the poker down, that the prize he'd hand over to you wouldn't be worth however many dimes it'd cost you to win it. When the dish with the pier painted on it was actually there glittering in your hands, it was just to let you know how much of a fool you actually were.

The marks didn't need to have their palms read, or the bumps on their thick skulls felt, to know what their future was. To go on shuffling under the strings of lights, past the buzzing neon and the bright fairground paint, fading from the salt air, shuffling past the unsmiling eyes, keeping their hands in the pockets, turning the dimes and nickels over with the tips of their fingers.

Even the kids ran out of steam, eventually. Just in the time he'd been standing there, Cooper saw a few of the youngsters who had come boiling up the pier like soda from a shook bottle, screaming and yelling in their excitement, now already exhausted, their high spirits dampened by the grownups' silence or the infrequent bursts of harder, more desperate laughter. The kind, coming somewhere out of the crowd, that was laughing at anything, a man determined in his dark silly heart to have a good time no matter what it cost him. The carnies could take care of that for him; they knew how, in the shadows behind the stalls. The scared children clung to their parents, being pulled along with them through the crowd.

"Come on." Fay tugged at his arm. Whatever guilt she'd felt at having made him come here had been sluiced away in the boredom of watching him just stand there and look around.

He let her lead him, pushing back into the thick of the crowd. Going farther out along the pier, he could see, through the gaps between the stalls, the ocean with its ragged smears of breaking waves reaching away, faintly luminous where only the moonlight touched them. Fay was up to something, he could tell: her firm grip on his arm, the way she dug between one person's back and the next, making their path open up before them . . . She had something cooking in her little brain. He wished they could have gone down to the beach instead. Wasn't that where people were supposed to go? When there was just two of them, and no money, or not much at any rate, and no place else to go. Away from the pier's lights, where anybody could look over the rail and see what all you were up to . . . what they wished they were doing.

There were probably people down there right now. Cooper looked as he shuffled along behind Fay, but didn't see anything except the waves lapping up on the sand. He knew there was an old wool blanket, stained with engine grease, back in the Ford; they could go back and get that and take it down to the beach, where those other, unseen people were. To just wrap it around themselves against the chill air while he held Fay in his arms . . . By this point, that was all he wanted anymore. Must be tired; he rubbed his brow with his free hand. Whatever he'd wanted when he'd started out, when he'd let her come along with him, that was almost forgotten. He would've liked to have listened to the waves coming in, one after another. Without ever having heard them, he knew what they would sound like.

They passed a carousel, unlit and motionless, the gate in the circling fence chained and locked. A couple of kids, fingers looped in the fence links, gazed at the horses, the rearing, teeth-bared heads and prancing hooves frozen in midstride, leaping as high as the brass poles impaled through the wooden spines would allow. Nobody had bothered to sweep up the ticket stubs from whenever the machinery had last wheezed into motion; the tattered bits sifted into the shadows under the platform. The parents didn't pull the kids away, but let them look as long as they wanted to.

The crowd had thinned out at the far end of the pier. Only about one light in five still burned in the overhead strings. The stalls here were closed down tight, some as permanently as could be done with planks nailed across the fronts. Cooper figured that as the pier had started to die, starving from the lack of the bright dimes rolling across the counters, whenever one stall had closed up, down by the brighter lights at the pier's entrance, one of these operations had shuffled into its place, the way crabs he'd read of would swap one shell for another one. If not a bigger one, then one hopefully more advantageous, where you might have a sooner crack at the marks shuffling past. Get their dimes, if they were going to part with any at all, before some other gaff did. Out at this end, you got only some kids, still excited at something they'd never seen before, running right up and climbing one step onto the railing so they could lean over on their stomachs and look at the water below. And a few couples, getting away from the crowd, a stroll to work up the mood for going down to the beach. The men looked annoyed at the kids' shouting and laughter.

"You know your way around here." He made it a statement, not a question.

"Yeah." Fay pulled him by the arm. "Vandervelde brought me here when we were out this way before."

It figured—the old man's idea of a wingding time. Probably broke his heart to find out that the carousel wasn't running. "Where we going?"

"Over here. There's something I want to show you."

She was practically running, holding his hand now

that there weren't all the ranks of people's backs to plow through. Fay stopped suddenly, a little out of breath; he could feel the flutter of her pulse as she pressed next to him.

"There." She pointed.

Cooper looked along her extended arm, past the point of her finger sticking out. On the side of the pier, flush into the farthest corner, a building blotted out a section of the night sky. Long and low, like an airplane hangar, with a corrugated-iron roof; the sides were built up of the usual wooden planks, like everything else on the pier. No windows. Something was painted on the side, but his eyes hadn't adjusted enough yet to the darkness to make out what it was.

"Oh." Now he saw. "It's a ride. One of those scary ones." Painted on the side of the building, in big red letters, was HOUSE OF FRIGHTS. A skeleton leaned over the top curve of the last *S*, grinning at him.

Something this big couldn't migrate down along the pier to where the people and the lights were; it was fixed in place. The back of the building actually jutted off over the end of the pier. He could see the moon broken and shining off the ocean, through the angled timbers that joined up farther down on the pilings. Around in front, a man sat on a stool reading a paper, bald, with a chewed-up stogie clamped in his mouth. A gaggle of kids was trying to peer around him, to see into the House of Frights' dark insides. The man paid them no mind, calmly folding the paper open to another page. The kids kept their distance, as though the House's guardian was possessed of the same malevolence, or so they wanted to believe, clutching one another to keep their courage up.

"You're not afraid, are you?" Fay looked up into his face.

"Oh, sure. Gotta watch out for this bad ticker of mine. One good scare and it'll just go pop like a paper bag." He tried to make his voice fit the joke, but he felt more sad than anything else. This is what she dragged me out here to see? Shit. The painted skeleton regarded him with its flat black eyes, and laughed. Nothing but some old shed, stuffed with papier-mâché on wires, an india rubber bat thrown right into your face to give you a thrill—probably had been as scary as some old toothless granny, back when they'd just built it. Now that the ocean salt had been working away at it—smart idea, that, building the thing right where you could feel the spray from the waves coming up from between the planks—along with just the decay of time that always ate up cheap things first . . .

"There's a dead body in there." She whispered it, important.

"They'd like you to think so." His heart fell inside him, grown that heavy. You fool, the skeleton told him.

He heard a rattle of machinery, gears and chains whining through a coat of rust. A little cart with a seat in it, like a section of a kiddie train, emerged from inside the building, pushing its way through an overhead tangle of some nasty, mosslike stuff. And a couple riding in the cart, the young man's knees up high, he was so cramped in the tiny space, his bony red hands clasping them through the thin fabric of his trousers. Beside him, the girl, with no shame— anybody could tell—tucked the loosened strands of her hair back into place, regarding herself in a little round mirror that clicked shut like a clam when she was done.

The fellow knew he was a fool, too. Just the way he ducked his head down, as if he were trying to disappear, even while he was helping his girlfriend out of the little cart. Her skirt brushed over another skull face painted on the front, with jagged bat wings coming up from under its white chin. A fool, spending his dime for a quick bit, maybe a hand slipped under and up, that'd be about all you'd have time for—couldn't take that long for the little cart to clank around its track inside the building. All you

got, and in the meantime there're others within spitting distance, if you grabbed the rail and leaned far
enough over, who were getting a lot more. Even if
they were just lying there, listening to the waves
rolling in. You—you got a rubber bat. Fool.

The fellow glanced over at him, one fool looking
at another, as the girl pushed through the little knot
of children. Her boyfriend caught up and they headed
together for the bustle of the crowd.

"No . . ." Fay squeezed his arm, pulling his attention back to her. "There *is*."

"Is what?"

"A dead body. In there." She didn't point this
time, but just nodded toward the low building.

Cooper sighed. "Who told you something like that?
And why'd you believe 'em?"

She went stiff; he'd offended her. "I knew it before anybody told me anything. I can tell. That's all."

That again. More of her spooky business. No wonder she went skipping along to places like this, stuck
out on the end of some falling-apart pier: she was
stuck on the subject. Cooper shrugged. "Yeah, well,
if you say so." He started to turn, to pull her around
and head back to where the other people were. "I'm
willing to take your word for it."

She dug in her heels, anchoring him. "Come on."
Her child's voice, with something else underneath,
like one untuned violin string. "I want to go in. For
the ride."

He felt tired. The whole thing, from the word go,
had been a bad idea. Soon as they'd rolled off of
Vandervelde's property . . . If there'd been one chance
in hell of having a good time, that old bastard would've
known somehow and just squashed him like a bug,
right there on the spot.

"He wouldn't take me." She said it with all the
force of some final, crushing argument. "When we
were here before. Said he didn't want to ride around
in no little box on wheels. You know what? I think he
was scared."

There you have it. The sort of thing a child who thought she was clever would say, to get you to do what she wants. He supposed she expected him to bluster right on up to the man sitting on the stool, reading his newspaper, pay the dime, and prove his fearlessness. You stupid little twat. Now he'd started to feel disgusted. Should just walk away, leave her standing there.

Then again, if this was all she wanted, to go clanking around on the little track winding through the House of Frights' interior . . . Jesus Christ, let her, go on and take her on the damn ride, get it out of her system. Maybe. Worth a shot, at any rate. Then they might be able to get down to something more worthwhile, even if no more than crawling back into the Ford they'd left in the dirt lot close by the pier's entrance, and just going to sleep. This whole deal had tired him out. She could curl up in the back seat and him in the front, and that'd be fine by him.

Turned out to be two bits, not a dime. "For each." The man sitting on the stool lowered his paper and stuck out the flat palm of his hand, waiting. Only when Cooper had peeled out one of the precious dollar bills from in his pocket, and gotten his rattling change in return, did the man get up and head over to the long, rust-specked levers that controlled the ride.

"Get in." He pointed to the little cart that the other couple had gotten out of.

Squeezed onto the cart's little bench—it had been painted black like the outside, but the passage of folks' hind parts had worn through to the wood beneath—with his own can pressed next to Fay's, Cooper looked over the side and saw the chain rattling in the groove below them. Some small donkey engine clattered in a shed next to the larger building. The man threw the lever over and the cart jerked into motion. Cooper raised his hand to fend off the dirty wisps of stuff around the ride's mouth; some kind of door, triggered by the cart, closed behind them, and they were in the darkness inside.

A screeching sound, metal against metal—he didn't know if that was intended as scary, or just part of the ride's machinery slowly falling apart.

He felt Fay lean close against his arm, reaching up to cup her hand around his ear, whispering. "He told me about it. About the dead body in here. He knows about stuff like that. How it got here, and stuff."

Something that was supposed to look like a spider— Cooper guessed—came dangling down in front of them, jerking around on a rubber line like a yo-yo. Only the thing had about half its skinny, wobbly legs missing, and wool stuffing oozed out of a rip in its side. Kids had probably done that, or just people batting it away from their faces. The light that had fallen on the spider disappeared behind a creaking shutter.

Fay went on talking in his ear. "See, what he told me—I asked him—he told me that there'd been this sideshow fella, with one of them traveling carnivals, and he'd bought this dead body. 'Cause it'd been a murderer who'd been hung. And they just let him buy the body for his sideshow. They'd do that back then. And the carnival fella took it to one of those taxidermists, who did it all up for him." She had to stop and catch her breath, she had been rattling on so fast. "And then he went around with the carnival, charging people a penny a look at this famous murderer. Until he got too old, or something happened and he didn't want to travel around anymore. So he sold it to these people here. And that's how it got in here."

He nodded, unseen in the dark. It sounded like something Vandervelde would know about, anything to do with buying and selling. Probably enough to have made him think for a while about the commercial possibilities in retailing corpses, see what the market was for that sort of thing. Add to the piles mounting up inside the safe in his office. Not that the story was true; some clever bastard had more than likely got it started, just to bring people with a taste for that sort of thing into the attraction. Like Fay here beside him. Just went to show that something like that actually worked, at least part of the time.

The little cart clanked on, pulled by the chain underneath. Cooper could feel the grinding machinery right up in his tailbone, through the wooden seat. A devil, made out of a department-store dummy painted red, with a farmer's pitchfork wired to its hand, swiveled out of its niche and gazed blankly at them. Cooper wondered how much farther they had to go.

"There—" Fay grabbed his arm and squeezed, hard enough to hurt. "That's the one."

For a moment he turned his head and looked at her, a black shape against the ride's general gloom. His heart felt even heavier, weighted with sadness for both of them.

"Look . . ." Her whisper became tighter, excited. "I told you—"

He looked around from her toward a lit-up section ahead. Something had rated a place of honor in the ride: it was bathed in electric light from either side. The scraping metal scream sounded here, too.

They slid through more of the phony-moss stuff that had obscured his view. Now he saw it standing there, waiting for him, with its hand upraised, its eyes gazing straight into his.

He almost burst out laughing.

That wouldn't have been a good idea, he knew. He bit his lip and managed to hold it inside. Beside him, Fay leaned forward, gripping the front edge of the cart, looking hard at the thing.

It looked like another store dummy, but not even as good as that. Dressed up in shabby trousers—with what were supposed to be bloodstains, Cooper figured —and an old plaid shirt, the figure had a little wooden gun wired to its raised hand, the fingers fanned out straight, not even curling around the toy's grip. A rope with a hangman's noose knotted in it dragged from the thing's other hand; whether that was some souvenir from its own rumored demise, or something that it was looking to use on someone else, Cooper couldn't guess.

They clanked under its flat glare. The face looked shiny like wax, with round blue marbles stuck in for eyes, the whites painted in around them. The biggest fool of them all, whether there was anybody inside there or not; Cooper got a charge out of it, almost worth the two times two bits it'd cost him to see it. *This poor bastard doesn't even know he's dead. He'll be waving his toy pistol around inside here for a long time to come.*

The chain pulled the cart past the dummy. Cooper settled back, still laughing inside. At some point in the ride, the track had made a *U*, and they were heading toward the front of the building again; Cooper could see the exit up ahead, and beyond it, the man sitting on a stool, still reading his paper.

He turned to look beside him, and the smile slid off his face. Nothing to laugh at. Fay had twisted all the way around on the wooden seat. Gripping the rear edge of the cart, she stared back behind them, into the darkness.

He looked. The dummy could just be seen, falling away, as though back down a hole as they rolled away from it. Farther and farther away, with its glass eyes staring at nothing.

Fay went on gazing back at the thing, long after it couldn't even be seen. Cooper sat with his hands on his knees, just waiting to emerge into the night outside.

9

"This is the stupidest thing I've ever done in my life." He said it just loud enough for her to hear. They'd been speaking in whispers, looking out for whatever watchman might be prowling around on the pier after midnight.

Fay ignored him. Crouched down, she peered through the fence that had been dragged across the neck of the pier, cutting off the amusement stalls on the other side. Dark enough at this hour, with every electric light switched off, that the black dress fell right into the night, became a part of it; he could just see the back of her neck and her pale hands holding on to the fence's twisted wires.

Cooper rubbed his own stiff, creaking knees. How he'd let himself be talked into something like this . . . When what he should do, if he had any smarts at all, would be to just stand up, turn around, and walk right back off the pier. But he didn't.

"I don't see anybody around." Her whisper. She had advanced the opinion before, when she'd told him what she wanted to do, that she didn't think they kept a night guard on the pier. What was there to steal? Pawning an armful of cheap stuffed animals wouldn't make enough to buy a cup of coffee. And if some tramp was stupid enough to bunk down out here, where the ocean wind sliced right through the planks, and built himself a little fire and wound up burning the whole place down, charred timbers falling with a hiss of steam into the water below—if that happened, most of the folks who were left to work the stalls would likely breathe a sigh of relief. Just to have finally been moved off this dead spot, one way or another. Take their gaff out on the road, where the pickings might be better.

Nobody had bothered to do anything with the fence, other than pull it into place after the last of the crowds had shuffled away, their eyes as hungry when they left as when they'd come here. Nothing too sturdy to begin with, either, just a mesh roll nailed to splintery boards; with what rust and general neglect had done since, a child could peel an opening big enough to skin through. As Cooper watched, Fay tugged on the fence and a triangle section lifted up from one corner. She scooted through on her knees and looked back at him from the other side. "Come on." She held it open with one hand for him.

Gone this far; might as well go the rest. Cooper grabbed hold of the fence section and pulled it farther open; a rusted nail groaned and popped free from the board. He picked up a splinter through the cloth of his trousers as he crawled through.

Without the gawking, butt-to-belly crowd, he could hear the waves lapping at the pilings below. The pier creaked, the way he'd read of big sailing ships doing, way out on the ocean; he could feel the tiny shift and motion in his feet.

He followed along behind Fay, the dark braid of her hair glinting with blue stars. Going past the shuttered stalls, they heard somebody snoring inside one: some pitchpenny barker, Cooper figured, who'd spent the night's takings on a bottle and had crawled into a nest of button-eyed teddy bears to sleep it off. The rasping gurgle fell behind them as Fay, with no apparent worry about being spotted, headed toward the end of the pier.

The man who'd been sitting on the stool was gone. The House of Frights was just a long black building now, without even the planks it stood on vibrating from the donkey engine clattering away in the little shed. You could just make out the smiling death painted on the side, leaning over the big letter *S* and watching whatever happened in the dark hours.

Maybe the ride operator was sleeping inside; there was room enough to have fixed up a nice little place, with even a stove to keep warm with and fix his meals on. The thought of it brought a smile to Cooper: bunking down in the spookhouse. Least you'd have somebody to talk to. Whenever you wanted. And they'd probably come up with better ideas than this.

He pressed his ear against a crack in the barnlike door, which had been swung over the ride's entrance. He held his breath and heard nothing.

Stepping back, he ran his hand over the rough boards until he found the metal hasp at its center. He tugged at the padlock dangling there, then turned around to Fay.

"It's locked." He shrugged, even though he knew she couldn't see him against the building. There; that's it: the way he spoke said that much, all that needed to be said. They might as well turn around and walk off the pier, slide through the gap in the fence, and head back to where they'd left Vandervelde's Ford. Enough of this jokey prowling around. Kid stuff.

She had an answer for him, in the shape of a crowbar. Cooper felt its rough, rust-specked surface as Fay laid it in his hands.

"Where the hell'd you get this?"

In the dark, her silhouette nodded toward the engine shed. "It was lying on the floor in there. That'll do it, won't it?"

He hefted the solid weight, balancing it in his palms. "Don't know. Should, I guess."

Now they weren't just prowling around; this was

breaking in. Fool. He levered the crowbar between the hasp and the door, pulled, and heard a sharp crackle of splintering wood. The hasp dangled free, the padlock swinging back and forth.

The noise had shouted through the night, louder than he'd expected. For a moment he held his breath, hearing only the roll of the ocean against the pilings. Then he bent down and carefully laid the crowbar at his feet. "There you go." Whispered, when he wanted to shout that, too.

The door gaped open. Fay leaned inside to look, then turned back toward him. "Come on." She squeezed partway through the opening and beckoned.

Even stupider—he'd entertained the notion of staying outside, keeping an eye out while she took care of whatever business her cracked brain had fastened on to. Not to warn her, but to hightail it away from there himself, if anybody—a cop or the ride's operator—had come snooping along. Let her ass get caught in the wringer; that'd solve a lot of problems, right there.

A lot of problems . . . If she just walked into the House of Frights—where she belonged anyway, in there in the dark—he could just turn and go, even if nobody was coming, just get out of there . . .

He took her hand and let her pull him inside, unresisting.

Couldn't see a thing inside, except a thin slice of moonlight falling through a crack in the roof. Cooper took a box of matches from his pocket and lit one. The sputtering flame was enough to make out the track in the floor, running farther into the building's depths. He dropped the match when it singed his fingertips, and the dark flooded back over them.

Fay pulled at his arm. "This way."

She moved fast, tugging him along behind her but without colliding with anything. Like going through a forest at night, it struck him, behind a dog following a trail, a sharper sense where you were blind. He reached out with his arm beside him, searching for the wall, and found nothing but empty air.

When she stopped suddenly, his chest bumped into her shoulder. "What's wrong?"

She didn't say anything, but just pressed her hand against his shirtfront. He could smell her faintly against the salt odor and musty, rotting wood planks. He fumbled with the box of matches from his pocket, stepping back from Fay in order to scratch one alight.

The match flared, sending wobbling shadows onto the walls. Fay's eyes, startled, snapped toward him. Then she turned, slowly, back toward the other thing in the narrow space.

In the dark she'd managed to locate the dummy, the one she claimed had once been alive. She must've kept track, Cooper figured, somehow, when they'd been rolling in that stupid little cart. Of just how far along into the building the thing was. Or else she did smell it, like a dog, a bloodhound tracking down what it wants. People got like that, he'd heard, when they were fixated on just one thing. One-track minds, stuff like that.

He pinched the end of the match with his nails, letting it burn long enough to watch Fay step over to the dummy. Its glass-eyed gaze stared straight on, over her head. The wavering light played over the wax face; it stayed dead, or never-alive, not even the illusion of a smile in the shadow of its mouth. Behind it, the knotted rope in its hand cast a dark loop in the corner of the wall.

The thing stood on a box pedestal. Fay was just reaching up to touch its face when the match singed Cooper's fingertips. The flame was out before it hit the floor.

Cooper lit the next match.

The dummy's hand, dangling its knotted rope, rose upward with the same metal creaking. Fay stood so close to the thing, looking up into its idiot blank face, that the hand could have been slowly coming up behind her back, like they were dancers in a waltz. When the music started, the dummy, whatever was inside it, could just step off the little box, and the two of them would twirl away, where the shadows merged together and became the dark again . . .

That's crazy. The flame, burning down to his fingertips, brought him back. Don't think shit like that . . .

The match stung him and he threw it away. It landed, still burning, on a scrap of paper on the dusty floor, a torn-off bit from a candy-bar wrapper or something like that. For a moment the flame leapt up brighter, the little bright tongue snaking up an inch, then dying back down to red-tinged ash. Cooper watched it go, not wanting to raise his eyes. Then there was another sound, a different, quieter one, and he couldn't help himself. He looked up at the dummy's face.

Fay had reached up to touch it. Her hand stroked the waxen cheek, the glass eyes staring over her head, the thing's shadow dancing on the wall behind it and growing bigger, merging with the dark all around as the scrap of paper burned down. Cooper watched the slow caress of her hand. In the shadow under her fingers, it looked as if the dummy's jaw was melting, lengthening . . .

Then he heard the sound again; a small, muffled scraping, as if away at the front of the House of Frights, someone was pulling out the rusted nails from the boards, the way he'd done when he'd busted open the lock.

Then the dummy's mouth opened, and the sound came louder, out of the hole filled with blackness, a crack in the stiff pink cheek running right under Fay's hand. As the thing's head tilted on the neck, the glass eyes pinning Cooper hard in their idiot gaze, she looked around at him, over her shoulder. Her face was wet with a child's frightened tears, yet she couldn't pull her hand away, even as a chunk of wax fell away, catching for a moment in the lace at her wrist, then to the floor. Where it had broken away, there was something dirty white underneath. It was moving, underneath the pink wax, opening the black mouth wider . . .

The tiny flame burned out.

He knew it had, even though he had his eyes closed tight; he could feel the dark wash back over his skin. The scraping noise stopped; he was glad for that, too. She hit something, standing over there by it. That was all it was, he told himself. Some kinda trigger, the springs and shit they got all rigged up for the ride. So when you go by, it twitches around and goes boo at ya. That's all. Maybe it hadn't worked in a long while, and got all froze up. Then she had hit the spot that made the thing work, and it had cracked and lurched and started coming to pieces. That's all. That's all, that's all . . .

His eyes flew open when he felt her take his hand. In absolute dark, he hadn't heard her come up close. But now he could feel her, the warmth next to him.

"It was so cold in there." She didn't say *in here*. Her voice trembled, still scared.

Her face was damp when he touched it. "Don't talk about it. Okay? Come on, let's get out of here."

She wouldn't move. "And . . . it was dark. Real dark." Under the fear, her voice had an edge of wonderment. "Darker than I've ever seen. I've never seen it like that." She clutched his arm, her fingers digging tight toward the bone. "They did things to it . . . to make it like that. So it wasn't just dead. Some of it was just dead, and some of it—what they did to it—it was like some of it hadn't ever been alive." A shiver, as she pressed herself into the angle of his arm and chest. "They made it deader than that."

"Shh. It's all right." Cooper squeezed her around the shoulder. The dark and the silence wrapped around them; outside the building, he could hear the slow roll of waves surging around the pier. "Come on."

He couldn't even see her, but felt her shake her head. "No . . ." The fright broke in her voice, crying out. "It's too dark." Her hands reached up to his face, pulling him down to hers. "I don't want to be in there anymore."

Then he tasted the salt on her face, in the corner of her mouth. She fell, and he held her, falling with her.

He made a pillow of the black dress, bunching it up and laying his head back down upon it. The moon had risen farther in the night sky, finding a narrow angle between the planks: just enough to see her cradled in his arm, one hand spread out on his chest, her head so close beneath his that he could turn his chin away and smell her hair. On the House of Frights' dusty floor, a bottle cap dug into the back of his thigh; he didn't care, for now.

She opened her eyes and looked up at him. Not smiling, but no longer scared, either. The dark had gone away, for a little while.

Even the dummy, the creaking thing of wire and wax and, maybe, bone inside . . . It and all the other dead things, the never-alive, they watched from their places along the walls, frozen in place, silent.

She raised her head, bringing her mouth up to his ear. And said something, a whisper, her lips brushing the little curved ridges inside, so that only he could hear.

She said it, and he knew he would remember it all his life. Even when he was an old man, he'd remember. *This is what they call haunted*—Cooper gazed up at the boards of the ceiling. Her cheek nestled against his collarbone. She'd done that, just by saying something.

Underneath them, the pier trembled as the tide drew at the pilings. They'd have to get out of there pretty soon, he knew, before the morning light came and someone found them. But not just yet. It wasn't time yet. He stroked her hair and let the soft words go on saying themselves, over and over.

10

When they got back, right at the edge of Vandervelde's property, she told him what her plan was. Cooper couldn't believe he'd heard her right.

He'd pulled off the county highway and onto the dirt lane running through the trees. He let the Ford's engine go on ticking over as they sat there, the shade from the tangled gray branches falling across the windshield. Leaning his arms on top of the steering wheel, Cooper looked over at her. "That your idea of a joke or something?"

Fay gazed straight back at him. "No. I've done it before."

"Jee-zuss." He shook his head. He'd figured Vandervelde was a stupid sonuvabitch, but he didn't figure on the old man being *that* stupid.

What Fay had proposed, as their way of fooling Vandervelde into thinking that they hadn't been tearing around all the day and night before, together in his car, spending his money—her idea was for her to get out now and let Cooper go driving on up to the house by himself, with the big wooden crate that he'd been sent to fetch in the back seat. Just as if that was all he'd done, gone out to the dockworkers' place and picked it up and brought it back, like a good dog with the stick in its mouth. While Fay went circling around the edges of the orchard where nobody could see her, taking her time; then a little while later, she could just come waltzing up to the house from a completely different direction. Just as if there were no connection at all between them, just sheer coincidence that she'd disappeared at the same time Cooper had been flying over the roads.

No way is he going to buy that. Cooper drew in his breath between his front teeth. "I don't know . . ."

"Well, I do." His doubting had made her angry. "I've run out on him before. Lots of times. He doesn't give a damn, long as I come back in a day or two. He knows I won't go very far away—there isn't anyplace for me to go *to*. Hell, for all he cares, he might not even realize I've been gone."

Cooper doubted that, too. That old grasping bastard?—he could barely stand to see somebody else eat a biscuit in front of him, with his mouth already stuffed full of them. Maybe he hadn't cared much about this little skinny house pet spending a couple of nights sleeping out in some nest of dry twigs and leaves, while her belly got empty enough to bring her crawling back to the house, back before there'd been any other man on the property other than his son Bonnie. But now that there was one— sure, he's going to think nothing was going on. Cooper couldn't stop one corner of his mouth lifting into something like a smile. Sure, he's going to believe that.

He watched her get out of the car, stepping down from the running board onto the dusty track. There was no point in arguing with her any further; even if her mind hadn't been made up, he couldn't have suggested anything else. Which was, he knew, the problem with thinking from inside your pants and not with what God gave you upstairs. You only thought so far, and no farther. Then that little bit of gristle that called all the shots went back to sleep, and you had to face the consequences. The only comfort being that you weren't the only fool in the territory.

Fay stepped back from the Ford and shaded her eyes with her hand to look back at him. "I'll be a little while. Like a couple hours or so—that'll do for him." A conspirator's smile. "He's so dumb; I promise you."

"Yeah, sure." Cooper dropped the car back into gear. "If you say so." He'd gotten back to that place where he didn't care what happened. If goddamn Vandervelde ripped his whole head off . . . Least I got something off the old bastard. Least I got that. He let out the clutch, the wheels rolling over a tangle of crackling twigs.

He looked up at the mirror, just as Fay stepped off the side of the lane and disappeared among the trees. For a moment the black dress was there, darker than the surrounding shade; then he couldn't see it at all.

No point in arguing. You could tell when there wasn't. The steering wheel bounced in his hands, working through the lane's ruts. No point—he hadn't even bothered asking the question that had been in his mind all the way back: why are you going back at all? He knew why he was; underneath every other thing that went through his mind, there was the trustee's warning, delivered right back there at the turnoff from the county highway when he'd first seen the trees and everything else that belonged to Vandervelde. Himself included, as of that time. If he went to the end of that invisible leash and came trotting back without even tugging at it, that was because he was at least smart enough to know the way things were. But how were they for Fay? Shit, times weren't *that* tough—there's always some place else for a woman to go, one way or another. And anyplace else, she'd be free of Vandervelde's slobbering attentions. Even jail, a woman's lockup . . . Cooper had considered that notion before, that she'd come out here on more or less the same deal he had.

But they didn't put women out on a road gang or down at some backbreaking farm, not even in this hard-faced territory. There was always some easy pull handed out to women. He had a fuzzy picture in his head of a bunch of them sitting around a long wooden table, stitching away at flags for schoolyards. Christ, *I* could do that. Especially if the alternative was having that old goat on my ass all the time.

So that couldn't be it. Besides—the Ford bounced across a deeper rut, jolting his brain to the top of his skull—he couldn't imagine what a little thing like her could have done to get locked up in the first place.

A puzzle. He'd have to think about it some more. Or maybe he wouldn't; he'd already gotten enough of what he wanted from her. He pushed the accelerator down flat, enjoying the rough travel and the dust cloud boiling up behind.

For a moment, when he brought the Ford around to the front of the house, it seemed as if Fay's little plan was working. Vandervelde stood with his legs braced apart on the gravel, as if he'd been waiting there, a couple of strides from the porch steps, since sunup, watching for him. When Cooper lowered himself out of the car, all Vandervelde growled was, "Took you long enough."

"Got a late start this morning." Cooper slapped the lane's dust from his sleeves. "I was worn out from all that driving." From the corner of his eye, he saw Bonnie, oil-smeared crescent wrench in hand, come sauntering out of one of the sheds behind the house. "But I got it here for you." He pulled open the car's door and whacked the flat of his palm on the crate's rough wood. "Here you go."

Vandervelde stepped over and peered in at the crate, nodding, satisfied, as if a big wooden box with indecipherable lettering stenciled on it were all he'd ever wanted in this life. "Get it out of there." He stepped back and nodded at Bonnie, who'd come up behind him. "Give him a hand."

They managed to wrestle it off the Ford's seat.

One splintery corner eluded Cooper's grasp; the crate dropped heavily onto the gravel drive. "For Christ's sake," sputtered Vandervelde, "be careful with it, will ya?"

Bonnie trotted off to the shed and came back with a pry bar. Salt-rusted nails screeched the same as had the ones holding the lock hasp back at the House of Frights, as Bonnie worked his way around the crate. When the last side came loose, he pushed the lid off onto the ground. He and his father leaned over the crate, the old man's stub-fingered hands rooting through the contents.

Cooper, standing back, could see past them to the little pasteboard cartons stacked inside. Water had leaked into the crate during its long transit from wherever it'd come; the blue ink on the cartons had smeared and run, and a damp, mildewy odor seeped out. Vandervelde picked up one of the cartons and tore it open; for a second, Cooper wondered if he was going to gobble up whatever was inside, as he held it up to his face and breathed in the musty smell.

"Go get my gun." Vandervelde had taken a couple of thick, squat cylinders out of the carton and rolled them around in his palm. "It's up on the porch."

Bonnie came back with a double-barreled shotgun. It looked old, a farmer's piece, not a sportsman's. Rust spots speckled the dark metal. Vandervelde took the gun, broke it open, and slid in the two shells. He aimed up in the air, over the tops of the orange trees.

The first shell was a dud, getting a muttered *Damn* from Vandervelde. The second went off with a satisfactory roar; a flock of pigeons scattered out of the branches as Vandervelde lowered the shotgun.

The gun's noise went on bouncing around inside Cooper's skull. He watched as Bonnie knelt down beside the opened crate, one hand plowing through the pasteboard cartons. "Wonder how many of these are no good." He peeled open a particularly warped-looking box and sniffed doubtfully at the contents.

"Who the hell cares." Vandervelde broke the gun open again and dug out the shells, one whole, the other nothing but the spent casing. "Still got a good deal on 'em." Cradling the gun in the crook of his arm, he dug out another couple of shells from the box in his hand.

So that was what he'd hauled all the way back here. The gunpowder smell drifted across Cooper's nostrils. God forbid they could've told him beforehand what it was. He tilted his head toward the crate. "Where'd all that come from?"

Vandervelde shrugged. "Dunno. I forget what those fellows told me. Poland, or some place like that." He said *Po-land* like some ignorant country rube. "Unclaimed freight." He said that with a wink. "Could be from just about anywhere."

"What, you do a lot of hunting around here?"

"Some." Vandervelde clicked the loaded gun shut and lifted it, the barrels aimed straight at Cooper's chest.

Bonnie laughed, like a dog barking. "Jeez, you really got him sweatin'."

The broad face was smiling behind the gun's two deep holes. Cooper could see Vandervelde squinting down, taking aim. The old bastard knew, or suspected, which would be the exact same thing for him. Cooper's mouth went dry, as if the sweat trickling over his ribs had been drained from there. This was the price for taking a piece of anything off the old man—and only a true, complete fool would have come strolling back here to pay up.

He wondered if he should just flop down on his knees now and start begging; maybe that was what Vandervelde, with his thick-knuckled finger around the shotgun's trigger, was waiting for. Just for him to hit the dirt, one way or another. But he couldn't move; he could just stare at the two black holes . . .

Vandervelde's smile got bigger. He swung the gun

away and pulled the trigger; the noise made Cooper's gut roll up toward his throat. One of the pigeons, which had headed back to its roost in the trees, fluttered in mute panic as the branches and leaves below it jumped from the shot.

"I wouldn't shoot you, son." Vandervelde lowered the gun, still smiling at Cooper. "Hell, you still got lots of work to do around here."

Kneeling beside the crate, Bonnie smirked and nodded in agreement.

Son of a *bitch*. Cooper pulled in a long breath. They were all just goddamn nuts. He shouldn't have come back; he should've just hit the road, taken his chances out there. At least out there, you did get a chance.

He could see past Vandervelde, toward the rear of the house. He spotted Fay, looking around from the corner of one of the sheds. Maybe all the firing of the shotgun had brought her around sooner than she'd originally planned. Cooper could believe that she'd wanted to see who might still be alive. She glanced toward him, then quickly crossed through the weed-choked garden and up the back steps to the kitchen door.

Vandervelde heard the squeak of the door's hinges. He turned his head toward the noise, then back to Cooper. Still smiling. "Naw, I wouldn't *shoot* you." He turned away, shading his eyes as he scanned across the treetops for more birds.

Strange inside the house that evening, when the three of them were sitting down to eat the food the diner lady had brought in and left, as usual. Sitting across from Bonnie, with Vandervelde over in the lord-and-master's chair at the head, those two shoveling away in that head-lowered manner that always made Cooper lose his appetite—that was what was strange. They tore through the sopping biscuits and the cold, greasy pieces of chicken as if the house were on fire and they wanted to clean their plates before the flaming roof fell in on their heads. And they didn't say a word about somebody else being in the house, who wasn't here at the table. Who was upstairs, Cooper could sense her right through the roof and up through the next story's floorboards. Up in her room, as though she were the pearl hidden away in the house's shabby oyster.

The not saying anything, that unnerved him. Though he'd caught goddamn Vandervelde one time, looking up from his plate and smiling at him, as though some particularly pleasant thought had just crossed his mind. So the sonuvabitch knew—knew something, or everything—and was just going on enjoying himself, pretending that everything was just fine and dandy, rolling on like before. Just to give Cooper the crawl up his spine, half guilt—for what? —and half just dreading whatever was going to happen next. The sonuvabitch.

Cooper pushed his chair away from the table. In this house there was no need for *Excuse me, thank you very much, good night all.* You just got up and walked away, leaden gut pushing against your belt buckle. Usually. Tonight he'd stuffed down no more than two or three solid bites. Heading to the door, he could feel Vandervelde's piggy eyes on his back, the smile curving back from the yellow teeth.

He hesitated at the bottom of the stairs. He'd heard the two of them, Vandervelde and Fay, their voices muffled across the house's walls and doors; impossible to make out what they said, though both had gotten louder at the end, first his, shouting, then hers going shriller. Then silence. And then only the old man had come down to the dinner table.

He'd probably beat the tar out of her. That was what Cooper figured. The old man had hauled into her for her running off and doing whatever else— everything else—he would've figured she had. Maybe that was the game. Cooper rubbed the wooden ball at the end of the stairs' railing, thinking about it.

Maybe that was what the old man needed to get it up, old and sick as he was: to get good and mad enough, and dance her around with his big fists, till his blood was rolling high enough to have a go at her. There were always fellows like that; out on the farms, when there'd still been farms out there, it had been easy to tell which ones they were, just by the eyes; they got swollen just like Vandervelde's, peering out at the world from their little secrets inside and assuming that everybody else in the world knew those little secrets, too.

So maybe Fay hadn't come down to the dinner table because she was too banged-up to walk. Or else she wanted to wait until the bruises, and maybe a black eye or two, faded a bit. That was like out on the farms, too. When Mrs. So-and-so didn't turn up at Sunday church, the other women in the pews would exchange those knowing little glances. Not that any of them would say anything about what they knew. Just part of life out there and the way it turned men mean. They all put up with it.

Cooper climbed on up the stairs, going lightly as he could, not wanting the ones down below to hear him.

Fay wasn't in her room. The door was open a crack; he pushed it farther and peered in. Nothing. He wouldn't have put it past her to be hiding in there somewhere, the closet or—Lord knows—under the bed. But he could tell, just from the quiet, the still air, that there was no one in the room.

He stood back from the doorway. Downstairs, he could hear the two men's coarse, guffawing laughter. At the end of the hallway, the door to Vandervelde's bedroom was closed.

And locked. Cooper pulled on the handle and felt the cold metal sealed in place. He looked over his shoulder to make sure that one of them hadn't come sneaking up the stairs to see what he was doing; then he laid his ear against the thin wooden panel in the door's center.

Maybe he heard something; couldn't be sure. But he knew she was in there. The way you can tell, just from the dust traced across the sill, as though you could hear the breath and the heartbeat over your own . . .

She was in there, all right. The old man hadn't finished with her yet.

He was walking around outside, letting the clean night air flush the stink of the house out of his nose and mouth. Looking up over his shoulder, he'd seen a light go on in Vandervelde's bedroom. He'd listened, but heard nothing; then the light had gone out. With his hands in his pockets, Cooper kicked at the gravel stones, looking out across the dark mesh of trees.

Somebody came up behind him. He knew it was Bonnie from the heavy tread off the porch steps and across the drive. He didn't look around, even when the other's breath was right on his neck.

"What's it like to screw a loony?"

The question, out of the blue like that, made his shoulders jump. He looked around. "What was that?"

Moonlight turned Bonnie's grinning teeth blue. "I said, how'd you like screwing a loony? You know, a craaa-zy person." Like some funnyman on the radio, squealing the word up to make it comical.

Cooper felt disgust seep under his tongue. "I don't even know what you're talking about."

"You don't huh? Sure you do. You had a whole night of it. I bet the two of you was just goin' away at it like stray dogs, all night long."

He didn't give a damn how much bigger the other fellow was. "Why don't you just shove it up your butt?" He turned away, gazing at the dark trees again.

Bonnie's laugh came from behind him. "Hey, you don't have to get all mad about it. You musta liked it; you don't want to talk about, that's fine by me." Could just about hear the grin growing wider. "But that's what she is, you know. She's one of those lunatics."

"Sure she is." He'd rather have been listening to the rats scuttling under the dead leaves. Instead of this shit.

"Don't believe me? Where da ya think she came from?"

Cooper glanced over his shoulder. "What's that supposed to mean?"

Still smiling. "You think jail's the only place somebody like you can get sprung from? There's other places, you know."

Other places inched up his spine. "Like what?" Though he knew what Bonnie was going to say.

"Like the nut house, whaddya think? You think you know so much. Maybe you know what's it like in one of those places. Maybe you're as nuts as she is."

He'd said *crazy* inside his head, but hadn't meant it. Not like that. He swallowed the sour wad of spit that had gathered in his mouth. *Crazy—crazy bitch.* Stuff like that. But you didn't mean it when you said stuff like that.

Bonnie knew he'd hooked him. "Yeah, my old man's on the board for the county place." Bragging. "Home, they call it. They keep it over there, the other side of town." He lifted his hand and pointed, off through the trees. "He ain't the only one who goes down there—they call him, most times—and looks somebody over. Some nut. So they can save money, see? There ain't no money for a buncha loonies to be laying around, eating three meals a day and not doin' shit for it." He snorted. "Not that they get taken care of that good. So if one who ain't quite as loony as the others can, you know, work out her keep—and there ain't no family to say no—shit's sake, of course they're not gonna mind some kind soul like my old man taking one in."

Crazy . . .

"She was still pretty clean when they brought her out here; she hadn't been in there that long. Shoot, I wasn't even sure if she was crazy or not . . . until she started talking all that strange sorta shit. You know." Bonnie's grin stretched across his whole wide face. "I bet she's told you all kinds of loony stuff."

Cooper looked over his head, up to the dark windows of the house. That explained a lot: why she came back here. Because there were other places that were worse. That was the comfort in this world: there was always someplace worse. And if people were smart—even if they were nuts—they did what they had to, to keep from getting caught and sent back to one of those "other places." No matter what anyone had to do, what they had to endure.

"So, like I asked you"—Bonnie's voice slid around his ear again—"how'd you like screwing a loony?"

Cooper looked at him. "Must be okay," he said evenly. "Your father seems to like it."

Bonnie laughed, his gut shaking. Finally he stopped, gulping in his breath. "Yeah, that's right." He nodded, starting to turn away. "How do you think he got a boy like me? Huh?" He winked and headed back to the house.

For a while longer, Cooper stayed out looking at the trees, until the cold had gotten under his skin; then he went inside, too.

11

"He locked me in the closet." Fay was sitting on the
ground, her arms wrapped around her knees. The
hem of the black dress dragged over the dead leaves.
"That's what he likes to do."

Cooper leaned back against one of the trees, his
hands behind to balance himself. He couldn't see the
house from here. They were in a private little pocket,
screened from anyone else's eyes by the tangled wall
of the orchard. He said nothing, just let her go on
talking in that soft voice of hers, as if she were
talking of nothing important at all.

"That's what he'd done the other times." Fay picked
up a twig and watched her hand draw it through the
leaves. "When he's gotten mad at me. Whenever I
ran away and—you know—come back. Then he puts
me in there. And just leaves me." Her voice sounded
dead, emotionless. The twig drew a line in the damp
soil under the leaves, crossed it with another.

He'd guessed—finally, after a couple of days—that
that was what was going on. After that first evening,
when she hadn't come down to the dinner table.
Vandervelde had loaded up a plate the next day,
from the stuff set out for lunch, and taken it upstairs, without saying a word about what he was
doing. With a jug of water and a glass, one of the

bunch from the drainboard at the side of the sink that were always clouded with a white, mottled film. The jug was brought down empty the next morning, but nothing on the plate had been touched. That went on for three days total. Late at night, when he was lying there looking at the ceiling, he'd heard the sounds of the two voices down in Vandervelde's bedroom at the end of the hallway; once she'd been begging him for something, Cooper could tell— probably, he figured, begging not to be stuffed back in that dark, musty closet. And then, when the voices died away, the footsteps, both Vandervelde's and Fay's, down the hall to the bathroom, the running-water sounds, the john flushing, and the footsteps back again. And, loud in the dark, echoing right through the silent house, doors being closed. And locked. He'd close his eyes when everything was quiet again, and try to go to sleep. There was not a whole lot he could do about any of it.

After three days of that, Vandervelde had apparently figured that was enough; they'd all been sitting at the dinner table, the three of them, the old man and his son already digging through their loaded plates, when Fay had appeared and sat down at her usual place. As if nothing had happened. Nobody said a single word about it, as if they all didn't know where she'd been, locked up right above their heads, in Vandervelde's bedroom. They're *all* fucking nuts, Cooper decided . . . again. Even—especially—Bonnie, who'd looked over at Cooper, smiled, and given him that same dirty, knowing wink.

She hadn't said anything through the whole meal, just shifted the food around on her plate in that child's manner she had. Then, when Vandervelde set his fork down rattling on the table, as if that were some kind of signal, she'd pushed her chair back and gone upstairs again.

Goddamn Bonnie's right. That was the worst part. Cooper had rolled himself a cigarette from his dwindling supply of tobacco. Pacing outside the house, the cigarette's orange spark cutting through the blue moonlight all around, he thought about all the business going on in there. Shaking his head, holding the stale tobacco smoke inside: Nuts as they make 'em. He'd gotten through that little bit of stupidity with his skin intact—so far—but he'd have to be more careful in the future. Have to. He let out his breath, feeling the burn right at the hinge of his throat. The old resolution: if he could've tacked it up inside his skull with a nail and hammer, he would have.

He hadn't been surprised when he'd heard someone coming up behind him. He'd known it was Fay. She had taken his hand and led him toward the trees. The little stub of the cigarette burned out against the gravel where he'd dropped it.

In the dark space under the branches, the moon just coming through in little slivers that dappled the sleeves of the black dress, she'd told him. Everything that'd happened.

"He just leaves me in there. And goes away. One time . . ." Her dead voice went on, describing something that had happened to another person, a thousand years ago. "One time, I beat on the door and I screamed. I just went on screaming, long as I could. Maybe it was the first time he did it, put me in there like that. And when I stopped to get my breath, I knew he was there, right there in the room; I could hear him walking around. And if I knelt down and put my face right to the floor, I could see under the edge of the door, and I could see his shoes. Real close, 'cause he was listening to me. But he didn't do anything. He didn't let me out or anything. So I started screaming again and pounding on the door; and the next time I stopped, I knew he wasn't there any longer. He just went away." A shrug. "That's what he likes to do."

His eyes had gotten used to the dark; he could make out the small movements of the figure sitting on the ground, the dry leaves and twigs in front of

him. The child in the black dress that always seemed
too big, and too old, for her.

"Did he hit you?" He kept his voice low; he didn't
want them, back in the house, to hear him and Fay
out here.

She shook her head. "Maybe a little. Like the first
time, 'cause I fought. So he had to, a little, just to get
me in there. The same way I beat on the door and
screamed. Then I learned that it didn't do any good.
That if he was gonna do it, he was gonna do it and
there wasn't any way I could stop him."

But she'd come back anyway. Even though she
knew what was going to happen, what Vandervelde
would do . . . Cooper watched her hands digging
with the twig at the point where the two lines in the
dirt crossed. That meant she'd come back to his
place, because there was some other place she was
even more afraid of. Someplace worse.

They had both been silent for a couple of minutes,
Fay watching her hands scratching at the earth beneath the layer of dead leaves; he gazed at her and
worked through his thoughts, turning them over like
cards that always said the same things. Then she
spoke again, her voice softer.

"I know what Bonnie told you." She didn't look up
at him. "I knew he'd tell you, sooner or later."

Cooper didn't like the way her voice had gone, so
quiet that he could barely hear her, even out here in
the night's silence. Maybe she might start shouting,
or just screaming, just the way she'd been talking
about. He'd have some explaining to do, about being
out here with her, if that happened. There had to be
a limit to how far old Vandervelde would let him
push his luck.

"Well . . ." He glanced back toward the house;
there was a light on somewhere inside, spilling out
across the front porch. "He did say some stuff, but I
didn't—"

"Oh, no . . ." She leaned across the little space
toward him, her face lifted with the moonlight streaks

shifting over it. "It's true. Everything he told you. I know what he said. It's all true."

That surprised him. Not that it was true, but the way she told him it was. Her voice hardly changed. That was scarier than the screaming could have been.

She was close enough to have kissed him if she'd wanted to. She held the twig in both of her small fists, pressed against her knees, the knuckles bloodless from the squeezing. He didn't know what to do, to say, but he couldn't even pull away from her. The trees' branches knotted close around them, the air still and trapped.

"That's why he does it." Words he could feel, her breath tracing at his ear, almost louder than her voice. " 'Cause he knows."

He wondered if he could just jump up, knocking her sprawling away from himself, and run into the house. Right, that'd be real smart—even if she didn't start screaming now, and shouting, and saying God knows what crazy shit about him, because he wouldn't be her friend any longer, he'd be one of them, and she wouldn't care what happened to him then—even if he got his ass out of this dead-quiet little space now, there'd be another one and another one after that. Maybe the thing to do was to keep her talking; maybe she could get it all out of her, like squeezing a boil, at least for a little while. She'd still be crazy, but he might have some time at least to think of what to do, to get out of here for good. Good and gone.

"He knows." Fay went on talking in the same low voice. "He knows what they do in those places. What they did to me."

"I don't know." Cooper shook his head, watching her. "I don't know what you're talking about."

"Yes, you do. Everybody knows what they do in there."

That low voice scared him. "Jesus Christ, I don't. Honest to God, I don't know."

"They lock you up." She wasn't even talking to him now, looking at him; he could tell, even in the dark, that her eyes were staring right past him, locked on something else far away. "They lock you up in little closets like that; they just shut the door on you. If they don't want to bother with you, or if they're tired of you, or if they just want to be by themselves without you around. The people they got working in those places—" Her voice burned, narrowed down to a red wire. "I could hear 'em sometimes, doing things out in the ward, on the beds with each other. Dirty things. They weren't doctors or nurses, not real nurses anyhow. They were just mean, and dirty, especially the ones at night, when there wasn't anybody around to watch them. Then they could do whatever they wanted. And even if you didn't make any noise at all, even if you just lay in your bed looking at the wall and not doing anything"—a child's bitter, deep grievance—"they'd still come and put you in there, they'd lock you up, and there wasn't anything you could do about it. If you screamed, or if you beat on the door, they could come and tie you up, like that." She gripped her ankles under the hem of the black dress, curling herself into a ball. "And they'd shove this rag in your mouth, the same one they used for everybody, it'd be all stiff where the others'd been sick on it, and they'd tie the ends behind your head. And they'd leave you like that. For a long time—till you'd dirtied yourself." She snapped the twig in her hands. "And then they'd smile. When they opened up the door, that's what you'd see, they'd be smiling down at you. Just waiting for you to make any little noise at all, so they could put you back in there and leave you again. Or if you'd learned your lesson by then."

As though she were talking about someone else. That had died. Cooper watched, unable to speak, to say anything.

She looked up at him. Dry-eyed. The moon streaked across her face. Already having learned her lesson. "That's why he does it. 'Cause he knows what they used to do to me back there. He knows I can't bear it." She reached out and laid her hand on top of Cooper's. "It's like when we were out there, out at that pier. And we went in that place, where that dead thing was. When I went inside it, it was like that. It was all cold and dark inside it, like it'd never been alive at all, but *I* was still alive, only it was so cold, and it just went on, it just kept going on and on. That's what it's like." Her hand closed, squeezing his. "When they'd lock me up like, or like he does—he knows I can't bear it, and when I start screaming, it's 'cause I can't stop myself. I just can't, even though I know they'll leave me in there longer if I do that, I can't stop it." Her fingernails dug into the flesh at the base of Cooper's thumb. "I tried to stop. I thought I could, but every time . . . Here, look."

She pulled the lace cuffs of the dress up onto her forearms. She held her wrists out toward him, the white skin underneath exposed to the moon. He looked for only a moment, before he closed his eyes, squeezing them tight. He could still see what she'd shown him.

Fay pushed the cuffs back down over the ragged scars. "I chewed 'em. I didn't have any other way to do it. To make 'em come open." She shrugged. "But they found me; they opened up the door—they must've, I don't remember it—and they found me with the blood all over me, and it was all over the floor of the little closet they'd put me in. I remember that, it was all wet, and it got cold where I was sitting." She rubbed one of her wrists with her thumb through the yellow lace. "Then they had me tied up on a bed for a long time, while it all healed over; they had to sit there and feed me with a spoon. I think maybe they were a little scared, 'cause I'd almost done it, and there might've been trouble for them. So whenever they did it, put me in there like that, they always tied up my hands first, so I couldn't get to 'em. 'Cept I did once, and I did it again, just a little bit, and made it go under the door. One of 'em stepped in it, the blood, you know, and that time I did hear 'em, they were all shouting at each other when they let me out." She smiled. "I showed 'em. I didn't care what they did after that."

There was no way of not listening to her, of shutting out that low, smooth voice, smooth like black stones in a river, rolled against one another for so long that the edges are gone and only the weight remains. The voice had been going on so long inside her head, Cooper knew, the same words over and over; maybe the first time they'd been part of the screaming she'd done, and then bit by bit, every time, they got rubbed smoother and smoother. That was what was going on when she sat there at the dinner table, looking down at her fork pushing the food around on the plate: you didn't hear them, but the words were rolling around inside her skull, shiny and dark, deep under the surface.

"I would've done it again. When he locked me in there." Now just a whisper. "But I wanted to see you again."

You get these things said to you and there's no forgetting them. Cooper could barely breathe around the stone in his chest. Her little confession, her secret.

"I just wanted to see you again. So I didn't do anything like that. After a while, I knew . . . if I just waited . . ."

That was what he'd been afraid of all along. That she'd open up that world of hers to him, and he'd be inside it. Where it was dark and so quiet. He opened his mouth, dry lips parting, but there wasn't anything to say.

The little space under the trees . . . he could see everything in it now, a pocket carved out of the darkness and the hollow branches. He wondered, if he shouted now, would they hear him back inside the house; it was so far away now. If he turned his head and looked back over his shoulder, the light trickling through the webbed trees would seem miles away.

"You hate him, too, don't you?"

A spark of life had come back into her voice. Hate could do that much. Cooper nodded. "Well—he's not too likable a character, then, is he?" He laughed, or tried to; the dark outside the branches swallowed it up.

She nodded, thinking, her gaze drifting past him toward the house. "I know you hate him. That's one of the reasons I wanted to see you again. Not just that"—she gave his hand a squeeze, as if reassuring him—"but because I knew . . . if we were together . . . we could do something. Something—about *him*."

That wire in her voice—this time it was cold. "What do you mean?" He figured he knew, but he wanted to hear her say it.

Tracing with her finger the cross she'd dug in the ground. "I know you hate him, 'cause he's got you out here same way he's got me. So you can't get away. They'll catch you if you try, and you'll be right back where he got you from. Or worse. I know; I know all about it."

"Yeah. So what? That's the way it goes, ain't it? If it wasn't that way, I'd be long gone from here . . . and so would you, I guess." Just say it, why don't you? Yelling at her inside his head. He wasn't going to say it for her.

She leaned toward him again, looking right into his eyes. "If he was dead, then it'd be different. Wouldn't it? Then he couldn't keep us here. Then we could go wherever we wanted. We could go together, just the two of us." She nodded slowly, still looking straight into him. "He's old and he's sick. He deserves to die."

That was close enough; she might as well have come right out and said it. Talking about killing the old man . . . Cooper knew it. Crazy talk. If he hadn't know before, that would've cinched it.

And stupid talk, too. "Look . . ." He was trying to be kind, keeping from shouting at her. "Look, you're right, you know; the whole world might be better off if the old bastard was dead. But it wouldn't do us a hell of a whole lot of good. If he's dead . . ." Cooper had started to feel crazy himself, or crazier, explaining stuff like this in a dead-calm voice. That's where being with Fay had gotten him: in her world. "If he's dead, that just means Bonnie takes over this place; he's old enough. And we'd be just as bad off, or worse. Bonnie might not be any meaner than his old man, but he's younger—he can get up to a lot more shit." That's what the look in Bonnie's eyes had meant, the narrow gaze and smile across the dinner table at Fay gazing down at her plate. Cooper could read that much, right off; the son was just waiting for the father to die, to step into his place, in more ways than one. Plus a big, stupid, cruel smile for Cooper himself; there was just a ton of fun Bonnie was looking forward to.

Cooper bent his head lower, trying to look into Fay's eyes, to see if she was catching what he said. "And that's just if Bonnie keeps us on, same as his old man had. He could just have us tossed back where old Vandervelde got us in the first place. Back in the county lockup, or the . . . you know . . . the other place." He didn't want to say *loony bin*.

Fay looked back at him. "But we wouldn't stay here. We'd go. We'd run away."

Jesus' sake—there was no talking sense with her. Cooper felt the stone in his chest grow heavier, wearying him. "What the hell would be the point of that?" He shook his head, slowly and sadly. "If that was all we were going to do, we could do that *now*. We don't have to have the old man dead to do that. We could just hit the road right now. Except I'm not going to." His voice had risen; he took a deep breath and let it sink back down. "I know the score on that one. And so do you. You really think that if Vandervelde were dead, Bonnie would let us just go skipping on out of here, without doing any of the same stuff his old man would have? Christ, all the people around here and up the highway are his friends, too; he'd have 'em *all* down on our asses. Bonnie would just love to be able to sic 'em on us. We wouldn't get ten miles in any direction from here before we got hauled in. And then we'd really be in deep trouble. Especially if we had something to do with the old man cashing in his chips." Just thinking about that gave him the sweats, chilling against his skin in the night air. He'd be lucky if he ever saw the inside of the county lockup again. These goddamn farmers wouldn't bother to drag him all the way back there, just settle his hash right at the side of the road.

"I know." She gripped his hand hard enough to rub the bones inside together. "I know all that. But it'd be different. We'd have money."

"Money? What money you talking about? Good Christ, if you saw me with money before, that was his money; that was Vandervelde's. And even if I hadn't handed it over to that fellow out there for that crate of shells we hauled back here, exactly how far do you think we'd have gotten on a crummy two hundred bucks? That wouldn't have been worth stealing, not for the way they would've taken it back out of our hides when they caught up with us. Because they would. Two hundred bucks wouldn't get us anywhere far enough out of here. You know what would happen with that kind of piss-ant money?" Cooper pulled his hand away from hers and jabbed his finger toward her face. "It'd disappear. Just like that." A snap of his fingers—she blinked and drew back. "You think it's a lot when you're holding it, but it just leaks away. If you're running and somebody's chasing after you, you don't have time to look after your money. You just gotta go, and keep going. Until you reach into your pocket one time, and all that two hundred bucks is gone. You got two nickels, maybe. And then there ain't shit you can do. Except wait for them to find you."

Fay had listened to him rattling on, waiting for him to shut up. "I'm not talking about that two hundred bucks." An edge of steel in her soft voice. "I'm talking about other money."

"Oh? Is that right?" He dug into his pocket and pulled out his own four dollars, all he had left, unfolded and held them up. "How about this, then? Because unless you got something buried under a rock out here, this is it. There ain't no other money." He crumpled the dollars into his fist; he felt like throwing them at her.

Her eyes narrowed. "There's plenty of other money. In his safe."

Why the hell am I out here listening to this talk? "You are absolutely right. He's got bales of it. Know what else you're right about? It's in his safe. That's why he's got bales of it, and we don't."

"But we could get it. If he was dead. We could get all we wanted. And then we could go."

Cooper sighed. "Look, when that old sonuvabitch dies, if he hasn't told Bonnie the combination to the safe by then, Bonnie'll be dragging it to town and dropping it off the bank building to bust it open. Because it'll belong to him then. It and everything inside it. Just like everything else on this place."

She strained forward, bouncing on her knees, excited as a child could be. "But don't you see? The old man would tell us how to open the safe. He'd tell us, and then it'd be all ours. You see, don't you?"

He shook his head. "No, I don't. Why the hell should he tell us something like that? There's nothing in this world you could do to get him to tell you that. Tight-fisted as he is, you'd have to . . ." Then he realized what Fay was talking about. What the whole conversation, out in the dark, with the trees' branches tangling around them, had been heading toward. He felt like a fool for having forgotten it.

But she hadn't. She wouldn't forget something that important. That was her whole life. "I could make him tell us." She could see in Cooper's eyes that he'd finally understood. "After he's dead. I could make him do anything then. I can do that; you know

I can do it. The way I can go inside things when they're dead. You saw me; you know it's true, don't you?" She didn't stop for him to answer. Her words came rushing on top of one another. "If he were dead—when he's dead, I mean—it'd be easy. I could just go . . . inside . . . and make him tell us how to open the safe. There's like pieces of things still inside when they're dead, pieces of what they used to be when they were alive. And that thing inside him would know, only I'd be inside there, too, and I'd be what made him open his mouth, and talk, and everything. For just a little bit. That's all we'd need—just so you could listen, and it'd tell you how to open the safe. Then we could take all the money we needed before anybody knew. We could take it, and we'd be long gone before anybody even knew he was dead." She gulped to catch her breath. "They'd never find us, not with all that money."

That was what it came to. All of her talking: it came to dead things. Cooper looked away from her, out through the trees. The moon had ridden lower in the night sky. It always came back to that, any time she spoke.

Her voice tugged at his ear. "And I know how to do it. So they wouldn't even know we'd killed him. They'd never know. He's so old and sick, see; he knows his heart's just about worn out. 'Cause of all the stuff he's done. It wouldn't take much to kill him. There's times—all the time, now—when he's with me, up there in his room, he gets so red and puffing, like he's gonna die right on top of me." She said it with no embarrassment, as though she were talking about someone else. "He makes me lie there and not move or nothing; that's the only way he can do it now. 'Cause he's afraid if he gets too worked up, his old heart will just burst. Even when he rolls off me and he's puffing and his face is all gray, I can't move, I can't up and go wash myself off, till he says it's all right. That's how old and sick he is."

She smiled. "But I know how. I know what I can

do, and he wouldn't be able to stop me, not then, not
while he was heaving away and sweating all over me.
He wouldn't be able to stop, not till his heart gave
out. He'd be dead. I could make that happen, too."

Cooper felt sick, his throat closing so he couldn't
swallow. He could see the old man, naked and pale,
his wattled skin the color of a frog's belly, with old
dark markings on it, the bruise of his belt buckle
embedded deep in his gut. The ponderous flesh
rolling up against her thin bones, the bowl of her
childlike hips, the legs glistening with the smear of
his sweat. Lying there as though she were dead—she
must think of dead things the whole time it's going
on. That would be where her thoughts would go.
Miles away from old Vandervelde's groaning and
ragged, phlegm-choked breath; out in the dark, out
here in the trees, the things under the blanket of
dead leaves, dark and giving way, becoming the damp
soil itself. He knew what her eyes would look like,
gazing at nothing across the pillow on the old man's
bed. That's what scared him.

She kept talking. "It wouldn't take much—I mean,
that part of it. Any woman could do it. 'Cause of him
being so old and sick. I think, when they get that
way, it must be like they know they're dying, they're
right there on the edge—and that gets 'em even
more worked up. If they can do it at all. Sometimes
he can't. But I could fix that . . . if I wanted to. And
then I could push him right on over. It'd be easy."

Easy. For her, he supposed it would be. Easy
enough.

"See, the way I figure it . . ." That child's voice,
talking about games. "I figure if he died right there
in his bed, it'd be night and Bonnie would be asleep.
There wouldn't be anybody around. I could just come
and get you, and then I could . . . you know . . . go
inside him. And I could make him tell us how to open
the safe. So we could just go down and take whatever
we wanted . . . and we could close it back up!" The
idea had just struck her. "So that dumb old Bonnie

wouldn't even know anything was gone. We could just light out, and in the morning Bonnie would find him— he'd find his father like that, and he'd know what'd happened, at least about that much. He'd figure I got scared and ran off and took you with me. He'd probably be so busy trying to figure out his own way of opening up that safe, he wouldn't bother none about us. And it'd be days later before he would get it open, and we'd be so far away by then—with the kind of money we'd helped ourselves to—he and his friends would never be able to find us. We could be up north, we could be all the way up in Canada by then. Someplace like that. There's no way he could ever catch up with us, even if he was smart enough to figure out that we'd been able to get into his father's money." She leaned back, her face shining with excitement. "You see . . . we could do it. You and me. We could do it."

She had stopped talking. Cooper let the night's quiet seep back into the little nest under the trees. Just the two of them, talking about these things. He already knew what he'd have to say.

She waited for him to say something.

"Look . . ." Keep it slow. Nice and easy; don't let her get any more excited. "You know the place you were in . . . back before Vandervelde brought you here?"

After a moment, Fay nodded.

"You know why you were there?" Slow, easy.

She said nothing.

He pulled in his breath, then pressed on. "You were there because there really is something wrong . . . with you." He tapped the sides of his head. "With the way you think."

Nothing. Just watching him and listening.

"You can't really do any of that stuff. You just think you can. There isn't any way you can . . . go inside dead things. And make 'em move around, and stuff. Nobody can do that. They're just dead." Cooper lifted his hand toward the surrounding trees, as if the dead things had been gathered there, all around them. "When things are dead, they're dead. You can't do anything with them. That's just what you . . . think." He was running out of words. "You know, inside your head. That's why they put you in that place. Because you were going around believing stuff like that."

Fay shook her head, eyes fastened straight into his. "No. They put me in there 'cause I hadn't learned yet. To keep quiet about it. What I could do. That's why—'cause they wouldn't believe me. So they put me in there like that. That's why I never tell anybody anymore—except you. 'Cause I knew you'd believe. You saw me do it."

"No." He closed his eyes, then opened them again. "No, I didn't. I didn't see anything like that."

Her eyes went wider. "You did—you did see it." Almost shouting at him. "I showed you!"

"You showed me a fly one time. In your hand. That didn't mean anything. It wasn't even dead to begin with. And then that thing, that dummy, out at the pier—that was just some old wires and stuff, and it went creaking because you stepped on something, a board or something in the floor they got rigged up to make it do that. That's nothing. That's nothing at all."

Before he could move, she clutched the front of his shirt, pulling herself up to him. "It was!" She screamed right into his face. "They were dead! I went inside 'em! I made 'em move!"

He couldn't hold back any longer. He scrambled to his feet, tearing her away. She fell back across the dry leaves. "You're crazy!" His own voice rose as he pointed his trembling finger at her. "You think about shit like that all the time, and you think crazy things." He took a step back from her. Maybe they heard him inside the house; he didn't care. "They should've kept you locked up. That's what they do with crazy people."

She pressed her face into the leaves, hands clutching at her ears.

He reached against one of the trees to steady himself. "And you can leave off making these crazy plans, too. You just leave me out of 'em, okay? Because there's no way I'd hook myself up with you. I don't care how much money he's got in his safe, I don't care if there was some way we could get a hold of it. I ain't going anywhere with you. You understand?"

It took a minute for him to catch his breath. Silence all around. He could hear the blood rushing up into his temples. On the ground in front of him, Fay had curled up into a ball, her knees pressed against the points of her elbows. Her fists, squeezed bloodless, hid her face from him.

She didn't move. The dead leaves clung to the black dress. Cooper backed away until he was out from under the trees' branches and he couldn't see her any longer. Then he turned and walked as quickly as he could back to the house.

12

The old man still had it in for him. You didn't have to be a genius to figure that out.

Cooper could tell just by looking at him. That sly smile across the dinner table, the pig eyes glinting as Vandervelde looked up from his plate; just watching him as the thick fingers tore apart a biscuit and smeared it through the gravy. The last couple of evenings, Bonnie had taken to smirking along with his father's smile, as though the two of them were in on some tremendous joke. Fay made her brief appearances at the table, saying nothing, looking at no one—especially not at Cooper, not now—and then left her food untouched after ten minutes or at most a quarter-hour, going back to her room upstairs. Leaving him to the others' heavy-lidded gaze and silent, waiting pleasure.

Why don't you just get it over with? He could have shouted it at them as he listened to Vandervelde's fork scraping across the plate. Whatever you're thinking, whatever you're cooking up about what you're going to do to me . . . let's have it. Instead of all this screwing around, grinning and winking and shit. Get it done with, whatever the hell it's going to be.

But he knew that was their fun. The waiting. They had all the time in the world just to keep him dangling. At least now it seemed—and it was something of a comfort—he didn't have to do it with Fay hanging around his neck. Whatever was going on inside her head—he hated to think of what it might be—at least she was keeping it to herself now.

"I got a little job for you. Something special."

Cooper almost dropped his own fork when Vandervelde suddenly spoke. Maybe this was it, the end of the waiting. "Is that right?" He set the fork down carefully on the plate. "What's that?"

Vandervelde had finished stuffing himself. He leaned back in his chair, far enough back that he could balance a half-empty bottle of beer on his rounded gut. "Oh, just a little bit of fun, that's all. Not a real job. Me and some of my friends from around here got a little sort-of business to take care of tonight." He tilted the bottle, head thrown back, and swallowed noisily before setting it down on the table. "I just thought you might like to tag along— you know, join in. Enjoy yourself."

At the other end of the table, Bonnie smiled. "Kinda like a hunting trip."

"That's right." Vandervelde probed between his front teeth, then sucked at his fingernail. "A hunting trip." He set his elbows on the table and leaned toward Cooper. "You should come along. You been working real hard." Smile and wink. "Real hard. You should have a bit of relaxation."

It didn't sound good, whatever it was they were dallying around. "I don't know. I don't think I'd be much of a hand at hunting. Never did any."

"Time you learned, then. 'Sides, this is dead-easy hunting. Shit, we already know what we're going to catch."

Bonnie laughed. A speck of food lodged on his chin; he wiped it off with the back of his hand. "You could say."

"You know . . ." Vandervelde tapped his finger against the empty beer bottle. "I'd really like you to come along." The smile grew wide over his yellow teeth.

That meant he couldn't say no. Whatever they were planning, refusing would mean something worse. It would mean he knew, they knew, everybody knew. Just what was going on.

"All right." Cooper picked up his fork and rubbed his thumb over a spot of grease on the handle. "Whatever you say."

Vandervelde had his shotgun with him. He carried it, broken open and unloaded, in the crook of his arm. Cooper could see the bulge of a couple boxes of shells—likely those Polish ones, or whatever they were—sticking out the side of his jacket.

"Get in." Vandervelde used the gun's rust-specked snout to point to one of the cars in the drive. The Ford and an older Hudson belonging to one of the other orange growers—they were already about filled, men sitting front and back. Vandervelde's poker-playing buddies and their older sons—Cooper recognized them, more from their laughter and braying voices than by the seeing them in the edge of moonlight sliding through the cars' windows.

He slid in next to Bonnie, behind the steering wheel. Vandervelde climbed in and yanked the door shut, butting shoulders with Cooper as he dangled the shotgun down between his legs.

"Let's get goin'," one of the men in back called out. Bonnie let out the clutch and swung the car around in the drive; the bottle being passed over the back of the seat sloshed across Vandervelde's hand as he took it. He threw his head back to drink, then handed the wet bottle to Cooper. One swig—he figured he had to. Bonnie smiled and shook his head when Cooper offered the beer to him; he was busy working through the gears, bouncing the Ford over the dark lane's ruts. The car got louder with the men's yelling and laughter, one of them thumping the floorboard with the butt of a rifle. Cooper took another swig and gave the bottle back to Vandervelde. Up in the mirror he could see the headlights of the car following after.

"Hey—hey, pal; ya better have one of these." One of the men in the back seat leaned forward and spoke right in Cooper's ear. He could smell the heavy, gassy breath, laden with beer. The man tossed something white and floppy up onto the seat back.

Cooper pulled the thing off his shoulder. At first he thought it was some kind of bag, for flour or sugar, flat and empty now. Then he saw the two holes on one side, bigger around than the circle he could make with his thumb and forefinger. He smoothed the doubled cloth out on his palm; a simple face, just two empty eyes, looked back up at him.

"M'wife sews these up. She's a damn good little seamstress." The Ford lurched through a deeper rut, sliding the man's arm across the seat top. His elbow dug into the back of Cooper's neck. He pulled himself closer, voice right at Cooper's ear; on one hand he had another of the sacklike things, a ghost puppet with his fingers waggling inside.

"See, lookit that. That's all hand-stitching." He waved the thing at Cooper, jabbing at the eyeholes with one finger. It had a drawstring around the open bottom edge; the two knotted ends dangled around the man's forearm, the ghost's skinny, boneless legs.

"Siddown, Rufe." The two other men in the back seat pulled on his belt. "Whyn't you just shut up and have another? He doesn't want to hear about your goddamn wife and her goddamn hand-stitching."

"Hand-fucking, more'n likely." The third man giggled. The rifle slid off his knees and thumped on the car's floor.

Their friend ignored them. He tugged the white sack over his head, twisting it around until one eye peeped through one of the holes. "Look at me." The cloth muffled his voice. "Look at me!"

Cooper looked at him. He'd already figured out

that the things made of white cloth were some kind of masks. He'd guessed as well just what kind of hunting party it was. You didn't need a mask to go hunting deer.

One of the other men had pulled his on. He grabbed the seat back and pulled himself up into Cooper's face. "Boo!" They all started laughing, just from the way Cooper looked at them.

Bonnie took a hand from the wheel and reached over his shoulder to shove the men back. "Knock it off, will ya?" He reached across Cooper to take the bottle from his father. The men in the back seat went on laughing through the white masks, clutching at one another and howling until they gasped for breath.

There were others waiting when the two cars finally pulled over to the side of the road and stopped. Cooper saw them standing in a bunch, about a dozen of them. Their heads were white shapes in the thin moonlight, except for a couple who had pushed the masks up on their foreheads so they could work away at the beers in their hands. A couple others had rifles, slung loosely in their arms, the barrels pointing to the ground in the easy way of men used to the feel of the wooden stocks in their palms. They nodded in greeting as Vandervelde and Bonnie and the others who'd come along walked up to the group.

Cooper followed after them. The men talked, their voices kept lower now, laughter clipped off to short barks. One of the men drinking cocked his arm to pitch an empty bottle out onto the road, then thought better of it and laid it down in the dust at his feet.

"You better go ahead and put that on."

Cooper looked around at the figure who had spoken to him. Recognizing the voice coming from under the mask: it was the trustee from the lockup. He pointed to the wadded-up white cloth in Cooper's hand. The trustee didn't have a rifle, but carried a piece of framing lumber, sawn off just short of a yard, with one end wrapped to make a handle. The squared edges along its length were dulled and splintered.

"They're going to be starting up now." The trustee didn't say *we*. It was someone else's hunting party, the men who owned the land and the trees, the younger ones who'd inherit them. The two of them, the trustee and Cooper, were brought along for different reasons. He unfolded the mask and drew it over his head, pulling the bottom edge down across his chin. When he breathed, the air smelled like cotton, sifting through the white cloth.

"Where they going?" Cooper's lips brushed against the inside of the mask.

He didn't get an answer. The trustee had already turned away and headed back over to the other men. He didn't need an answer, anyway; he knew where they were. He'd been out this way often enough by himself, carrying the little black payout book under his arm, its inked-in lists of names and boxes filled and weighed. Even if he generally cut through the orchards to get out to the pickers' camp, instead of going the long way around by the roads, he recognized the cardboard shacks and sagging triangular shapes of the tents nestled together in the dry gulley. He could smell the ashes of the dead cooking fires this far away.

The men, the orange growers and their sons, started down the trail to the camp. Cooper watched the backs of the white masks, bobbing disembodied in the darkness. He could just make out Vandervelde stopping to dig out a couple of shells from the box in his jacket pocket and loading them into the shotgun. The barrels clicked into place, and the stocky figure rejoined the others heading down the slope.

"Come on." The trustee prodded Cooper with the piece of wood. "You don't want to miss anything, do ya?" His voice sounded grim, no smile under the mask.

The shouting had already begun by the time they reached the camp. A torch made of kerosene-soaked rags had been lit, sending a wavering orange glare around the shacks and tents, the men's shadows elongated, dancing toward the ring of old cars farther out. The younger men made whooping animal calls, racketing open the night; the wail of babies scared awake joined in underneath. A woman, one of the picker's wives, appeared at an open tent flap; she held a squalling infant tight to herself as she knelt and gaped at the strangers' shapes moving around the camp. She drew back, herding her other children, staring openmouthed, into the tent's darker corner.

One of the cardboard shacks tilted and collapsed, pushed over by a waist-high kick. A man, stripped to the waist, tried to crawl out, his forehead bleeding; another kick sent him sprawling. The man's wife hugged a nest of worn-thin blankets to her breast and screamed.

Standing at the edge of the camp, Cooper saw a couple of the orange growers lifting a picker up between them, his arms pinioned behind him. The man folded, his head jerking down below his shoulders, when the butt of a rifle snapped into his gut. His head jerked back up with a stroke to his chin; a bright trail of blood dribbled down his throat. The man with the white mask and gun stepped back, admiring the picture.

The camp grew brighter; one of the tents was burning. The flames licked over the squares of a bunched-up quilt, the cotton underneath the stitches smoking and charring with crawling edges of bright orange. A numb-faced man and woman crouched at the edge of the camp, watching with two kids sheltered behind their arms. The rope holding the tent up burned through; the canvas collapsed, sending up a cloud of sparks that swarmed in circles like insects.

Cooper saw the trustee come strolling back toward him. Sweat drawn out by the fire plastered the mask to the trustee's face. He started to say something, shouting over the yelling and laughter of the men beyond him, when a deep, sharp-edged roar filled the air. The trustee looked back over his shoulder. In the middle of the camp, Vandervelde let off the shotgun's second shell.

It was some signal they'd worked out before, Cooper figured. The animal whoops died out. The man who'd taken the rifle butt in the gut hung like a deadweight between the two masked figures holding him up. They dragged him toward the trail leading out of the camp, the man's feet scoring a pair of lines through the dust.

Cooper stood aside as they hauled the man by him. The eyes had rolled up white in the man's face; his neck and chest were smeared wet, the blood ink-black in the dancing light.

The others followed behind, clapping one another on the shoulders and laughing. None of the pickers, standing or crouching at the edge of the camp watching, said anything; the women quieted the babies in their arms. One child picked up a stone and drew his arm back; an older brother grabbed him and pulled him back into the dark.

Someone was looking at him; Cooper turned and saw the trustee again. For a moment, the eyes peering through the mask's eyeholes met with his. The trustee said nothing; he turned and slung the piece of lumber with the taped handle into the smoke of the burning tent. Then he followed after the other men, up the trail to the waiting cars.

"You shouldn't have made trouble." Vandervelde squatted down and poked his finger at the thing in front of him. "We don't a-*preee*-ciate people who make trouble like that."

The thing was still alive. It'd still had the face of a man—one of the pickers to whom Cooper had paid out the little bits of money—when they'd dragged him out of the camp. One eye had swollen shut now, and the blood and dirt obscured his face as com-

pletely as the white masks hid those looking down at
him.

He managed to hunch himself up on one shoulder, dragging his elbow in the straw on the barn's
floor. His hands had been tied behind his back after
he'd gotten in one good swing right into the throat
one of the men who'd been carrying him to the car.
He'd been slumped down in their arms as if he'd
been unconscious, then had sprung to life. There'd
been shouting, and a scuffling pile of bodies, fists
and boots flailing, right at the side of the road.
When it was over and they'd loaded him into the car,
his face looked like raw meat.

"You see . . ." Vandervelde sighed as if stricken
with all the cares of the world. "When you go making trouble for people—talking about unions, and
strikes, and stuff like that—you just make people . . .
unhappy. For no good reason at all."

The man's tongue moved through a wad of red
spittle. "Why . . ." He swallowed, throat straining.
"Why don't you . . . you go get fucked . . ."

A gargling rasp. Cooper hadn't expected the man
to be able to talk at all. He hung back behind the
others, all still wearing their masks. His hands pressed
against the splintery planks of the barn door.

The one good eye in the red face locked on the
squatting figure. "Know it's you . . . tell you by
your . . . fat . . . gut."

Another weary sigh. "Now, you shouldn't have
said that." Vandervelde rested his arms on his thighs.
"Maybe we could have just let you off with a little
warning—a lesson, sort of, about what kind of things
you should say and you shouldn't say. But if you're
going to start saying names . . ." He shook his head.
"Going around lying about what happened to you . . .
I don't know if we can let you do that. People might
believe you sometime."

The man on the barn floor couldn't stand; one leg
was skewed around at the knee, his bare foot twisted
inward. The straw had become red and sticky, cling-

ing to his back as he pushed himself up on his elbow. For a moment his face was near the same level as Vandervelde's; his head lolled back, then snapped forward. Spit streaked with red rolled down the side of the white mask, just under Vandervelde's eye.

"Come on," called one of the other men in the barn. "What're we waiting ar# for with this sonuvabitch?" He lifted the jack handle from one of the cars circled outside.

Vandervelde stood up. He touched the red smear soaking into the cloth. "You know . . ." Voice soft, playing at regret, but with a smile sliding underneath. "You're just not very smart." He stepped back.

The circle of men surged forward, lifting the things in their hands. Cooper staggered, pushed out of the way.

Through the legs of the men, he could see the face, the eye that glared up at them, the mouth spitting out words that were nothing but bubbling red foam.

Then he was outside the barn, tearing off the mask, trying to swallow in enough of the cold night air to keep from being sick.

13

"They had some folks come out here, over from some of the big towns." The trustee had one of the white masks in his hand; he looked at its blank face as he talked. "From over around Anaheim, south of there, where some of the really big growers are. They came around here, going around to all the growers, talking up this Klan business they'd got going where they were. That's where Vandervelde and his buddies got all their ideas about this shit from." He brought his hand up inside the mask and poked his fingers through the eyeholes.

The other men, the growers and their sons, had all left. They had come out of the barn, not laughing, but smiling, drawing breath deep into their lungs, their faces flushed as if they'd all run a race in the middle of the night; they'd pulled the masks off and used them to wipe the sweat from their foreheads. Then they'd piled into the cars, pitching out a last few empty bottles at the trees by the side of the road, gunning the engines, gravel spitting under the wheels. Cooper had been able to hear them a long way off, heading back out the county highway to their homes, until the night was quiet again. Must be long past midnight, he figured; the moon had gone low in the sky. All that screwing around with that poor bastard—

must've eaten up hours, though any little bit of it, like the stuff that had gone on in the barn, had flashed by in minutes.

Vandervelde hadn't told him to get in the car. Just left him sitting on the wooden lid of a dry watering trough, in the darkness yards away from the barn door. Cooper had thought he was alone, everyone else gone, until the trustee had sat down next to him.

The trustee had his makings; from the corner of his eye, Cooper could see him methodically assembling a cigarette. A safety match flared up for a moment, casting the other's face all orange and deep-shadowed, then flicked away and went out in the damp underbrush surrounding them. The trustee contemplated the burning end of the cigarette, then went on talking.

"They didn't care much for all that foolishness those other folk were up to." He tapped ash down onto the mask laid across his knee. "All that dressing up with silly-ass pointy heads and parading around with banners and all kindsa shit. Those folks had all these photographs, thought everybody'd be all impressed with 'em, of them having their whole god-damn Main Street filled as far as you could see with their pointy white getups; the mayor and everybody belongs to the Klan over in those parts." The trustee pulled on the cigarette, then dug a piece of wet tobacco from between his teeth.

Cooper leaned forward, rubbing his hands, trying to bring some warmth up in them. It had taken a while for his head to clear from the fumes of beer sweat and battering laughter packed in so close inside the barn. He swallowed and managed to find his voice. "Didn't know they had that many black folk out here."

The trustee snorted. "What the hell's black folk got to do with it? Anyplace you got farmers, big farmers, big enough to have people working for 'em, then you're gonna have people fixed up to kick some asses. If it's black folk you got working for ya, then it's gonna be black asses that get kicked. And when it's white folk, these Okies and shit, then it's white butts that're gonna catch it. Shit, it's cheaper than paying 'em what they need to live on. And a whole lot more fun."

Two fellows sitting in the dark, watching the moon creep through the tree branches, and bullshitting about the way of the world. Cooper shook his head. He'd kept from being sick, but a sour taste that he couldn't get rid of had risen up his throat and into his mouth.

" 'Course, Vandervelde and all that bunch were too goddamn tight to be sending their money off to a lot of folk they didn't even know, just so's they could call themselves Klan. They just figured having the masks and kicking the butts was enough for 'em." The trustee blew on the end of the cigarette to make it glow brighter. "Seems to have worked, I guess. We don't usually get anyone come around trying to stir things up." He pointed with his thumb back toward the barn. "That fellow was the first in a long time. He should've cleared out before the end of the picking season—wasn't too smart of him to hang around this long."

Bullshitting, and listening to the crickets' rhythmic trill out in the dark, and the things rustling in the dry leaves under the trees. Just as if there weren't something behind them in the barn that was leaking slow blood into the matted straw.

Cooper rubbed his arms. He still felt cold. "Now what happens?"

"Well, now, all the fun's over, isn't it?" The trustee nodded toward the empty dirt lane leading away from the barn. "They all had their little party; now somebody's gotta clean up after 'em."

You could see that one coming. That was the little job old Vandervelde had been talking about. Cooper had wondered just what it was going to be. Nobody—

Vandervelde or any of his buddies—had given any sign they'd wanted him to join in the butt-kicking; that was fun reserved for themselves. Not to be shared with the hired help.

The trustee glanced over at him. "What'd you think they brought you along for?"

Cooper shrugged. "I don't know. Thought maybe they just wanted me to see . . . what happened to people who make trouble around here."

That got a laugh. "Shee-it. If they wanted to show you that, they'd show you on your own thick skull. That's how you get an education around here." He stood up, tossing the cigarette stub onto the ground. "Here's what the deal is. There's something in there that's gotta be taken over somewhere else. And someone's gotta take it there. Something like that gets found on the property of one of the growers, it's kinda hard to ignore, even for a place like this. There's people down in the town who like to stick their noses in things, make a big fuss about stuff that don't concern them. These growers may own just about everything in sight around here, but they can't get away with just anything, least without going to a little effort about it. That's where you come in."

Cooper looked up at him. "I'm not touching it. They're the ones who killed him. I didn't have anything to do with it."

"That may well be." The trustee watched his own hands folding up his makings in a little pouch. "But if that poor bastard, or what's left of him, gets found out here, and people start saying unfortunate things about who might've killed him, and what oughta be done about it—you really think it's gonna be all them growers, or a couple of 'em, or even just one of 'em, winds up being taken down to the courthouse? You better wise up, son; you know things don't work that way around here."

It was all becoming a little clearer. Cooper stared at the mask that had fallen to the ground when the trustee had stood up. It all figured now . . .

The trustee could read his thoughts. "You're catching on. You've already done a spot of work for these folks, just by coming along while they had their fun. Now if somebody's gotta pay for all that good time . . . Somebody comes across that fella out here, it's real easy now to say it was you that done it. That's all they need, just somebody like you."

The mask with its empty eyes looked back up at him. "Why would I do something like that? I didn't even know the sonuvabitch."

Even in the dark, the trustee's pitying gaze was visible. "Oh, they wouldn't have to come up with a good reason for you. Maybe they could say you'd been cheating the man. When you went out there to the camp with your little payout book. Maybe you'd been short-weighting him and pocketing the difference, and he'd found out and faced you down about it. That'd be reason enough for you to kill him."

"Who the hell would believe a story like that? As if I could do something . . . like that—" Cooper pointed to the barn. "Mess somebody up like that. Shit, there was a dozen or more men beating up on him."

The trustee smiled. "You're right; nobody'd believe it. Small fella like you. They'd just have to say they believed it. And then you're screwed. You wouldn't have to worry about the county farm no more. You're talking death row now. But a poor sorry bastard like you, that nobody gives a fuck about to begin with, you'd only wind up sitting there a coupla months, anyway. Folks in this state don't see a lot of sense in wasting food on a dead man. Or as good as. They'd hustle your case right along."

That's what the mask was saying, crumpled up on the ground by Cooper's feet. With the blank white cloth where a mouth should have been: *Fool.* What Vandervelde had playing at all along—maybe he hadn't had any other reason for keeping him around. Just until he came in handy. Like this.

The trustee reached down and wadded up the

mask in his fist. He stuck it in his back pocket like a handkerchief. "Now, you can be as prissy as you like about getting your hands dirty. It's no skin offa my ass. You can leave him in there if you want to, and let somebody find him, and see what happens 'cause of it. Or . . . The irrigation ditch, the big one that the feeders run off of, it's over there a ways." He pointed off through the trees. "It's all cement for that section there; and it gets pretty silted up this time of year. Mud's maybe four, five feet deep in places. Now, if you were to take our friend there, just drag him on out and . . . you know . . . drop him in, maybe take some of them big cement chunks they left lying around when they poured the ditch, kinda load him down so as to put him down nice and deep . . ." He nodded, sucking in his breath through his teeth. "Might not see him again for a long time. And when somebody did, maybe some kid poking around, the sheriff could just come out and took a look, say the fella musta been stumbling around drunk, slipped and fell, cracked his head open—that's all."

That's all. Cooper stared at his hands clasped in front of him. All it'd taken to get to this point.

"I'll see you around." The trustee slapped him on the shoulder. "You think about it awhile, whatever you want to do."

Cooper looked at the other man. "You're not going to help me . . . with him?"

The sad smile again. "I don't have to. That's your little job. Me, I do enough things for these folks around here—things like telling people like you what the deal is—that I don't have to worry. Now if you're smart, you'll do the same: just make yourself . . . useful. Let some other poor bastard get the shitty end of the stick next time."

Cooper watched the trustee walking up the dirt lane, up to the road. The dark swallowed the other man up, and he was alone.

* * *

If you're going to do something like that, you should do it while it's still dark.

Cooper pulled open the barn door—nothing but weathered boards barely held together by rusted nails—and looked inside. Somebody, one of the growers' party, had left a lamp hanging on a hook. Little danger of fire, if the lamp had fallen and broken: the barn had been abandoned so long ago, the straw had rotted to a wet, dark-brown matting on the plank floor.

The lamp was guttering down, reaching the last of its fuel. Dull orange shapes bound with shadow fluttered against the walls. Cooper found himself looking at an old harness, the leather cracked like mud, and a coiled-up chain soft with dust and cobwebs dangling from a nail by the door hinge. He knew he was putting off looking at the thing in the middle of the floor.

At first, in the wavering light, he couldn't even see it—just the dark, still-shining wet on the tangled straw. For a moment he had the wild hope that there wasn't anything there, nothing solid; like when you take a swollen tick off a dog's neck with a drop of gasoline, and then you stomp the little ugly grapelike thing into the ground, and there's just a smear of blood in the dirt. Like that. As if all the growers and their sons had beaten the troublemaker—Cooper had started calling him that inside his head—beaten him right down into the planks beneath the rotten straw, so that there wasn't anything there except the wet stuff seeping away, drying out so that the flies wouldn't even crawl around on it anymore. That would've been nice—nothing to drag out to the irrigation ditch—even though he felt disgusted with himself for wishing it. That was what living here, with Vandervelde and all the rest like him, did to you. You could wind up like the trustee, talking cold and nerveless about the best way to get rid of something dead.

He'd been wishing for it too hard; that was why he hadn't been able to see it there. Wind slid through the open barn door and stroked the flame inside the lamp. The shadows bled away from the straw mounded in the center of the floor. He saw it then. The loose stalks clung to its limbs, as though it were a scarecrow that hadn't been stuffed into its raggedy old clothes yet. One hand sticking up, the fingers curling around air—it had slipped and fallen, it was an old drunk who needed somebody, some kind passerby to give it a hand back up onto its feet.

An old drunk. Cooper squeezed his eyes shut. That's all. If he just walked over there—like walking through a room to your bed when you've already turned off the light, and you know just where everything is so you don't hit your shins against a chair or the little chest where you keep your clothes—just walked over there with the lamp's dim glow edging under his eyelids and grabbed the hand raised up toward him . . . *I could drag him. With his eyes still closed. Out in the dark. And not even see him.* Blind, he stepped away from the door.

He shuffled through the damp straw, feeling ahead with the edge of his shoe. Once he tapped against a plank warped away from the joist beneath, and his heart jumped with the hollow sound the wood made. His eyes flicked open for a moment, just long enough to see the glow of the lamp hanging on the far wall, and just ahead of him a thing tangled in straw that looked ink-black in the yellow light. He swallowed the sick taste inching up his throat, closed his eyes hard, and slid his foot forward again.

A couple more steps and he hit it. Something soft that made no noise. It weighed against his shoe, a man's weight. In his head, he still had the picture of the raised arm, the hand with its fingers curled. Waiting for him to come and take it. Like a patient old drunk, happy to lie out in the mud in an open field, the tall grass swirling around him, singing under his breath as he watched the moon sail through the clouds ... Cooper kept his eyes closed and reached out in front of him.

Nothing. Too far up, as if he'd talked himself into believing the hand would reach up and grab his, the old drunk grateful for someone coming along and finding him. Cooper leaned forward, moving his hand in a slow, blind circle.

It brushed against the back of his fingers. He froze, his breath jerked back into his throat.

Just some old drunk ... In the dark behind his eyelids, he told himself again. That's all.

He moved his hand, bringing it around the other, his palm fitting into its, the space between the thumb and forefinger ...

Pleased to meet ya. He suddenly felt like laughing. How ya doin'? Long time no see. He gripped the hand in his and pulled.

The weight of it surprised him. The arm raised, straightening as he leaned back, then stopped. As though the body it was attached to were nailed to the floor.

Maybe the old drunk didn't want to go home. Leave me alone ... Go 'way ...

The hand was wet. He hadn't noticed at first, but now he did. Something sticky clung to the skin of his palm. He could smell it now, too; it didn't smell like an old drunk, of spilled beer and beer soaking out in sweat. It smelled like the pen behind the shed where he'd seen his father lift the pig up on the hook and slit its shining belly open, and reach his hand inside while something red and steaming puddled around his boots. It smelled like that, and shit, the way the bed in the little room upstairs had smelled when they'd taken his sister away wrapped in a sheet, and his father had burned the old mattress and lifted him up to show him his sister sleeping in a box on the kitchen table, sleeping even when he called her name and thick black smoke came billowing up from the fire behind the house ...

His throat clenched and he felt as if he were going to be sick again. He let go of the hand. It wasn't some old drunk singing to the moon; it was the troublemaker the growers had dragged out here and beat to death. He let go, but his hand wouldn't pull free, the wet stickiness on its hand clung to his and he could feel the weight of its arm flopping about as he waved his hand back and forth, trying to break loose. He shook it harder, clenching his teeth, and the sticky hand pulled free with a soft tearing noise. The straw slid out from under his feet and he couldn't stop from falling, twisting about to keep from landing on it. His shoulder hit the bare planks, hard enough to jolt his clenched eyes open.

Cooper looked right into its face, as if morning had come and woken them in bed together, and this was the face on the pillow next to his. It smiled, the white teeth glistening in the lamplight. There was no pillow; something black had leaked through the teeth and soaked into the straw, until there was a puddle of it slowly spreading. And it wasn't smiling, Cooper could see it now; a flap of skin had been torn away from the cheekbone, down to the jaw. The bone above the ear was flattened and shoved in, a hard-boiled egg before you start to pick the pieces of the cracked shell off; something specked with the black stuff, soft and raw-looking, pushed its way through.

On his hands and knees, Cooper gathered the sour taste in his mouth and spit it out. The smell of his being sick mixed with the slaughtered-pig smell and the mattress of the dead little girl.

Emptied of everything—he turned his head and looked at it as if the part of him that had been afraid had been spewed up with the rest. It did look as if it were smiling: a skull's great wide smile underneath the ruined flesh. He felt nothing now. He lay on his side, away from the black sticky straw and his own mess, and gazed numbly at it.

Easy to go on lying there. He felt so tired; he

could have fallen asleep and let whatever remained of the night drain away. When the sun came up, someone could find him there, still sleeping with the troublemaker's body a few feet away, and he wouldn't care; you get that tired finally.

He didn't know how long he'd been there. He could see through the gaps in the barn's wall that it was still dark outside. He pushed himself up, rubbing his eyes. Stiff, he got to his feet and stepped over to the body. He grabbed hold of the upraised arm by the wrist, then reached farther down to get the other one. He pulled, putting his back into it. The body came free of the black straw and slid across the planks. He backed toward the barn's open door, dragging the troublemaker with him.

It was easier outside. The loose gravel around the barn rolled underneath the troublemaker's weight, his heels digging two long lines as Cooper pulled him toward the trees.

Working his way backward, he looked over his shoulder, trying to make out a path toward the irrigation ditch. The body's legs had started to catch in the tangled brush around the tree trunks, slowing him down. He had to stop and catch his breath, gulping down mouthfuls of the cool night air while the loose arms dangled from his grip. If he looked down, he could see the ruined face with its lopsided grin peeled back to the hinge of its jaw. It didn't bother him so much now. Just some poor dumb dead bastard. He just wanted to get it out to the irrigation ditch and be done with it.

He tried to remember exactly which way the trustee had pointed. The barn was hidden now by the trees and the night's dark. The image came of him still dragging the troublemaker's body around in a big looping circle through the trees when the sun came up; he could almost laugh, just thinking of it. He pulled up on the thing's arms, lifting the shoulders free of a snaking root on the ground, and dragged it farther along.

* * *

The trees thinned out. Looking over his shoulder, Cooper could see an open space, blue in the moonlight. A straight line of something gray, a yard wide or so, dropped off into black.

He let the troublemaker's arm go, flopping onto the ground, and breathed a sigh of relief. There was a smell of brackish water on the night air. His muscles were worn out, his own arms stiff and trembling from dragging the body through the trees. But another few yards to go, and it'd be done. The big effort to make then, he knew, would be to not just curl up on the ground and melt into sleep; tired as he was, he'd have to drag himself up onto the road and hoof it back to Vandervelde's place. To a real bed, as if that mattered now.

As he drew in his breath, each one slower and longer, the ache in his arms ebbing, he looked out past the open space and the ranks of trees on the other side. In the distance, the hills were etched with a faint red line. That close to morning—the whole night had been eaten up in dealing with the poor sonuvabitch on the ground in front of him. He'd have to hurry along now, to get some distance between himself and this place before it was light.

He had the body at the cement lip of the irrigation ditch; a couple of yards below, the mud was speckled with mosquito hatchlings, shimmering the water where it had collected into little pools. The rough concrete butted into the ground at an angle steep enough to push the troublemaker's body into a sitting position, the head lolling forward, chin on chest. With its face in shadow, it did look like a drunk sleeping the booze off, hands flopped palms-up beside it—if the line drooping from the slack mouth to the shirtfront had been clear spit instead of clotted black in the moonlight.

No place to stand behind it, on the rim of the ditch, and pull it over; he swung his leg around and stood beside the body, figuring out a handhold on the awkward weight.

A voice spoke behind him. Soft. "I knew you'd come here. I've been waiting."

He spun around, his heart hammering up into his throat. Fay stood there. The black dress made her invisible in the night, except for her pallid face.

"Sweet fucking Jesus." If it'd been a man, even as big as Bonnie, he'd have swung his fist. The sharp wash of being startled had ebbed in his blood to a red-visioned anger, as if the sun had leapt up the other side of the hills and poured over them. It faded a little as he looked at her. "What the hell are you doing out here?"

She pointed past him to the thing lying up against the concrete lip of the ditch. "I came to see."

It figured she would have. Cooper shook his head. One way or another—however long it took—he was going to shake himself free of this loon. *Promise myself.*

He glanced behind himself at the troublemaker. It still sat slumped forward, its broken face hidden in shadow. She must have sniffed it out, like a blood-hound catching a trace scent on the air, the smell of something dead. He could believe that of her, nuts as she was on the whole subject.

"I knew what they were going to do tonight." As if she had read his thoughts. "Vandervelde told me."

Cooper looked back at her. "He did, huh?"

She nodded. "He always does. He tells me lots of things." Her gaze shifted, looking over the edge of the ditch to the black mud below. "That's how I knew you'd be out here. They dumped the other one—a while back, before you came—they dumped him out here."

That figured, too. They were all too dumb, or lazy, Vandervelde and the rest of them, to come up with more than one story, since they didn't give a fuck whether anybody believed them or not. And if they stuck some other poor bastard with a story that wasn't going to wash anymore, that wasn't any skin off their asses.

He could've been breaking his back for nothing, dragging this thing out here ... or even getting himself deeper in shit. That was a thought that went on needling at the back of his head. They'd all think that was pretty damn funny. They were probably all laughing about it, at him, right now, back at one of the growers' places, passing around the beer and cracking wise about the two poor dumb bastards they'd left behind, one dead, the other good as.

Fay's voice broke into his black musing. "I wanted to show you. That's why I came out here."

"Show me?" Cooper stared at her. The way she had said it tightened the skin along his spine. "Show me what?"

Her voice went softer as her gaze drifted away from him. She looked across the rows of dark trees toward the hills. "So you'd believe ..."

He could barely hear her, even in the stillness of the night's last hours. In the bushes, the crickets had stopped; the stifling air from under the gray branches weighed against his shoulders, pressing him into the tiny space with her. And shrinking ... He could smell the stiff, aged fabric of the black dress, a smell of dust, warmed by the white body within. As if he were lying with her again, on the floor of the building trembling with the waves surging against the pier, her breath mingling with his ...

But he couldn't breathe. There was no air inside the night's walls, drawing around them. He stepped backward, away from her. His heel struck something soft, the thing lying on the ground.

Before he could fall, a hand gripped his ankle.

It squeezed tighter, holding him fast, pressing together the bones under the skin. He didn't want to look down, but couldn't stop.

The troublemaker raised its head, turning its raw

face up toward him. The grin, the teeth exposed by the flesh ripped away on one side, shone through the spattered tarry black. Its hand tightened, hard enough to cut off the blood to Cooper's foot.

They didn't kill him . . . The only words shouting inside his head. Didn't kill him, he's not dead . . .

In the corner of his eye, he could see Fay looking away toward the distant hills, the red line etching them sharper and brighter now.

The thing on the ground leaned forward, using its grip on Cooper to pull its spine away from the lip of the irrigation ditch. The other hand reached for him, blindly, the fingers straining toward his leg.

Not dead. The words were in his throat, choking him, but wouldn't come out. They battered inside his skull, the night's silence broken and dancing with the roar of his own blood.

Fay could hear. She turned toward him, her gaze level and blank.

The troublemaker's other hand flew and seized him, the fingers digging into the flesh behind his knee. The face lurched up toward his waist as the arms bent, drawing the thing toward him.

The lopside grin opened, the teeth pulling apart. Something wet and red moved inside the mouth. He could see the air bubbling from the throat. A word, something that it wanted to tell him, to shout into red morning light bursting through the hills and battering against him, the red wave surging against the pier until the ground trembled miles away . . .

He fell backward, the hands still gripping his ankle and knee. His own fingers dug into the damp soil, through the shiny layers of rotting leaves. A sob burst from his lungs as he bent his head down between his hands. He could taste the salt of his tears mingling with the dirt pressed against his mouth.

The hands loosened their grip. He raised his head; behind him, he could see the troublemaker, its arms entwined with his legs. The face was still turned up, yearning to whisper its secret to him.

He kicked his legs free and scrambled to his feet. At the irrigation ditch's edge, Fay stood watching him.

The troublemaker rolled onto its side, the red face smearing against the ground. Its hands flopped onto the ground, fingers curling over the blackened palms.

He backed away, her gaze still locked upon him, then turned and ran, the branches of the trees tearing at his eyes.

14

Bonnie got on his ass about it. For leaving the troublemaker's body there on the edge of the irrigation ditch instead of toppling it in as he was supposed to.

"I don't know why we keep you on around here. You can't do shit right." Bonnie had the hood of the Ford open, leaning over the engine and fussing around with a set of wrenches. He did that whenever he was in a sour mood, whether the car needed any work or not.

Cooper knew what he was talking about, without it being said aloud. And didn't give a fuck what Bonnie thought. He'd raised his head less than an hour ago and found blood smeared on his pillow, deep scratches on his face and neck still stinging. From the branches of the trees ... He hadn't even felt them when he'd scrambled to his feet and started running, away from Fay and the thing stretched out on the ground.

A good thing nobody had been out on the roads early in the morning; he could imagine the sight he'd made, tramping along the side, gasping for breath after the run, blood welling up and trickling down his face. Nobody had been up when he'd finally made his way back to the house; as he'd climbed the stairs, he'd heard Vandervelde snoring away behind the bedroom door, making up for a long night of his own. Exhaustion had brought a couple minutes of sleep at a time to Cooper, broken by that other red face with the lopsided grin, lifting up from shadow. He'd jerk awake, sweating, fingers digging into the thin mattress, afraid to close his eyes again, even in the morning sunlight slanting through the window.

He ignored Bonnie; behind him, as he walked across the yard toward the trees, he heard Bonnie snort with disgust and the clank of his tools as he turned back to the Ford's engine.

The payout book sweated in his hands as he came to the edge of the yard. Another little job that Vandervelde had come pounding on his door about, shouting in a bad-tempered, too-loud voice. Cooper could see how hung-over the old man was, just from his squinting, red-tinged eyes.

This late, getting on toward noon, the trees were nothing to be scared of. The bright sunlight poured through them, dust motes drifting in the shafts of still air. He could step right in among them, letting them close in behind his back, and keep walking, the dead leaves crushing underfoot, even if he knew he could close his eyes and see that red face grinning, locked in the dark inside.

The sonuvabitch wasn't dead. That was all there was to it. Cooper kept walking, heading out toward the pickers' camp. When he thought about it, he felt his own jaw clamping tight and the pulse of blood at his temple. As if the troublemaker had been playing a joke on him; they'd all been in on it, the trouble-maker and the ones who'd beaten him, and Fay. Just to give him a good scare—that was what it felt like, though he knew it wasn't true. Nobody gets that much tar kicked out of him just for the sake of a laugh.

He wondered if the troublemaker was still alive now. He doubted it—not all busted up like that, with all that blood lost and his skull caved in. Out there by the irrigation ditch—that must've been the poor

bastard's last gasp, a little spark that'd finally worked
its way up to the surface. Just some kind of weird
luck that it'd happened when Fay was there, going
loony on him, and his own head had been all muddled up from everything that'd gone on before. All
of that just to scare the piss out of him—one of
God's practical jokes, elaborate as hell.

The troublemaker had probably crawled off into
the bushes and finally got around to dying the way
he was supposed to have. Sonuvabitch ... Remembering his fright brought a simmering anger up behind Cooper's eyes.

Or else the bastard had been dead all along and
it'd just been one of those things, like you hear about
happening at wakes or at a funeral parlor: the body
suddenly sitting up in the casket and putting the
widow in a faint. The muscles contracting, or something like that. He could still feel the way its grip had
clenched on his ankle, like an iron band tightening.
The god*damn* sonuvabitch. Cooper swore under his
breath, his heartbeat slowing again as he walked on
through the trees.

When he reached the camp, he got the joke.
Vandervelde's joke. But he didn't feel like laughing.

The camp was deserted. The pickers had cleared
out during the night. Cooper could smell them still,
the sour odor of sweat and dirt, the dirt that worked
its way right into the skin like a tattoo because there
wasn't a place or the time or finally even the desire
to wash it off. Runny-nosed kids with big, watching
eyes, and babies too skinny to cry—you could catch
the ammonia whiff of the honey ditches the folks
had dug, not deep enough, out behind the bushes.
When the wind blew right, the growers' families driving by on the county highway, their wives and daugh-
ters would wrinkle their noses at the stink.

Whatever the pickers were—barnyard animals that
wore clothes, as the growers said, or something
else—at least they weren't fools. Cooper gave them

credit for that. They were gone, pulled up stakes and out on the road, heading somewhere else; it took only one of them getting his head kicked in for the rest to learn the lesson.

The picking was about done, anyway. Time to move on. The packinghouses and boxcars rolling out of them were already stuffed with oranges; what the growers were paying to get the last ones ripening at the foot of the hills wasn't enough to keep from starving while you scrambled up and down the ladders out in the orchards. The growers' kids and the ones from town could come out and get them, perfect for lobbing with a satisfying splatter at the sides of the trains heading east.

Cooper walked into the middle of the deserted camp. At the edge sat one old car, so beat-up and dust-covered that he couldn't even tell what make it was. One tire was shot, the thin rubber shredded away; the car sagged into the ground at that corner, like a draft horse that had broken its leg, waiting for the bullet behind its ear to put it out of its misery. A kid, five years old or so, dirty-faced, big-eyed, watched from behind one of the fenders, then scurried into the bushes when he saw that Cooper had spotted him.

The burned tent was still there, rags of blackened canvas fluttering around charred ropes on the ground. And one of the cardboard shacks, the smallest he'd seen there, hardly more than a couple of boxes, barely high enough to sit up in. A woman lay on a mud-stained quilt inside, shielding her eyes with her forearm from the sunlight cutting through the joins of the cardboard.

That was when he got the joke, as he stood looking down at her. He knew who she was without even seeing her face. He could remember, from when he had come out to the camp with the payout book before. She was the wife of the dead troublemaker.

Goddamn sonuva*bitch*. He could see the smirk on Vandervelde's face; that's what the bastard had been smiling about, through his red-eyed hangover, when he'd told Cooper to head out to the camp. All the rest of the pickers had been paid yesterday, everything settled up before the hunting party got together that night. Except for one of them, who hadn't been there when Cooper had been checking off names from the book and handing out the dribbles of cash into the waiting, calloused hands. His wife, the woman lying now inside the little cardboard shack, had said he'd be back that night, he was off tracking down a rumor of a full-time job, a real one, as a mechanic down at one of the packing sheds to the south; you could pay him when he got back. Bullshit, Cooper realized now; the fellow had been off in some other camp, spouting off his union talk. Stupid bastard hadn't known that he'd come strolling back after sundown, right where the growers with their white spook masks would be calling on him.

Dumb shit. Cooper felt a certain comfort in knowing that there were bigger fools than himself running around in the world.

The woman hadn't moved all this time he'd been watching her. He could see her breathing, the rise and fall of her breast underneath the cotton dress, faded so that the little blue dots in the fabric were barely visible. Skinned down, hardly any meat on her at all, the way they got, living on the road and one camp after another, stretching a bag of flour into biscuits that got tinier and tinier as the little hoard of money shrank and vanished. Her forearm, turned toward him, was streaked with ash from one of the dead cooking fires. You could tell somehow that she wasn't asleep, even if her eyes might have been closed under her arm—too rigid, a tremor in the muscles, a fist clenched so tight into itself, the way nobody sleeping could ever do. Nightmares didn't last that way; you had to be awake to be miserable this long.

"Hello." He felt stupid, but couldn't figure what else to do. "Hey—I got something for you."

The woman in the shack didn't move. He knew she'd heard him. And everything else. If Bonnie had been ragging his ass about screwing up with the trouble-maker's body, then it must've also gotten around to her. The county sheriff had probably come around and told her, or else sent the trustee to do it.

If he hadn't already felt like a shit—Jesus, he'd been dragging her dead husband through the trees less than twelve hours ago—he could've just wadded up the money, tossed it in to her, and turned on his heel and left. But that was the joke, what that sonuvabitch Vandervelde thought was so funny. Get a man's blood on your hands, then send you out with a couple of measly dollars for his wife. So you'd have to be the one to have to face her and have her spit right in your eye. He was ready for it, couldn't blame her if she did.

He waited another moment before speaking again. He opened the book and took out the two bills. "It's money."

All that was needed. He felt a new sickness that made him want to close his eyes, to be anywhere else but here, when she moved her arm from her face and pushed herself upright. Her eyes fastened on him. Then on what she saw in his hand, as if she were hungry for more than just food, as if she could stuff the money itself into her mouth and swallow it whole.

With the palm of her hand, she pushed her hair out of her eyes. "How much?" The words were sharp-edged and cold.

This was a bad territory she'd found her way to. He figured she'd been different before, somewhere else. He held up the two dollars. "Just what . . . was owed. That's all." He couldn't think of anything else to say. "It's what I came out yesterday to pay your husband."

She knelt at the open end of the cardboard shack, looking up at him. Waiting.

From his pocket he took his four dollars, folded

into a square, slick with his own sweat that had seeped through his trousers. He unfolded them, laid them on top of the two dollars from the payout book, and held them down to the woman.

Her hand snatched them from his. On her knees, she scooted back into the cardboard's shadow, like a snail poked with a twig. Her spine arched as she bent over the money, spreading the bills apart.

Cooper still felt sick as he watched her. He didn't know why he'd given her his own four dollars; his hand had just dug them out of his pocket, without a single thought moving inside his head. Maybe some part of him had figured she could use it more. Or else that he was in such deep shit now, four bucks wasn't going to help him any.

"That sonuvabitch. Goddamn bastard."

He heard her muttering as she looked at the money in her hands. Her eyes narrowed into red-rimmed slits as she stared at the greasy bills.

"Now what am I supposed to do? You tell me that—just what the hell am I supposed to do now?"

She had turned her fierce gaze on him. Crouched down in the shack's dark, her head bent low, she looked like a dog, whipped and kept hungry to make it mean.

Cooper's tongue moved inside his dry mouth. "I don't know."

The woman wasn't going to let him go with just that. The money he'd given her wasn't enough. He could imagine her teeth ripping open his throat, the hungry dog going for the meat off his bones.

"I told him." She slowly shook her head. "That sonuvabitch. I told him not to mess around with all that bullshit. All that union shit. I told him it was nothing but trouble, that they'd do him for it. Do him good and proper. But he wouldn't listen, not him; sonuvabitch thought he knew everything, better'n anyone else." Her voice worked itself shriller. "Wouldn't listen to a goddamn thing I said; he'd just go off with them organizer bastards, letting 'em fill his head up with shit. Unions and crap, like there was a chance in hell folks would put up with crap like that. Then they took off, they're long gone from here, left him behind to get what was coming to him. Just like I told him would happen. The stupid sonuvabitch."

He'd expected grief: that when he'd walked up on the shack and had seen her lying there, she'd reached the numb point past her tears. You could only weep for so long. Now he wondered if she had at all: maybe when the sheriff had come around and told her about her husband's body being found, she'd leveled the same look, thin as a knife edge, and started spouting the same stuff. What she'd been storing up for so long inside her gut, ready to spill out on anybody who got within range. The poor bastard she'd married was probably better off dead. Maybe that was what he'd been working toward all along. One sure way of getting out of this bad territory, and you didn't have to worry about ever coming back to it. Maybe not such a fool, after all.

She wasn't even that old, if you could look past what this place and the road coming out to it had done to her. Barely out of her teens when things had gotten so tough, for her and everyone else. Maybe she'd been happier somewhere else. He would've liked to have believed that.

"I told him." She looked through Cooper as if her poor fool of a dead husband were standing behind him. "I told him, anything happened to him—and I knew it was going to, I knew it—I wouldn't account what I'd do. What'm I supposed to do—you tell me." She focussed on Cooper again. "I got two kids to feed, and six dollars ain't gonna do it for long." She crumpled the bills in her chicken-boned fist. "That's why I told him. I told him I'd kill those children first. I ain't going to watch 'em starve." Spit flecked her lips as she screamed at him. "I'll drown 'em, I'll wring their necks, and I'll bury 'em—I told him that!"

He started backing away from her and stepped in

the cold ashes of the cooking fire. The woman wasn't looking at him anymore, but at the dollar bills trembling in her hands. He was going to say something, but couldn't find anything. All the way to the edge of the camp, and back among the trees, he expected to hear her voice shouting after him. But there was nothing. He walked, the dead leaves crumbling beneath him.

Bonnie had finished with the Ford by the time Cooper got back to the house. He was sitting on the running board, with the usual beer in his hand, a couple of empties at his feet. He wiped his mouth with the back of his hand as Cooper walked across the gravel drive, carrying the payout book.

"Did you manage that all right?" Bonnie's sneering voice followed Cooper as he mounted the front-porch steps.

Cooper stopped, hand on the screen door's knob, and looked around at him. "Yeah. It's all taken care of." He kept his voice flat and cold; he was still angry at being sent out on a shit job like that.

"Glad to hear it." Bonnie smiled as he rolled the bottle between his palms. "Glad you can do something right. Maybe the same thing that happened to the last bookkeeper we had out here won't happen to you. He couldn't do things right either. And then, he had a little accident. Amazing how bad you can hurt yourself if you're not careful." He tilted the bottle at his mouth, head tilted back, throat working as he swallowed.

The sonuvabitch—that was supposed to scare him, Cooper supposed. A little warning, make him think they'd beaten up some other poor bastard they'd had out here from the lockup. Maybe even dumped him out there at the irrigation ditch. Only thing was that it worked. Cooper felt a knot inside his gut tighten. Thinking about the way the troublemaker had looked, there in the barn, with its lopsided smile leaking blood. This was a bad place to be because people like

Bonnie and his old man got to do exactly what they wanted to do. It was like living inside their heads or something, with no way to get out.

Bonnie had already forgotten him. He rolled the bottle between his hands again, gazing across the yard to the trees. Cooper watched him for a moment longer, then pulled the screen door open and stepped into the house.

Vandervelde wasn't in his office when he passed by the doorway. He threw the payout book onto the desk, scattering the papers on it.

"See, that's why we gotta do it." Fay touched his arm, bringing her face close to his. "We don't have any choice about it."

After dinner, he'd slipped out of the house and gone walking among the trees. Just to get out of the house and away from them. Fay had tracked him to where he'd sat down on the dead leaves, his back to the tree trunk. Listening to the things rustling under the leaves until she'd shown up, the black dress a silhouette against the darkness. In some way he'd been glad that she'd come out after him.

"They get mad." Her hand tightened on his arm. "About things like that." He had told her about Bonnie's smiling remarks, the bookkeeper who'd been out at the place before. "Just so they can hurt somebody. That's what they like to do."

Cooper snorted. "Hurt, hell—they do more'n that. What about that poor sonuvabitch last night? They hurt him right into his grave." The face, with its smile even bigger and uglier than Bonnie's or Vandervelde's, leered up in his mind again.

"That's what I mean." She had knelt beside him and now scooted closer. He could feel the press of her knees against his leg. "That's why we gotta do something. Now. Before they get it in their heads to do something to us."

Too late for that, Cooper figured. Those sonsabitches had already locked it down inside their skulls that

some deep shit was in store. That's why they bring
you out here. Then they got a nice long time to
think up the exact nature of the shit.

"Sure thing." He nodded. "Let's just jump up and
go get the old boy's shotgun, and let fly at 'em. Blow
their heads clean off. Then all our troubles would be
over." It didn't sound like a half-bad idea to him. He
could imagine the weight of the gun in his hands
and the way old Vandervelde's face would look, not
smiling anymore, that sonuvabitch, when he'd be
looking at the two black holes pointed at him. Not a
bad idea at all, as long as you didn't care what happened to you next.

Fay didn't catch the sarcasm in his words. "Then
you will?" Her voice leapt, excited. "You'll do it,
then, won't you? You will, I knew you would—"

"Do what? What the hell are you talking about?"

"You know—I told you about it. What we could do
to get away from here. To get the money out of the
safe, and take care of him, and—all of that. I told
you."

"Jesus Christ." He shook his head, feeling the tired-
ness wash through him. She was on it again, just as if
he hadn't made it clear that he thought she was nuts.
Knew it. For a while he'd hoped that some of that
had drained out of her head, that his rough talking
and not going along with all that looniness had maybe
burst open some of the black, grim balloons floating
around inside her head. Evidently not. She'd gone as
wide-eyed and little-girl breathy, all excited at the
fun game she'd thought up, as she'd been before.

"Look . . ." He wasn't angry at her now, just sad.
"I don't want to hear about that stuff anymore. I
don't believe it. You understand me? I just don't
believe any of it."

She drew back from him, drawing herself up. "But
you know it's true." Her voice soft and cold. "You
saw it. You saw me do it."

There was no point in talking to her, in trying to
make her understand. You'd have to make her not

nuts, at least for a little while. And you can't do that; nobody can. But he tried.

"I didn't see anything like that." Carefully, slowly, as to a child. "I didn't see it because it didn't happen. All I saw was some fellow I thought was dead—I thought they'd killed him—and he wasn't. He wasn't dead yet. So when he came to, just for a little bit—it scared me. I wasn't expecting it. So it was just natural for me to get a little rattled. You understand?" He lowered his head to look into her eyes. "Just because something scares somebody, that doesn't mean they believe . . . something crazy about it. All right?"

He shouldn't have used that word. *Crazy.* Fay's eyes drew down to slits. "You saw it." A hard whisper. "You know you did."

Around them, in the little space hollowed out from the trees, the darkness pressed tighter. The way it had before, when she had been this close to him. He felt it pressing against his shoulders, sealing him to her. The air between them became thick, a warm thing that crawled from her breath and chilled to ice in his lungs. She didn't have to kiss him now for him to know just what her lips would feel like against his.

Tired, tired of arguing with her. He would rather have wrapped his arms around her, or let her take him in hers, and sink to the ground, the dead leaves a blanket over them. Under there, where the things moved in the blind earth. Tired of everything.

"All right." He closed his eyes; the dark moved back a little until he could breathe again. When he looked again at Fay, she was a silhouette against the black, beside him. "Whatever you say. I don't care."

She knew she still hadn't won—not yet. "You'll see." Kindly, enough to make him think that she did love him. "When I do it with him—you'll know it's true then."

Maybe he would; the prospect didn't scare him. "Sure—you go ahead." With him . . . He'd almost forgotten about old Vandervelde. That was another world, back at the house.

"Tonight—" The excitement filtered back into Fay's voice. "There's no point in waiting."

"I suppose not." He lifted his lead-weighted hand and rubbed the side of his nose. What was there to lose? Not much, he figured. Her loony plans . . . Now he remembered: she was going to do it, the other thing, the dirty stuff, to him in bed. So the old bastard's heart would give out. So what if she couldn't do the rest, that was just her brain rolling around loose inside her head, that stuff about getting inside the dead body and it telling them how to open up the safe. So they could fill their arms with his money. If she just wound up giving the old boy a heart attack and nothing else . . . Shit, he didn't see where he was any worse off for it. Maybe Bonnie wouldn't have the same pull around these parts that his father had. Cooper might find himself back in the cozy little county lockup, or maybe one of the other growers, who wasn't so flat-out demented as these folks, would take him on. All sorts of things could happen.

Whereas only one thing was going to happen here, sooner or later. The red face in his memory smiled all lopsided and wet and promised him that.

"Go ahead, then." He leaned his head back against the tree. Maybe he could sleep here for a little bit. He'd need it; there likely wouldn't be any chance later tonight, back at the house. With all this shit going on. "You go and do what you want."

With his eyes closed, he heard her get to her feet and walk away, the branches brushing against her dress.

Lying in his bed, he could hear them. In the house's dark, deeper than the night outside. Doors opening and closing, and the soft sound of her bare feet in the hallway. Through the walls, faintly, he heard their voices and Vandervelde's grunting laughter.

Cooper closed his eyes. Everything had gotten silent, enough so that he could have slept. If sleep had been possible at all . . .

Then he heard her screaming.

He'd only taken his shoes off when he'd lain down. He didn't bother with them now. Fay's screams continued as he pulled open the door and stepped out into the hallway. The air split open with the sound of her fright. She couldn't be faking it, not like that. It broke down into sobbing and gulping for breath as he ran to Vandervelde's bedroom door.

She had pulled the sheet partway off the bed to cover herself; the rest was tangled around the old man's legs. Her eyes, wide and staring, caught his for a moment as he stood in the doorway. Then Bonnie came up behind him—he'd heard the footsteps racing up the stairs—and shoved him out of the way.

Bonnie stood looking down at the naked figure of his father. The old man was on his back, spine arched, the dark hair matted to his chest and legs with sweat. His fingers dug into the mattress, drawing a thick knot into his fists, the knuckles ridged and white.

Cooper stepped slowly to the side of the bed and looked down. The old man's face was suffused with blood, trembling with it, as if the pressure inside would start leaking it from the corners of his eyes. Jaw clamped, lips drawn back. Cooper thought the yellow teeth would break against one another, until they parted and Vandervelde's swollen tongue welled up, smeared with red saliva.

The eyes locked right on to Cooper's. Behind him, he could hear Fay sobbing. But that was miles away. Here, he could see the old man, still inside there, behind the eyes.

The tongue moved, trying to say something. But only a line of red dribbled from the corner of his mouth and onto the pillow.

15

The doctor who came out from the town told Bonnie he could get a nurse to look after his father. Or they could take him on up to the city, to a regular hospital. It wouldn't matter much either way.

Cooper listened to them as they talked inside the house, Bonnie and the doctor, a gray little man who looked like a doctor, the way you could make a hedge look like a horse by clipping away everything that didn't fit. Cooper sat on the front porch, watching the sun come up and letting their voices drift out to him.

After a while, the doctor came out, carrying his black bag. Unshaven, no tie. One of the growers having a stroke had been important enough an event to pull him out of his own bed. He walked past Cooper without saying anything, climbed into his car, and chugged back down the dirt lane to the county highway.

Bonnie stood on the porch, drawing the cool morning air deep into his lungs, shoulders back so he could drink up even more of it.

"What're you going to do?" Cooper looked over from where he sat. "About him?"

A shrug. Bonnie rocked back and forth, heel and toe, his hands slid into his hip pockets. "We can take care of him right here. Ourselves. Ain't no point in putting him in some hospital, or getting one of them private nurses to come out, just to keep him washed and fed. Shit, that doc already told me just about everything that's gotta be done." He snorted in disgust. "Folks hire a nurse or dump somebody in a hospital just because they don't want to get their own hands dirty." He turned his head and smiled at Cooper. "That doesn't bother me none."

Tell me something I don't know; Cooper looked away from the other's gaze. He already knew just how much Bonnie looked getting his hands dirty.

"Besides . . ." Nodding slowly, Bonnie studied the trees stretching in ranks out to the hills. "It's not gonna be very long for him." His voice went softer. "Not long at all."

Cooper glanced over at him. The bastard might just as well have said it out loud: just waiting for the old man to die. As he had been all along, the way any son his age, waiting to get his hands on his inheritance, would be. Only now he could smell it coming within days.

Christ, he was practically counting up the trees. Cooper watched him looking over the little world between here and the highway. Everything that would be his. Everything that had been the old man's. Bonnie was already tasting it inside his mouth, Cooper knew.

And everything—he also knew—meant him, too. For Bonnie to do whatever he wanted with.

The sun had risen a little higher, breaking across the tops of the trees. He watched Bonnie gazing straight into the red glare. And smiling.

"Now we gotta do it. We don't have any time to waste."

In the space among the trees—it had become theirs, like a kids' hiding place—Cooper looker around at Fay. The moonlight slid through the low branches and striped her white face.

"Do what?"

"You know." Whispering, wide-eyed. "We gotta finish him off. So we can do what we planned."

That's what it had come around to. He should have been able to see it coming. That's what happens when you throw your lot in with crazy people. It just gets worse.

He shook his head. "I never heard you say anything about *finish him off*. I don't know what the hell you're talking about." He wished he didn't.

Her voice went into pleading. "You know—he's gotta be dead. I can't make him do anything while he's still alive. Even having that stroke—with him just lying there like that—he's still alive inside there."

This was a grim business. All this talking about death and stuff. Enough to make you sick. The spit under his tongue got bitter just thinking about it. Should just get up and walk away from her. He studied the leaves between his feet. Loony bitch.

"Well ..." He shrugged. "Not much I can do about it, is there? You were the one thought all this up. You were the one said you were going to . . . you know . . . take care of him."

"I did." Her voice rose in pitch. "I did it. But it wasn't like I thought it'd be. I thought he was going to die, and then he didn't, he just kept . . . pulling at me, and his fingers, they were like hooks or something, I couldn't get away from him—" She was close to crying. "And then his face, and his eyes, they got all red like that . . . I didn't know it was gonna be like that. And I got scared."

That was almost funny, in a bad way. For somebody who spent so much time thinking about dead things, she didn't have any idea in her head about what they went through to get that way. It was the process of dying that had scared her. "So you started screaming, and all."

She nodded, looking miserable. "I couldn't help it. It just scared me so bad, seeing him like that. And not being able to get away from him. Till he went all rigid like, and he wasn't looking at me anymore, he wasn't looking at anything. But I could hear him, way inside, he was trying to say something but he couldn't get it out. Then he let me go."

More than she'd bargained for. He felt a bit of satisfaction in that. Usually, crazy people just made everybody else suffer the consequences of what they did. And her starting to scream sure hadn't been in the plan; he'd been genuinely startled when he'd heard it. Things like this were supposed to be done in silence, tiptoeing around . . . like murderers. Cooper smiled to himself. Just like murderers.

"But he didn't die." Fay said it with a child's disappointment, a Christmas box that turned out empty. "That's why you've gotta take care of him."

Cooper's smile withered. It wasn't funny now, if it had ever been. "You're talking about killing him. That's what it is."

"That's what I was talking about before. And you didn't mind it then."

He shifted uneasily away from her accusing glare. "You said *you* were going to. I never said *I*'d do anything like that."

"You have to do it. You have to. There isn't any other way."

Her voice pressed against his ear and on inside his head as he looked away from her. Out to the dark shapes of the trees. The night hadn't tightened around them the way it had before, when she had been talking about these things. But he remembered how it'd been, that little airless world with nothing but her soft, insistent voice inside it.

"You'd be doing him a kindness. Like the way it was with that cat—you remember that? When Bonnie broke its spine, and it was crawling around on the ground, and you killed it. 'Cause it wanted to die. It hurt too much."

He remembered. He closed his eyes and could see

the animal dragging its hind legs, the wild look of pain and terror in its eyes, the red trail welling out of its mouth.

Fay went on. "Well, that's how it is with him. It wouldn't be like killing him at all. The doctor said he's only gonna last a few more days, maybe a couple of weeks at most. Just lying there like that. You'd just be putting him out of his misery."

He turned his head to look at her. "I don't care about that." The old bastard had made enough other people suffer; if he rotted inside his own body for a while, that'd serve him fine. Not going to cry any tears over him.

"That's all right. That doesn't matter. Just as long as you know that it's not murder. Not really."

Cooper studied her for a moment. Trying to be sane—that was the sad part. Like an actor in the movies. She'd studied for the part, figured out the lines, what she was supposed to say—to talk, to reason things out, to make plans and explain them to someone else—all without knowing that her own head was screwed on backward. That would be the worst part of being nuts: you wouldn't know you were. You would just keep rolling along on that little private course that always led to some darker place, where there finally wouldn't be anyone else to talk to. A little road that never turned around and came back.

And you're doing so much better? You're the one listening to her right now. He wondered how far down that little road he'd already gone with her.

Then again, it was something to think about, in the time he figured he had left; maybe it was what you had to do, to become in this bad territory. Where everybody was nuts. The only one who hadn't been was that troublemaker out there at the pickers' camp, and look where it'd gotten him. Gotten the stuffing kicked out of him, that's what. Maybe you had to go as crazy as the rest of them just to survive, to even have a chance of getting out.

What've you got to lose? Cooper looked past Fay, out toward the dark behind her. Even if she couldn't raise the dead, get inside poor old Vandervelde and get him to tell them the combination to the safe—he hadn't gotten so crazy that he believed shit like that—still, if the old man were to die, have his misery ended, as it were, before Bonnie had had a few days' time to figure out everything he wanted to do . . . if, say, the sheriff or somebody else from the town had to come out here and sort things out . . . Cooper nodded, biting his lip. Could be, could be. When things got all confused, you had a chance. That much he'd learned. The slow pace at which Bonnie's brain worked, chewing away at one thought at a time, like a cow on old hay—shit, he could be back in that nice cozy county lockup before Bonnie knew what'd happened. The county farm, all that stuff the trustee had warned him about, that wasn't so fierce a worry now. Besides, if he could get away from here, and away from Bonnie . . . The other growers had seen him taking care of things and making himself useful. Just like the trustee had said was the smart way. Some other job in these parts, without all this crazy shit going on all the time— that'd be all right. As long as it was somebody else's butt getting kicked.

Nothing to lose. Smart fellow. All you got to do is kill somebody.

"It'd be easy." Fay's whisper. She knew he was thinking about it. "He can't fight you or anything. He's just got one arm he can still move, and not much. You could put a pillow or something over his face, so nobody'd know you did it." Softer. "It'd be easy."

Easy . . . He wondered if anybody had ever talked themselves into going nuts. Maybe that was how they all got that way to begin with.

He turned and looked at her, against the gray trees and the dark behind them. "All right."

He went up to Vandervelde's room while Bonnie was there feeding him. Bonnie had a bowlful of something that looked like cornmeal, or the stuff people mash up for babies, but smelled like chicken broth. The woman from the diner had fixed it up to the doctor's instructions and brought it over with the usual covered dishes.

Cooper watched as Bonnie spooned up a bit of the stuff and brought it up to his father's mouth. After a few more spoonfuls, Bonnie looked around at him standing in the doorway. "Something you want?"

He shook his head. "No—not really." He stepped into the room, alongside the bed. "Just came to see . . . you know . . . how he's doing."

Bonnie grunted. "Oh, he's doing just fine. Can't you tell?" He dropped the spoon back in the bowl; half of the stuff was still in it, uneaten. From where he sat on the edge of the bed, Bonnie reached down for a beer on the floor. He tilted his head back to drink.

The last bit Bonnie had fed the old man was still in his mouth, dribbling out the corner of the slack lips. Cooper stepped over to the bed and looked down at him. The sheet pulled up across the bare chest was damp with sweat. The trickle of pulp and saliva made him look even more like a giant infant, the fleshy jowls wobbling loose from the bones somewhere underneath. But a sick baby, one that had been that way for a century, never growing up but aging anyway. The flesh gray, darkening with unshaven stubble. The eyes rolled, his gaze fastening on Cooper. A wheezing noise came past the tongue lolling against the yellow teeth. His hand, the one he could move, grabbed Cooper's sleeve and twisted the cloth into a knot.

"This is probably what he wants." Bonnie held up the beer bottle. "Instead of that other crap."

The strangled word, whatever the old man was trying to say, bubbled at the back of his throat. Cooper looked down at him, not pulling away, letting the locked fingers tug him closer. The old man's eyes were wide open, with webs of red veins spread across the whites. Inside, in the dark at the center, Cooper could see his own face, tiny and watching.

He's afraid. That was what the old man was trying to say; Cooper could see it in Vandervelde's eyes. He was screaming, but the gurgling noise in his throat was all that could come out. The poor sonuvabitch is scared. Cooper felt sorry for him. He hadn't expected that; he'd thought the old bastard would be up here, stewing away in his own juices, mean as ever even if he couldn't do anything to show it, like a wasp in a jar that you shake just so you can hold it up and watch the powerless fury, the stinger jabbing at the glass.

And to feel sorry for him . . . That was the real surprise. After all the old fucker had put everyone else through . . . Getting just what he deserved . . . Still, this was too much for him to pay.

She's right. Cooper saw it now. It would be a kindness. You'd do the same for a cat.

"You come up here just to gawk at him?" Bonnie lowered the beer, his face heavy and sullen.

Cooper didn't even bother looking at him. He shook his head. "No." He hadn't known why he'd come into the old man's bedroom—maybe to work his own anger up to a point where he could happily do the next thing in Fay's little plan. But it was different when he saw him lying there, frightened like that.

The trembling hand pulling at his sleeve felt like a different one, the one that had locked onto his ankle out by the irrigation ditch. Like some poor bastard trying to claw his way out of there, trying to crawl into death, a cat with a broken spine.

"What the fuck . . ." Bonnie drained the bottle

and tossed it into a corner of the room. "It ain't gonna be long, anyway."

Cooper pulled his arm out of the old man's grasp. For a moment the hand struggled in air, reaching for him, then fell back to the bed, bunching the sheet up in its fist. Cooper stepped back from the bed until the eyes couldn't follow him, then turned and walked out of the room.

They waited until Bonnie was asleep, and then for a while after that. He could hear Bonnie's drunken snoring, farther down the hallway, from his room. For a time he'd been concerned that Bonnie might sleep in his father's room; he'd slumped into a chair he'd dragged from downstairs, working away at one bottle after another as he gazed heavy-lidded at the old man, until he'd enough of a skinful to put him under. Cooper had glanced through the room's open door and seen Bonnie there, his eyes closed, head slumping down on his chest. But an hour or so later, he'd heard his shambling, drink-leaden steps down the hallway, shoulder bumping against the wall, and the collapse onto the bed in his own room.

Fay had already come into Cooper's room by then, sneaking out of her own, pulling the door open just wide enough to slide through. To wait with him until it was time. She sat on the edge of his bed beside him, her face turned away, listening, her white hands folded together in the lap of the black dress.

"There he goes." She leaned closer to him to whisper. With the light out and the room so quiet that the sound of Bonnie flopping onto his bed came clearly to them. She touched his hand. "We should wait a little while. Till he's really asleep."

It didn't take long. In a few minutes they heard his deep, rasping snores—the way drunks snored, gurgling back in their throats, as though all that beer were sloshing inside a barrel.

"Come on."

She led the way. Down the hallway . . . The door to Vandervelde's room stood open. He could hear the old man's breathing, each gasp fighting for air.

Fay pushed the door all the way open. In the corner of the bedroom, a lamp had been left on by Bonnie. The empty bottles in the corner glowed in the dim light. Cooper looked over at the shadowed figure in the bed. Beside him, Fay turned her face away in disgust. The stale air in the room smelled like shit; the sheet was wet where it clung to Vandervelde's gut and thighs.

Cooper stepped over to the bed. The stink filled his nostrils. That sonuvabitch Bonnie, letting his old man lie in his own filth like that. He could imagine Bonnie dragging the old man down to the yard and hosing him off, when the smell got too bad. Or maybe Bonnie just didn't think it was going to be that much longer for him, anyway.

The old man's eyes looked up at Cooper. Still frightened. He could see it in them. The gurgling noise, tongue thrusting against the teeth; still screaming, down inside where nobody could hear him.

"You'd better hurry." Fay came up behind him and whispered in his ear. "There isn't much time."

The poor bastard. It'd be a kindness. The hand, the one that he could move, rose up from the sheet and reached for Cooper. He stepped back from it and the fingers groped an inch away from his shirt. You'd do as much for a cat. The hand strained toward him, trembling.

Cooper bit his lip, then looked around at Fay. "I need something." He kept his voice low, barely breaking the room's quiet. "You know, like a pillow or something."

"Just use his." She nodded toward the figure on the bed. "That'll do all right."

He hesitated a moment, then reached down and grasped the edge of the pillow. Vandervelde's head lolled to the side as he tugged it out from underneath. It came free, and Vandervelde's head, face turned to the side, fell back to the mattress. He saw where the dribble of food had been left to dry in the fold of the old man's cheek next to his mouth. A trickle of saliva moistened the crusted patch.

"Go on . . ."

She was the one who was scared; he realized that now, just from the edge in her voice. As if she wanted to scream, too, right in pitch with the old man. Because he wasn't dead. If he'd been dead, she would have known what to do, but not like this. Crawling around still alive, like that cat trailing its legs in the dust, screaming . . .

"Go on . . . do it!"

He gripped the ends of the pillow in his hands. From the corner of one eye, Vandervelde looked up at him. The noise he made gasping for breath went faster; for a moment Cooper thought the old man might die just like that, the heart finally splitting open with the strain, the lungs unable to draw enough air inside. Then he knew it wouldn't be that easy. For either of them.

Reaching down, he turned Vandervelde's head so both eyes were looking straight up at him. The other's hair was damp with sweat; his hand felt stained with grease when he took it away from the side of Vandervelde's skull. He wiped his hand on the pillow, then took the end again and held it down in front of himself.

A couple of inches away from the old man's face . . . He could see the eyes shift from him to the pillow and back again. The old man knew what Cooper was doing; he could see that, too. The wet noise down in Vandervelde's throat grew louder; the word was there, ready to burst, the tongue curling back to tear it out. He couldn't hear what Fay was saying behind him. If he bent down, put his ear close to the other's mouth, then he might have known.

The face disappeared under the pillow, and he

could no longer hear the wet, gurgling noise. He drew a long breath, then straightened his arms and pushed his weight down into the mattress, his fists locked onto the ends of the pillow.

Vandervelde's hand flew up and grabbed his arm. Cooper looked and saw the fingers digging through the sleeve, squeezing into the flesh above the elbow. He heard Fay draw in her breath with a little cry; he looked over his shoulder and saw her shrink back, staring at Vandervelde's white knuckles. Cooper turned his face from her and pressed the pillow down harder.

He kept on pressing until the hand let go and fell away from his arm. It floated for a moment, upraised, showing him the creases in the palm, shiny with sweat. Then it flopped back against the sheet.

Cooper looked down the length of Vandervelde's body. The chest with its damp-plastered black hair no longer rose, struggling for breath. He lifted the pillow up.

Vandervelde's eyes still stared upward, his mouth open, the tongue thrust over the bottom teeth. But nothing moved; the eyes looked past Cooper, up to the ceiling. The word had died in its throat.

Fay touched his arm, looking around him to the bed. Her eyes widened as she looked down into the face.

She nodded slowly. "He's dead—"

Cooper pushed himself away from her. "Is he?" His voice came out harsh, the words sharp-edged. "You tell me." He dropped the pillow onto the floor by the bed.

She bent over the face, as if to kiss it good night.

Behind her, Cooper watched as she looked into its eyes. For a moment he felt sick, his stomach churning up into his throat; then a red pulse of anger welled up, washing everything else aside.

He could go now, he realized. With no regret, about her or anything else. If that was what Vandervelde being dead was supposed to mean. Now the old bastard *was* dead—he knew it, could feel it, the thing in the bed where the old man had been—and he didn't care what happened next. Because nothing was going to happen. His arms ached with the strain of holding the pillow so tight over the face. There wasn't going to be anything except this loony woman going loonier, eating up whatever was left of her brain while she tried to hear what some pile of dead meat, going cold and stiff like a slaughtered bull, was going to tell her.

Could just walk right on out of here. And she'd still be standing there by the side of the bed when the morning came, staring down at the dead thing's eyes. Maybe even hearing it talk. In a voice only she could hear. She'd be there listening to it when Bonnie, or anybody else, came into the room, to see what was left there from the night's business.

With one hand, he kneaded the muscles of his other arm. He could walk, and just keep on walking. Leave her here. Maybe they'd think she had done it, had smothered the old man. Like killing kittens— you didn't need much strength, you just had to keep on. They'd think she did it, and he could just keep on walking down the highway until he was long gone from here.

He couldn't decide if that was the way it would go. Things didn't move inside his head the way they should have: like a rock had settled behind his brow and nothing could get past it. He bent his head down lower, squinting to block out the light from the lamp in the corner.

She'd talk, though, wouldn't she? That'd be the problem. There'd be no shutting her up; she'd spill out all that crap about her being able to get inside the dead and make them do things, and that's why she'd made this plan with him, and talked him into killing the old man, on and on—nuts as all get out, but good enough to put him right there in with her, in the same deep shit. They'd find him and show him what a fool he'd been for getting hooked up with her.

Cooper squeezed his eyes shut, trying to think. She was still over there, by the bed, he knew, falling into the dead thing's eyes. If he could work it out, make everything fit together . . . What if she didn't talk? Or couldn't? Taking care of old Vandervelde had been so easy. To do the same for her wouldn't be much harder. He could imagine his hands fitting around her thin neck, the tips of his fingers meeting beneath the fall of her hair, and then just pressing together, her mouth opening up and the tongue welling up inside, the same word Vandervelde had tried to speak trapped down at the root of her throat. Maybe she'd be able to get it out, and he'd know what it was.

He opened his eyes and looked at her. That was crazy thinking; once you got started, it was hard to stop. Killing her, leaving two bodies up here instead of one, what the hell good was that supposed to do? He shook his head, trying to clear it. Crazy as her . . . You got to be careful.

"Hey . . ." He spoke softly. "We'd better get out of here. Before Bonnie wakes up, or something." He reached out and touched her arm. "It doesn't matter. He's dead. That's enough." He felt sorry for her, for her poor addled brain in love with the dead. Hopelessly. His hand folded around her arm and he pulled her toward himself. "Come on."

She turned her face toward him, and he dropped his hand from her. She smiled at him, the corners of her mouth slowly lifting. Her eyes were blank depths where he could see himself, small and lost.

As she smiled, he heard the other voice. Of the thing on the bed. It groaned, something wet rattling deep in its throat.

It's dead. She kept on smiling at him. Triumphant, she seemed to be tasting it in her mouth. He's dead—Cooper heard himself shouting, but the still air in the room stayed silent, locked around them.

Fay turned away, looking back toward the thing on the bed. He could see past her to where it lay, the pallid face gazing up at the ceiling. As he watched, the mouth opened wider, gaping, the lips pulling back from the teeth; a string of saliva stretched, then broke. The tongue moved, thrusting out, then curling back on itself. In its throat, the groan choked, strangling around the word that was still there, lodged like a stone inside.

16

The old man was dead. But the thing on the bed moved.

Its hand rose and reached for Cooper, the heavy, blunt fingers straining to touch him, to fold around his arm. The noise it made inside its throat rose in pitch, a soft cry.

He's dead. Cooper knew it. He'd killed him. He'd felt the old man's lungs fighting for air through the pillow, the word that wouldn't come out muffled underneath. His own arms ached from it, the blood slowly draining back into his hands. But if the thing on the bed, the thing that had been Vandervelde and was now just meat turning cold and blood thickening in the silent veins—if it moved and tried to speak, to say the word still trapped in its throat . . .

Fay smiled at him. She looked at him from miles away, her eyes filled with dark, the night outside the house flowing through and washing over him, a tide rocking the pilings beneath the house.

The thing that had been Vandervelde groaned, the hand still groping blindly for him. Cooper looked at the blunt fingers curling, reaching.

The room that held the thing, and them with it: it was her world. He knew it; she had brought him inside, wrapped the dark things from inside her head around him. The wall at his back, pressing in closer: that was her skull, the curved inside. You could look out the windows, the rims of her eye sockets, but there would only be more dark outside. More of her world.

This is what it's like to go crazy. Cooper watched the dead thing's hand reaching for him. To be like her. She had finally brought him all the way inside. Now he knew.

He closed his eyes and felt something touch his hand. Fingers closed around his and gripped tighter. The blood under his skin chilled, the warmth drawn away by the dead flesh.

"I . . . I can't," Fay spoke, her voice breaking.

Cooper opened his eyes and saw that it was her hand holding his. Her mouth parted as she gasped for breath. He wondered numbly what it was she couldn't do. Here, in her own world.

She squeezed his hand harder. "It's all . . . red in there." She looked away from him, to the swollen, gray face of the thing on the bed. "Inside him. I can't make him . . . talk. I can go inside him . . . like I did with all those other things . . . the dead ones . . . but it's all wrong inside him. It's all red and torn in there."

To talk of dead things. Cooper lifted his head up from the empty quiet that had swallowed him. "It's the stroke he had." His voice was level, deadened. "It's like something bursting inside. In his head. That's why."

Fay drew back from the side of the bed. Away from it. The eyes of the face staring up had clouded with a gray film. "I can't make him talk . . . He can't tell us . . ." Her voice sounded as if she were about to start crying.

What were you supposed to say: There, there. It's all right. Hug and a kiss. You gave it your best shot.

Cooper bent his head down to get away from the faces, hers and the thing on the bed. Crazy thinking—that was what it was like inside this world. You talk about dead things, and what you can and can't do with them. Learn to live with them . . . His laughter caught in his own throat.

The noise it had been making, the choked cry, ended; its jaw worked, the swollen tongue thrusting over the bottom teeth. Then that stopped, too. The mouth gaped open, silent, the clouded eyes gazing upward at the ceiling. Only one thing moving: the arm had fallen back and its hand scrabbled at the sheet, the fingers curling, drawing the sheet into its fist.

Fay suddenly turned toward him, her face shining with tears. But her eyes were wide, excited. "His hand . . ." Her whisper tautened to a wire. "He can still move his hand—"

For a moment, Cooper couldn't understand her. What was so important about that? He looked away from her, to the thing on the bed. The fingers curled, then flexed open, fanning as far apart as possible, then clenched into a fist again. The knuckles whitened as the hand squeezed tighter.

"Don't you see?" Fay stood beside him, gripping his arm. "He's still in there. He's dead, but I can make him move. What he could move before he died. That part—inside his head—that part's still all right." She nodded toward the bed. "See?"

Cooper looked. The hand spread out, palm down, on the mattress.

"Make it point." He bit his lip. "At me."

Her face paled, white and bloodless, as she gazed at the thing on the bed. As Cooper watched, the hand made a fist, rising an inch from the mattress. Then the index finger slowly straightened. It trembled, pointing toward his chest.

"All right." He looked from the hand to her. "So what?"

"He's still in there. Don't you see it?" Her voice rose. "He's in there, and he knows how to open the safe. He just can't tell us! But he can *do* it."

Maybe it was true—along with everything else. Cooper didn't know anymore. And even if it were, how much time was left to them? He felt like he had been in this little room, inside her world, for years. With the dead things. But outside, that other world had to be still moving. There couldn't be much of the night left to them.

"So . . . what are we supposed to do, then?" His brain was frozen, like an animal caught in the glare of a car's headlights. The numb sickness had risen from his gut to eat up all his thoughts. "Get him like a pencil and paper, or something? So he can write it out?"

Fay's brow creased as she bent her head down. "No. I don't know if I can make him do that. It's like . . . he doesn't have words, or things like that, inside him anymore. It's just red, and all changed where that was. But . . ." She bent lower, shoulders hunched, as if she were listening to its whisper. "But he knows . . . in his arm. Like that part remembers . . ."

He considered this. More crazy stuff, a piece with the rest. In this world . . . "I don't—see what good that does—"

She turned her gaze on him, fierce with impatience. "We can take him down there—to the office. That's what good it does." She pointed to the thing on the bed. "All you gotta do is carry him down there, put him up next to the safe. I can do the rest. I can make him do it."

Finally he understood. His stomach clenched at the thought, the imagined feel of the thing's cold skin. To drag that off the bed and lug it downstairs. Somehow the weight of it, the dead flesh like a slaughtered cow, would be more than when Vandervelde was alive. He couldn't have pictured himself putting his arms around the old man in a wrestler's bear hug and lifting him clear of the floor; he'd just been too goddamn big, with a big man's heavy muscles under those layers of fat. And now, dead—with the flopping arms and legs, and the head lolling on the thick neck—there was no way he could move something like that.

"You got to." She had read his thoughts. "It's the only way." Her eyes locked on to his. "You killed him. We did. Now we gotta get away from here. And we need that money."

Killed him. The clouded eyes stared up at the ceiling.

"It's the only way."

Once you had become crazy . . . become part of that dark, narrow world . . . there was no stopping. The hand on the bed turned, the fingers uncurling to show its gray palm to him.

"All right." He took a deep breath. "You get the door. We got to do this quiet as we can."

He stepped closer to the bed and brought his hand under the dead thing's arms. Sliding back until his grip was beneath its shoulder blades. The clammy skin sank around his fingers as he lifted the body up from the mattress. Its head lolled forward as he raised it into a sitting position. The face brushed against his cheek, the eyes rolling to meet his. Cooper turned his head away, nausea welling in his throat; a smell of rot, the gas from its innards, breathed out of its open mouth as the folds of its gut pressed together.

"Come on—" Across the room, Fay's whisper sounded. "Hurry up—"

His arms circled around it until he could touch the ends of his fingers. He straightened his knees, pulling the weight onto his own chest. Its arms flopped down beside his as he staggered backward, drawing it along with him.

The skin, damp with its own sweat, started to slip from his grasp. He hugged the body tighter, his hands straining against the knots of its spine. The face was above his for a moment, the stubbled cheek rasping against the corner of his eyes. The legs finally drew free of the bed, dropping from the edge onto the floor with a muffled thump.

He held still for a moment, bearing the weight against himself, and listening. Beyond Fay and the door she held partway open, and down the unlit hallway—faintly, muffled by distance, the soft rasp of Bonnie's snoring continued. They hadn't woken him up—at least, not yet. Cooper hugged the dead thing tighter—he could feel its soft belly pressing against his own—and took a step backward. He twisted his neck as far as he could, to look behind him.

"Wait—" Fay held up her hand.

He stopped while she stepped quickly beside him. The sheet from the bed was tangled around the thing's legs, stuck to its thighs by the mess Bonnie had left his father lying in. The outhouse stink hit Cooper; he turned his head away as Fay pulled the sheet free and tossed it back onto the bed.

"All right." She touched his arm. "Come on."

The face lolled to one side as he lifted. In the moonlight slanting through the window, Cooper saw the eyes, slitted down the way they'd been when Vandervelde had been alive, watching him. Underneath the gray film, they were dark at the center, dark as hers.

Cooper lowered it to the floor of the office, squatting down on his haunches to bring it sitting against the safe. His knees pressed against its belly as he pulled his arms out from behind it. The gray-jowled face dropped its chin against the matted hair of its chest. Cooper scooted back from it until there was room enough for him to grab his own knees, bending his head down between them and gasping for breath.

The hallway had been the least trouble. He'd just had to take one trembling step backward after another, the dead thing's heels sliding along the bare wooden floor, until he'd reached the head of the stairs. Then it'd gotten tricky. The last half-dozen or so of the stairs, it'd slipped free of his grasp, pinning him for a moment to the rail, then thumping heavily the rest of the way down, the soft fat of its arms flopping against the boards. It'd landed facedown, shoulder wedged against the bottom step.

Dragging it into the office had taken the last of his strength. Each breath burned into his lungs. He lifted his head, his arms dropping beside him.

Fay leaned over the desk, switching on the lamp. She turned the green-glass shade until the light fell on the safe and the thing slumped down in front of it.

"Come here."

He turned his head at the sound of her whisper. She motioned him to come to the side of the safe where she had knelt down. The hem of the black dress fell across the dead thing's lap.

His legs wobbled underneath him when he tried to get up. On hands and knees, he crawled to her.

"You gotta hold him up." She pointed a couple of feet away from the safe. "So I can get his hand up to the dial."

The dead thing's smell, the oily sweat on the cold skin, had already seeped into his hands and across his chest. He could feel the wetness smeared across his throat, chilling in the night air. The clouded eyes gazed from under the bruised-looking lids, watching him as he knelt in front of it, still trying to slow his own heart.

Cooper squatted down beside it and worked his shoulder under its arm, one hand circling around in back. He pulled it away from the safe, supporting the cold weight against himself. The hand flopped against the safe door.

Still dark outside. Cooper looked over to the window, away from the thing's face beside his and the sight of Fay kneeling down in front of it. Maybe they hadn't been at this, dealing with dead things, for hours; he couldn't tell anymore. Maybe only a few minutes, an hour total, since they'd heard Bonnie start to snore, and they'd sneaked into Vandervelde's room. Maybe no time at all had passed; maybe in this world it would just always be like this, a world squeezed down so small you were pressed right up against the dead things. Smelling the still breath, the stink of rotting, right at their gaping mouth, your own flesh so numb from the weight laid upon it that you couldn't tell it anymore from the cold, gray flesh next to it. You were just a part of that world now, where it was always dark.

From the corner of his eye, he saw Fay reach out and touch the thing's face. She grasped its jaw and turned it, moving the head around on the thick, loose-skinned neck. Until it was looking away from him and over toward the safe. The head lolled forward, a line of spit dangling from the gaping mouth onto its chest.

Fay pulled her hand back and sat with it folded, the other in her lap. Cooper watched as she rocked forward on her knees, holding herself straight, trembling as she leaned toward the dead thing. Her eyelids half-closed, thin crescents of white behind the lashes.

Then it happened, again. He had watched it, when the thing had just been lying there on the bed and she had gone into it. And he had felt then, just watching, that one world had shut behind him and another had taken him in. Into the one where the dead things could turn their clouded eyes toward you and open their mouths, whispering the word they had choked on in that other world.

But now he wasn't just watching; he had his arm around it (*another poor old drunk; come on, buddy, we'll get you home*—he wanted to scream out his laughter) and had its flesh weighing against him. He could fall under it, and the naked limbs, the heavy, wobbling gut would bury him beneath, an embrace like lovers. The face would whisper that word into his ear for an eternity, the dead thing's sweat mingled with his own.

He gripped it tighter, his fingers digging in toward its ribs. If he kept its weight balanced on his hip, he could manage it. Under its skin, clamped against his own, he felt a tremor, something moving.

Fay closed her eyes all the way. In the edge of the lamplight, her face paled to white.

Its eyes opened, the dark lids drawing back to show the red webs.

The arm, the good one, raised. The hand dangled loose from the wrist.

She's in there. He could feel it in the flesh tightening under his grip. She was inside the thing, moving in the red spaces inside its skull. Cooper turned his head toward it and saw the heavy-jowled face, mouth still gaping open, roll on the thick neck. Its gaze leveled on the safe door, on the dial at its center.

He could see past its cheek. The hand flopped against the metal, fingers spread out. A couple of inches away from the dial, slowly, the fingers curved, then straightened and curved again. An animal with its spine broken, crippled, drawing itself up the flat surface. The blunt fingertips found the edge of the dial.

He closed his eyes and listened. In the room's silence, he heard Fay's breathing, deep and slowing. Beside him, the dead thing exhaled the sour air from inside, its ribs compressed by Cooper's grip. Faintly, the sound of metal sliding against metal, like silk, and even softer, the muffled click of the lock's tumblers falling.

Then the room was silent.

"Put him down."

Her whisper ... Cooper opened his eyes. She gazed straight at him, waiting. He turned his head and saw the hand sliding away from the dial and down the safe's smooth metal. The arm turned at the elbow as the hand fell against the floor.

He backed up on his haunches, laying the body down as he went. Carefully, he cradled the back of the head in his hands and eased it so it made no noise.

"Go ahead." Fay nodded toward the safe. "It's open."

He touched the handle beside the door. Once before, when he'd been alone in the office, he'd tried, pushing down the rounded lever; it had moved an inch and stopped cold, the solid finality of the mechanism traveling up his arm and into his shoulder.

This time, he pushed down on the handle, and it kept moving. It swung through a quarter-circle and stopped when it pointed straight down. He pulled and a line of brighter metal, glistening in the lamplight, sparked like lightning around the door's edge. The door swung open, sliding on its hinges.

"Sweet . . . fucking . . . Jesus." He hadn't been breathing, all the time the metal of the door's handle had been in his grip. The pent-up breath rushed from his lungs as he sat back from the open safe. He put his hands behind him for balance; one palm came down on the dead thing's bare leg, but he didn't pull it away. For a moment, while Fay scooted next to him, he stared at the inside of the safe.

Her hand reached past him, into the safe. She drew out a stack of bills, bound with rubber bands, and handed it to him.

The bundle was an inch thick, easily. More money than he'd ever seen in one place. He fanned the ends with his thumb. Tens and fives; old ones, well-handled, with that smooth, worn feel of other people's sweat, all mixed together, in no particular order. "Damn." It felt like a brick in his hand; he could smell the money.

"Look at this." Fay hauled a paper bag out of the safe. She passed it over to him.

More. The bag was stuffed with money, some of it bound, the rest crumpled and loose. Cooper reached in and brought out a fistful. That sonuvabitch . . . Some butt-end-of-nowhere little orange grower didn't have this kind of shit plunked down in a safe in his house. The old bastard, the corpse laid out on the floor behind them, had been up to something else, that was for sure.

Or maybe all of them, all the growers out here. Maybe the paper bag, and the inch-thick bundle, and all the rest still sitting in the safe, maybe that hadn't been just Vandervelde's. People dealt in cash when they didn't want other people—the law, mainly —to know what they were doing. You didn't have to be much of a sharpie to be wise to that. Cooper smiled to himself, admiring the larceny in other people's hearts. Maybe a little under-the-table business with the railroad folks? Not all of them, maybe just the ones manning the scales down at the loading dock. Shipping weight that never existed except on the freight manifests. Or something else like that. There were a million ways to make cash breed in the dark, once you knew how. And somebody around here had known. You clever sonuvabitch. Cooper looked over his shoulder at the face staring up at the ceiling. You had to hand it to him.

"There's hundreds here. Thousands . . ."

He was about to stick his own face down in the paper bag's opening, just to inhale even deeper the rich smell of the money, when the overhead light snapped on. Looking down at the bag's contents, he wondered why Fay had done that. Weren't they supposed to be doing this on the sly? Not turning on the lights and all, letting everybody in the world know what they were doing? Then he heard her startled gasp and realized she was still sitting there on the floor next to him.

Cooper twisted around where he knelt. Bonnie stood in the doorway, his hand still on the light switch.

"What the fuck—" Bonnie was stripped to the waist, his feet bare. His eyes were red and puffy from sleep and alcohol. "What the fuck are you doin' down here—"

Cooper clutched the paper bag to his stomach and watched as a confused rage contorted Bonnie's face. *Must think he's still asleep, dreaming . . .* He could see it in the other's bewildered eyes. A nightmare scene: the dead old man stretched out on the floor,

mouth gaping wide, and the safe open, spilling out
its treasure into their arms.

"Jesus fuckin' Christ!" Roaring, Bonnie strode across
the room and jerked Cooper to his feet, his shirt
bunched in the other's fists. The bag fell and spewed
its contents across the floor. Cooper felt himself lifted
higher, clear into the air, then thrown against the
desk. The edge snapped into his spine, a ball of
white light bursting behind his eyes. The lamp crashed
to the floor in a flurry of papers as his arms swept
across the desktop. As he slid down, back arched
around the jagged pain behind him, he could see
Bonnie standing over Fay, his hand raised, then swinging down to send her sprawling.

Then someone was screaming. But not Fay . . . A
deeper cry, breaking in shouts of fear, unable to
draw a full breath. For a moment, Cooper thought it
must be himself. But he wasn't afraid, not the way
the screaming voice was. The pain along his spine
dizzied him, the room tilting on its side. He raised
the side of his head from the floor and peered
through a red haze.

It was Bonnie screaming. Head back, lips drawn
white, the cords in his neck tightening. His eyes
stared down, to another figure that clung to his
waist.

The old man, the dead thing, grasped Bonnie with
its good arm, drawing itself up to show the gray face
and clouded eyes to its son. The mouth opened
wider and the gargling whisper sounded from deep
in its throat. It wanted to tell its son something, one
word, an echo of the scream tearing open the room's
silence. The arm circled tighter around Bonnie's waist.

A few feet away, Fay had pushed herself up with
her hands. A trickle of blood seeped from the corner
of her mouth, bright against the skin paling even
whiter as she stared, eyes slitted, at Bonnie.

Inside him, Cooper realized as he gripped the edge
of the desk. She's inside him again. It was her

inside the dead thing, making it move, whispering the word trapped in the thing's throat.

Bonnie pushed against its arm, but it wouldn't let go. The blunt fingers dug red trenches into the soft gut; it held on as Bonnie shoved his hands against the face, his palms sinking into his father's open mouth. They fell together, Bonnie landing on his back, with the dead thing pinning his legs and stomach, the gray-stubbled chin lodging against his breastbone. Bonnie's hands scrabbled futilely at the floor, trying to pull him out of its hold. His screaming had turned to a child's whimper.

"Come on." Something tugged at Cooper's shoulder. "Come on!"

He turned his head and saw Fay standing next to him. She grabbed his arm and pulled.

"Let's go. We gotta get out of here—" Shouting at him.

He stared at her, trying to understand what she meant. There wasn't any way out; the whole world was in this room, all that was left of it. Wouldn't they always be in it, creeping across the floor with the dead things, their mouths stuffed with the black money? He wanted to wrap his arms around her, pull her down to him, whisper in her ear; the red word was in his throat now.

"Get up—"

She managed to pull him to his feet. The pain along his spine had become a dull throb, washing with his pulse up to the base of his skull. He looked away from to the others, the great naked bulk of the old man, the black hair on his shoulders and back tapering to matted points above the white buttocks, the heavy legs entwined with his son's, as though in some brutal mating. Bonnie's face, just visible past his father's, was wet with tears; he beat feebly with his fist against the gray, wobbling jowls.

Something broke inside Cooper. He wiped a trembling hand over his face, then grabbed Fay's arm. "You're right—" He drew her away from the desk. "We've—we've got to—"

"Come on—" She led him toward the door.

The night air hit him like cold water; he gasped, pulling it deep in his lungs.

"Hurry—" She urged him toward the car in the drive.

The keys were inside it. His breath eased out of him in relief; he couldn't have gone back inside the house to find them. His hands shook as he started up the motor.

He killed it twice, trying to get the car into gear. On the seat beside him, Fay shouted at the dark beyond the windshield. "Get going!" She hit the dashboard with her fists. With a lurch that snapped them both against the seatback, the car moved, scraping gravel underneath as Cooper swung the steering wheel around.

Halfway down the dirt lane, he fumbled on the headlights; he'd almost run the car into the ditch before a low branch had smacked against the windshield and he'd pulled back into the rutted dirt.

No one on the county highway this time of night. He held tight to the wheel to keep his hands from shaking. Fay leaned her head back, looking up at the roof liner, her breath gradually slowing. He kept on driving, leaning over the wheel to peer into the dark.

He had no idea where they were when he pulled over. Just a wide space off the road, shaded by overhanging trees so it was hidden by the moonlight.

"Why you stopping?" She looked at him.

"Gotta rest a minute." Gotta think, he wanted to shout at her. He wiped his face with his hand and rubbed the sweat off on his trousers.

Amazing, the messes you could get into. The scene back in Vandervelde's office crawled through his head. He wasn't numb now; he felt like throwing up, seeing the dead thing in his memory, feeling its cold flesh in his hands again. Jesus Christ—he shook his head, beyond weariness. His arms still ached from dragging the body out of the bedroom and down the stairs.

Crazy—just crazy. If she opened her mouth again, he'd hit her. He didn't know if he'd be able to stop, or if he'd just go on, beating while he screamed, echoing inside the car's narrow space. His hands shook as he thought about it.

That was what it was like inside her world. Dead things—you got right in there with them. Hugged them to you like your wife, got down on the floor with them. That was crazy—that was what she'd taken him in there to show him.

"And for what."

He realized he'd mumbled the words out loud when she touched his leg and he jerked away from her. He stared bitterly out the side window at the strip of highway turned gray in the darkness.

"For fucking what." He tasted the salt welling up under his tongue. "For nothing."

All that—killing the old man, dragging him around like a side of beef in a meat locker, going through one nightmare after another, going fucking crazy—to get here, sitting in a stolen car God knew where, waiting for daylight and whoever was going to come chasing after you to kick your tail. Right into the ground. He closed his eyes and laughed. Some smart bastard, all right.

"It wasn't for nothing." Fay spoke quietly. "Look."

He turned and looked. She held up the paper bag from the safe. She raised it higher and turned it upside down. The money poured out on the seat between them.

17

He let himself sleep for a couple of hours. He figured he could afford that much. Besides, he had no choice; he was too exhausted to drive anymore. When Fay had dumped the money out of the paper bag, he'd had to hold on to the steering wheel with both hands, leaning his forehead against the column, just to keep himself upright. He'd wept, laughing at the same time.

Not really sleep, anyway. More just passing in and out of dreams, like running a fever, his muscles cramping and jerking with the weight of gray flesh that pressed against his, fighting to get out from its cold grasp, then snapping awake to find himself in the car, the dark night still wrapped around it.

Fay had curled up like a child in the other corner, her legs tucked under her. In the first thin light of morning, Cooper looked over at her. Face peaceful, mouth slightly parted, breathing the way a child does; one of her hands draped down from the seat, the backs of her fingers grazing the paper bag on the car's floor.

Cooper scraped the crust from the corners of his eyes. Quietly, so as not to wake her, he pushed the door open and slid out.

He stood, taking a piss against a tree out of sight

of the car, and thinking. There was a lot of thinking to do.

Like a big-time military general or something—you got to assess the situation. Then you could figure out what you had to do. In the cold morning air, steam rose from the base of the tree.

First of all—he closed his eyes, laying everything out neat inside his head—all that business back at the house: that had been a fucking disaster. Not so much from being a nightmare and one piece of loony shit after another, though that was bad enough; he could still go a little sick and dizzy if he let himself think about some of the things that had happened, that he had done, but a disaster because of screwing things up so badly. He couldn't believe it. What the fuck had he thought he was accomplishing? Dragging poor old Vandervelde's body downstairs to the office like that . . . Even if they had wound up getting the safe open and the money out of it. He shook his head, opening his eyes for a moment to study the bark of the tree. What had been the rest of the plan cooking away in Fay's head? For him to drag the body back up the stairs and dump him in the bed, so Bonnie wouldn't know what had been going on while he'd been snoring away?

God knows. That was the problem with having dealings with crazy people, with becoming one of them, even for a little while. They had brains like rats, seeing one thing at a time, the next little thing they want. That was how they got caught. A rat'd crawl into a bottle, squeeze itself right through the neck, to get to that raw onion, if that was what it wanted, had fixed its little rat brain on. And then stuff itself so full it couldn't get back out, and a farm kid could poke it to death with a stick, right inside the bottle. Same way with these crazy folks: they went after what their brains locked on, and they didn't think about what happened next. They didn't think about consequences.

Cooper smiled grimly. That's why they call them crazy, isn't it? He shook off the last drops and buttoned his fly back up.

So, where did that leave them? He walked back to where he could see the car and Fay sleeping inside it, and stood regarding it. A stolen car, a good car—you could put a lot of miles on it, the way Bonnie had kept it up. And not too recognizable; there were a lot of Fords on the road, or enough of 'em, at least. But still, a nice, new car that people would be looking for, the friends of the Vanderveldes all up and down the highways. That was the real problem: Bonnie would put the word out on them and the car. It would've been real nice if he'd had a heart attack or something like that, maybe even a stroke like his old man, from the shock of all that had happened in the office last night. Instead of just having the piss scared out of him ... Cooper got a laugh out of that, remembering the way Bonnie had started to scream when his father had grabbed hold of him like that. It was funny, long as you didn't start screaming yourself.

No such luck, though. Bonnie was built like an ox, with an ox's heart, like his old man before he'd rotted himself out with all those years of daily drinking. Once Bonnie had gotten over his fright—and how long would that take? It was his father, after all—he'd be hot on their tails. Looking for blood. Just as brooding mad as his father got in his prime.

So, the car—they had that. Better, he guessed, just to get in and drive, get in as many miles as possible before the word went out along the grapevine. Rather than try to get rid of it, get something else; that'd take too much time, be too suspicious. With his nerves shot the way they were, he didn't think he could pull that off: anybody'd be able to tell that there was something funny going on.

The car and the money. That was the most important thing. You could do all kinds of stuff with money, that kind of money. That much of it. If you could just get someplace with it.

And Fay. That was the other thing to consider.

Cooper looked at her; from a few yards away, he could just see her head tilted to one side, against the seat back. Still sleeping; she looked the prettiest that way . . . (His mother, looking down at his little sister in her crib, and saying, They always look like angels when they're asleep. Only it was the narrow box on the kitchen table and she was saying the same thing and he was hiding behind the door and listening . . .) You wouldn't know it, to look at her . . . the stuff that went on in that world behind her white brow.

At least I'm not in there. Not anymore. Not in that dark world, crawling around on the floor with the dead things. Smelling their rotting breath, listening to the whispers choking in their throats. He'd gotten out, gotten this far.

Stuff like that didn't happen in this world. Cooper scuffed the side of his shoe through the dirt, digging out a couple of pebbles. In this world . . . Say, when Bonnie pulled himself together, when his father was just a dead body again, nothing inside it making it move and grab hold of the living, Bonnie wouldn't let crazy shit go spinning through his head. He'd just naturally think his old man had been alive, that they'd dragged him out of his bed while he'd still been breathing and somehow got him to open up the safe for them. The last thing old Vandervelde had done, Bonnie would figure, had been to grab on to his son, probably begging for help, if he'd been able to speak. Then he'd died.

That was what Bonnie would figure. You'd have to be crazy to believe anything else. Cooper stood gazing at Fay inside the car. He didn't want to think about it anymore. He'd been there, in that little world with her, where that crazy stuff happened, and he didn't want to go in there again. Maybe in that world somebody like Fay could go inside the dead, make them move and do things. But he was outside now; he didn't have to believe the things he'd seen.

He was alive . . . When he'd dragged him out of the bed, the old man had still been alive. Cooper didn't believe that, either; he'd felt the cold flesh, the soft weight of the body. But that was how it must've been. You had to believe that, or be crazy. Like Fay.

She woke up when he pulled the car door open. Blinking, she looked across the seat at him. "Where are we?" She rubbed the corners of her eyes.

"Where we stopped last night." Cooper slid in behind the wheel. "I thought it was better to wait till we figured out what we're going to do. 'Stead of just driving around in circles."

"We oughta get going." She leaned forward, looking past him to the sun rising in the distance. "They'll be coming along after us pretty soon."

Not completely crazy, he supposed. She knew that much about how things worked in this world. He ran his hands along the curve of the wheel. "Where you suppose we should go?"

"North. We should go north." She rubbed her face to bring some blood up into her cheeks. The wisps of hair that had come loose during sleep were tucked behind her ear. "They got less friends farther north you get."

"All right." The simplest plan so far: just keep on driving, see where it takes you. If they could get a long ways north, to a city, someplace like San Francisco, then maybe they could just ditch the car, roll it off a cliff into the ocean or something, and just lay low. In a city, you could hide; that's what they were for. As long as they had the kind of money in the paper bag.

And as long as Fay . . . didn't do anything. Anything crazy. Going on about how you could make the dead sit up and do things—that'd get you noticed, even in the city.

Something to think about. He started up the engine. "Might as well get going, then." He dropped the car back into gear and pulled on the roadway.

*   *   *

"You got any idea where we're at?"

Driving for close to an hour, the sun well up. Cooper didn't recognize the road, anything along it; somehow, during the night, when they'd been flying away from the Vandervelde place, he'd gotten off the county highway. Probably better that way, he figured; less likely to be seen by anybody, one of the growers or anybody else who might recognize the car. This road, narrower and more potholed, wound up into the hills overlooking the valley filled with neat rows of orchards. Except for a couple switchbacks, the road had worked north; the sun had stayed on his right as it rose, slanting in through the car's side window and across his face.

Getting low on gas, though. He'd been hoping they would come across some small town where they could fill up and maybe buy some food. His stomach had started to growl; all that work during the night, the heavy lifting and all, had burned up everything inside him.

Fay nodded. "There'll be a fork a little way ahead." She pointed out the windshield. "You'll want to bear right. The other road goes back down into the valley."

He looked over at her. "You know this territory around here?"

She shrugged. "Kinda. I was born near here, lived my whole life in this place." Her face was set, emotionless. "One of the reasons I wanted to get out."

Yeah, I bet. If your family didn't own a big chunk of land, if they weren't growers or they didn't have some money-maker in one of the towns, like a store or being a doctor . . . He'd seen enough of the way things worked in these parts, to know what a hard grind that'd be. Bad enough to be poor back where everybody had dust in their mouths; to be that way out here, surrounded by folks like Vandervelde and his buddies . . . you could go nuts, just as a reasonable proposition.

"There some place along there?" The fork had appeared ahead; he nodded toward it. "Where we can get gas and stuff?"

"Coupla miles."

Not much, when they came to it: a couple of stores and a gas station. The air smelled like pine, as though the road had climbed enough to enter into the low reaches of the mountains. Cooper pulled the Ford alongside the pumps and stopped.

"Here." He picked up the paper bag from the floor of the car and rummaged through it, pulling out a five and a couple of singles. "Whyn't you go on over and pick us up some groceries? You know, nothing we got to fuss with, just whatever we can eat while we go. Maybe some fruit or something like that." He handed her the money.

Standing by the pump, he watched her cross the street and go into the store, a little bell on a curl of metal jingling as she pulled the door open. A kid with an old man's face, as if he'd been squinting down the road all of his seventeen or eighteen years, watching for something wonderful to come rolling along, slouched over to him.

"You want'r filled up?"

"That's right." Cooper had taken a couple of dollars from the bag; hand in pocket, he rubbed them against each other.

"Y'up here to see somebody?" The kid had a hopeful tone in his voice. It didn't have to be for him, whatever happened. Just as long as something, anything, happened. He stood back from the pump, wiping his hands on his grease-stained overalls and looking slyly from the corners of his eyes at Cooper.

He shook his head, watching the gasoline slosh up in the pump's glass cylinder. "Just heading on through." *I killed somebody last night . . .* He could tell the wistful-looking kid that, make his day.

"Sure gone out of your way, t'get to anywhere else." The kid unscrewed the Ford's tank cap.

"Got lost, I guess." Cooper leaned his back against the car. Killed him with a pillow. And when he was dead, we made him get up and dance around, and give us all his money. "Afraid I don't know my way around these parts too well. You wouldn't have a map handy, would you?"

The kid shrugged, staring down at the nozzle in his hands, a shimmer of vapor floating up as the gas went in. "Could get ya one." Glum. He'd been hoping for something more from strangers than that. "Be right back." He left the nozzle hanging on the Ford's spout as he shuffled through the dust to the station's tiny building.

Cooper looked across the road to the store. Through the window he could see Fay inside, picking up things and carrying them in the crook of her arm. Looked like a loaf of bread, some cans, a bottle of milk. A fat man in a white apron watched her from behind the counter at the front. Cooper turned away, folding his arms across his chest.

The gasoline had bubbled down to the bottom of the pump's glass cylinder when the kid came back out, a folded road map in his hand. "Jeez—" Half way to the pump, the kid let his mouth drop open; he stared wide-eyed past Cooper, the map fluttering from his hands to the ground.

At the same time, Cooper heard the shouting: Fay's voice and a man's. From across the street. He turned and saw her in the doorway of the store, her face contorted as she screamed, struggling against the fat storekeeper's hold around her waist. She fought to get away from him, clawing at the thick arm against her stomach. Behind her, the storekeeper's face was red and sweating.

"Golly—" The kid was both stunned and delighted at the scene. The commotion brought other people out onto the street, all gaping at the struggle in the store's doorway.

Cooper couldn't move. They know, all he could

think. Already, out here in the middle of nowhere, Bonnie must've gotten out the word. And the store-keeper had spotted her, known who she was, what she'd done, and had grabbed her. Sweet Jesus, maybe there was already a police bulletin or something like that gone out on them; the Vanderveldes were up there high enough. Steal from one of these high-and-mighty growers and you were in deep shit before you could turn around.

Another figure came out from the back of the store and joined in the struggle: the storekeeper's wife, fat as him, her round, sour face set in determi-nation as she grabbed hold of one of Fay's arms and held on. All three of them fell together, Fay landing across the storekeeper's gut as she scrabbled to get away from him.

The kid didn't want to miss out. He closed his mouth, trotted, then ran across the street. Another man from farther down the street joined him in grabbing hold of Fay's shoulders; the storekeeper, gasping for breath, flopped the backs of his pudgy hands against the doorsill.

Cooper heard the shouting and Fay's screaming. Nobody looked around toward him.

He bent down and picked up the road map the kid had dropped, folding it in two in his hand. The commotion from across the street went on as he tossed the map into the car, then took the gasoline nozzle from the car and hung it back upon the pump. He twisted the cap back into place; from his pocket, he took out the money he'd slid in there earlier. Looking over his shoulder, he tucked the bills into the pump's handle. Then he got into the car and started it up.

Nobody turned around to watch as he pulled out of the gas station.

He looked up into the mirror as he started picking up speed, heading down the road. The kid and the other man had pulled Fay to her feet, her arms pinned between them. Her hair had come undone, a black web tangled across her mouth as she shouted at them. With a wild strength, she jerked her arm free from their grasp and started running after the car. He couldn't hear her, but he knew she was shouting his name. For a moment he saw her face, then they had grabbed her again, pulling her back. The road dust billowed up behind the car, and all of them were hidden from view.

A couple miles out of the town, his hands were trembling so badly he had to pull over and stop.

He leaned his forehead against the steering wheel. The vibration from the motor worked into his skull. He turned his head, looking across the car's floor.

The paper bag was still there, right where he'd put it when Fay had gotten out of the car. He could see a couple of green bills sticking out the top.

"Jesus Christ." He said it aloud, no one along the silent road to hear him. It'd been that easy: just start up the car and go. And a great big part of his problems was solved, just like that. He'd gotten free and clear, all the money except for the little bit he'd given her to go into the store with—everything. Except her. He'd gotten rid of her.

If it'd been a matter of having to do it himself, of pulling over, say, somewhere along these back roads and grabbing her and putting her out of the car—he knew he'd never have been able to do it. He wouldn't have been able to lay his hands on her, have her that close, her face looking right into his, the skin of her arms in his hands, fragile underneath the black dress—to touch her, and then go ahead and do it. And not because he would be afraid of her. Something else. He closed his eyes, rolling his brow against the wheel. Under the car's murmur, he could feel the waves surging against the pier. She whispered, his ear touched by her lips.

He lifted his head and gazed at the bright world sifting through the dust on the windshield. Now

there wasn't any time to waste; you couldn't expect a
lucky break like that again. The people back there
had done for him what he wouldn't have been able
to do. Have to get moving. He rubbed his eyes.
Moving, and keep moving. Once they'd gotten her
down where she couldn't get away, tied her up or
something, they'd call the county sheriff, tell him
what they had on their hands. Bonnie must've gotten
over his fright pretty quick; the sun probably hadn't
even been up and he'd been getting the word out.
And now Fay wouldn't even have to say anything at
all; they'd know the other guilty party was nearby,
still on the loose with the stolen car and the money.

They'll be looking for me. The sheriff and everybody else. He could imagine how excited the kid at
the gas station would get, blabbing about the car that
had been right there at the pump. And waving around
the two dollars, everybody in the little town crowd-
ing around to see the money that people had killed
to get.

So they'd know that he was up here, on these back
roads. He'd really have to make some time now. For
all that money in the paper bag to ever do him any
good.

He couldn't afford getting lost, either. A picture
lodged in his mind, of finding himself driving right
back into the little town, everybody waiting for him,
the county sheriff included. He didn't have the fog-
giest idea where he was; he could easily wind up
going around in a circle, getting nowhere except
right back where he'd started.

Take your time. He wanted to just dump the car
back into gear and push the accelerator to the floor,
go flying down the narrow road, but he forced himself to take a couple of deep breaths. He picked up
the road map from the seat beside him. It was old
and well-handled, he saw now, the creases worn and
feathery. The kid at the gas station probably hadn't
meant to give it to him, just use it to give directions.

He unfolded it and spread it across the steering wheel.

A dot had been circled in pencil, right on one of the thinnest lines wavering across the map. The paper was blackened around it, from one oil-stained finger after another having traced out routes. He could just make out the town's name: Tippedge. That must be it; the map showed a fork just south of the dot. And it was in the right place, the hills shading off into the mountains at the right-hand side.

He traced a line up the map with his fingernail. As long as he could keep heading north . . . It was all he could think of to do. He folded the map back up and dropped it beside the paper bag.

His hands had stopped trembling. He put the car into gear and eased back on to the road.

Toward dusk Cooper spotted a farmhouse a little ways up from the road, at the end of a rutted dirt lane. Or what had been a farmhouse. It looked as though it were about to fall in on itself, with a swaybacked roof and gaps where shingles had blown away in the wind. Through the windshield, he could see a trail of smoke drifting up from the chimney; somebody still lived there. The land around the place was choked with weeds, coming right up over the house's windowsills. A rusted harrow showed its spine, a carcass picked clean by crows.

He'd been driving all day, winding along the back roads through the hills. His stomach felt as though it were eating itself, knotting up with hunger. Afraid to stop anywhere. Anytime he'd had to go through a town, when there hadn't been any way to circle around it, he'd carefully slowed the car down, keeping his eyes straight ahead, not even glancing up at the mirror to see if anybody was noting his passage. And all the time, braced for a shout or the first low note of a police siren working its way up to a scream.

Where the dirt lane came down to the road, he stopped the car. He studied the house; now he could see a light, the dull glow of a lantern, in one of the windows. It didn't look like the sort of place any friends of the Vanderveldes would live—more like just some poor broken-down dirt farmer. That'd do, he decided. He turned the car up into the lane, the wheels jouncing in the ruts as it climbed up to the house.

There was somebody inside the house: he could tell, after he'd knocked on the door, chips of faded red paint flaking around his knuckles, and stood back. The splintered planks of the porch buckled under his weight. He could hear whoever it was moving around inside, and see the shadow passing across the lantern.

The door pulled open, the hinges scraping through a skin of rust. Just far enough to show an old man's face, squinting leather. He peered up at Cooper without saying anything.

Cooper pointed back to the Ford sitting in the weeds. "I was driving by. And I was wondering . . . if I could buy some food from you." The eyes in the weathered face glanced past him to the car, then locked back on his face. "You know, if you had anything . . . that you could sell."

"Stores're full of stuff." The old man worked his mouth as though the words were something sour he wanted to spit out. "If you got money to buy it."

"Well . . ." Cooper nodded. "I don't really know my way around here. I'm just kind of heading on through. The town I went through a little ways back, everything was already shut up for the night." That was true; he'd seen them pulling down the shades in the store as he'd driven past. "I got money. I can pay you."

The old man looked him over again, then pulled the door open wider. "Come on in here." He drew back from the doorway, turning and shuffling into the house's dark interior.

A couple of rooms—Cooper spotted a sagging bed

through another doorway—and a kitchen with an ancient stone basin and hand pump. He stood waiting on a threadbare rug, worn to the same color as the dirt trod into the wooden floor, as the old man rummaged around.

"There's eggs." The old man called to him through the kitchen doorway. "I got my own hens here. That do?" He came back out, his gnarled hands cradling the half-dozen eggs; he spread them out on the table in the corner, along with a couple of wrinkled apples and a half-loaf of bread. The bread made a dull thunk when it hit the table. "Four bits sound fair to you?"

"Sure—guess so." It'd been a long time since he'd thought about what food cost. He'd been eating at Vandervelde's table since they'd pulled him out of the county lockup. He took a dollar bill from his pocket and held it out.

The old man plucked the dollar from his grasp and examined it, holding it by the corners. He looked slyly over it at Cooper. "Ain't got change for you." He smiled, pleased with himself.

"That's all right. You keep it." Cooper picked up the apples and dropped them into his jacket pockets. He was about to ask the man if there was something, a rag or an old newspaper, that he could use to carry the rest out to the car. He spotted the telephone on the wall. A wooden one, with a crank on one side and the earpiece hanging on the other. He pointed at it, turning his head to look at the old man. "That thing work?"

The old man snorted. "I don't ever use the sumbitch. Ain't got no use for it. My boy had it put in, had 'em run the wire up here. He makes a pile of money, more'n he's worth, down in the city." The city, as if there were only one. "Does something with people's feet, people got more money'n brains. Went to school for it, and everything. So he has 'em put that thing in here, expects me to call him and his fancy-bit wife up and let 'em know I'm still alive."

"Could I use it?"

The old man scratched his head. "I dunno."

"Then we'd be even. For the dollar."

A grunt and a sour look, as if Cooper had stolen the dollar back somehow. "Yeah, all right, go ahead. I don't give a fuck." He stumped back into the kitchen, muttering.

Cooper stood waiting, with the earpiece laid against his jaw, while the operator put his call through. Wasting time, he knew, but he had to find out. Just what they knew, how close behind they might be. He tapped at the wooden box with his fingernails.

A man's voice crackled through the line. "Sheriff's office."

He'd gotten the sheriff himself; it was all the sheriff did, just about, answering his own telephone; any other bit of work he left to the trustee, busy making himself useful. When Cooper had been in the lockup, he'd seen the sheriff lounging back, feet up on his desk, shooting the breeze with one of his cronies on the other end.

Cooper cleared his throat. "I think, uh, you might have one of my family in your ... you know ... custody."

He could hear the amusement slide into the sheriff's voice. "Yeah?" Delighted at someone else's troubles. "Who might that be?"

The sheriff hadn't recognized his voice. No reason why he should; the trustee had been the only person at the lockup who'd ever spoken to him.

Cooper leaned closer to the telephone. "A ... cousin of mine. A young woman named, uh, Fay—" He realized he didn't know her last name. "I think maybe she got arrested or something up in that little town called Tippedge."

"Oh, yeah, her." The sheriff knew who he meant. He chuckled, sounding nastier than a real laugh. "Sweet little Fay. Yeah, we picked her up this morning. Those folks were pretty happy to see us come around and take her off their hands." A creaking noise, a swivel chair turning. "You her cousin, you say? Didn't know she had any family left, least who'd lay claim to her."

"Well . . . I don't live around here. I haven't seen much of her for a long time." He coughed and wiped his mouth with his hand. "Was there a man or somebody with her? That's what I heard. What happened to him?"

"Maybe. There was some fellow, let her off at the gas station. Probably just some poor bastard who picked her up hitchhiking. She used to do a lot of that, back when she lived out there with her folks, and she was still running around loose. Got into a peck of trouble that way; the fellow in the car probably doesn't know how lucky he got off."

It wasn't adding up. What the hell was he talking about? "So . . . what's the charge? What're you holding her on?"

"Well, we wouldn't have been holding her on anything, if she hadn't made such a ruckus out there. Shit, she just about gave some of them folks a heart attack or something, the way she carried on. And all they did, the people run the store, all they did was ask her what she was doing out there. 'Cause, you know, they all thought she was still in the hospital." The sheriff's voice went low, sly. "You know the one I mean. Where they keep people like her. And she just went wild, hollering and stuff. Guess she thought they were gonna throw her right back in there. So, the way she was screeching, the storekeeper figured she must've escaped from the place, you know, climbed the fence or something. He grabbed her, and things just went from bad to worse. Well, hell, you're family; you know how she could be."

Still didn't make sense. He had to figure out some way of making the sheriff tell what was really going on, short of letting him know who he was. Or maybe the sheriff already knew and was playing with him. He hadn't thought the fellow was smart enough for that. "Now, wasn't she out working for some folks? Taking care of a little girl, or something like that? I mean, instead of being locked up."

"Oh, yeah, well . . . that's true enough." The chair squealed again; Cooper could picture the sheriff leaning back in it. "Out at the Vanderveldes' place. I never thought that was such a good idea, her being sorta . . . loony, you know. No offense. You know what I mean. But they didn't seem to mind. Well, when we got back here with her, we called out to the place. I didn't get to talk to old Vandervelde himself, but I talked to his son, and he told us we should just hang on to her for a while; he'd come by in a coupla days to sort everything out. He didn't have any idea why she'd gone kiting off like that. Just slipped out in the middle of the night. Probably just jumped her trolley again, you ask me."

He was talking as though Vandervelde were still alive. He doesn't know . . . Cooper's brain felt as though it were about to burst, trying to figure it all out. Bonnie hadn't told him yet? The only reason Bonnie would do something like that, keep his father's murder a secret was because he didn't want anybody getting in his way, even slowing him down for a moment. Interfering with his own taking care of things. Cooper bit his lip, feeling his gut clench, hunger forgotten. For what Bonnie wanted to do, it'd be best—and easy enough—to keep a dumb county sheriff like this one in the dark.

And then Bonnie would get around to Fay later, at his convenience. After he'd taken care of her accomplice. Bonnie was clever enough to get all the information he needed, where she'd been arrested, out of the sheriff without letting him know what he was up to. Him and his friends.

A lot would depend on what Fay said. Whether she kept her mouth shut, as she apparently had so far. This was the way criminals thought, real criminals, not just fellows who thought they were so damn smart. He couldn't figure it out. Maybe it'd be better if she just told them everything she knew: that old man Vandervelde was dead, probably still out there lying on the floor. How long could Bonnie keep it a secret, anyway? The doctor was supposed to come back out in a day or two, see how the patient was doing.

Means he figures he's got that much time. And it's enough . . . The stone in Cooper's belly crawled up into his throat. Maybe it'd be better if the sheriff knew; he might have a chance if the sheriff got him first, locked him up in a nice, safe cell.

Safe for how long—that was the real question. Even if Bonnie didn't figure out some way to get his hands on him—and he'd have lots of pull with the people who could do it for him—you were still talking about going up on murder charges. In a place like that—shit, anyplace—some poor sonuvabitch gets tagged with killing a rich man . . . it was like killing twenty people. Even if they could only gas you once for it.

"Anything else I can do for ya, fella?"

There was nothing to lose in talking to her. "Do you think I might have a word with my cousin? It'd be really kind of you."

The nasty chuckle again. "Well, now, that'd be a little difficult to arrange."

"I'd really appreciate it if you could."

"Well, I'd be happy to just bring her on out here to the telephone, let her have a little talk with her family. I mean, I don't mind a bit. But I'm afraid your cousin Fay's not going to be talking to anybody."

The stone grew cold, became ice. "What do you mean?"

The sheriff could hardly keep his laugh from breaking through. "She didn't take too well to being locked up. I guess she never did. When I couldn't hear her screaming back in the lockup anymore, I thought maybe she'd settled down a bit. But my trustee went back there a little while later and there was just a pool of blood all over the floor. She chewed her wrists out. Can you beat that? The doctor said it wasn't the first time, from the looks of it."

Cooper said nothing.

"I sure am sorry, fellow." You could hear the smile in his voice. "These things happen sometimes, though. You want to make some arrangements for claiming the body?"

He hung the earpiece on its hook. When he turned around, he saw the old man watching him.

"Bad news?"

A moment passed before he could speak. "I don't know." He shook his head slowly. "I just don't know."

Cooper couldn't figure out anything to do with the eggs, and the thought of sucking them raw—he'd seen people do it—made him sick. He wound up throwing them into the dark and hearing them splatter against the trees. Crouched close against the little fire he'd built, he wolfed down the apples from his pockets, then broke the stale bread into pieces. It dried his mouth, like eating dust, but he managed to get it down his throat.

When it had gotten dark enough, he had pulled off the road. Just long enough to eat and rest a little. There was no way he'd have been able to sleep— useless to try. You'd just lose time that way. And he didn't have any to spare. If he had any at all . . .

He snapped a dead branch in two and fed a bit of it to the fire. He'd needed it for light more than warmth. Not because of anything out in the night—he could laugh, thinking he'd ever been scared of something like that—but because of what he saw when he closed his eyes. Inside there.

That sonuvabitch sheriff. Pool of blood . . . Couldn't hardly keep from laughing, could he? He was probably laughing right now, fit to bust. About how he'd strung along some fool on the telephone, getting him all set up just so he could pull the rug out from under him. Chewed out her wrists . . . A real joke. That was the way they all were out there; because they thought it was funny. Can you beat that? Laughing their heads off.

Cooper stared into the flames. One way or another, for better or worse, Fay wasn't a problem anymore. He couldn't help feeling relieved, though it made him feel even sicker, right down at the base of his gut, to know that was how he felt. At least he wasn't laughing about it, like those bastards. He had to give himself at least that little bit of credit.

Hearing their laughter was better, though, than the other thing, the whisper underneath. That was why he'd built the fire, but it didn't help. He kept his eyes open, the glare of the flames stinging them and making them water, but he could still hear the slow surge of the tide, the creak of the pilings. Where he had lain down with her, on the ground with the dead things close in the dark. In his arms. She turned her face against his, her lips brushing his ear, and whispered . . .

The branch broke apart in his hands again, the splintered edges gouging his palms. He peeled the bark away and threw it on the fire.

He saw the beetle then, the small shape with its legs tucked up against its belly. In a tiny space as wide as itself, bored into the wood. He poked it with his finger. It didn't move; it felt so light when he prodded it out onto his hand that he knew it was dead. Dead and dry, like ash. He held the still creature on his palm, then closed his fingers around it.

Then it moved, its legs tickling against his skin. Startled, he threw it down on the ground, getting up from his crouch and backing away from it. He rubbed his palm against his trousers to get rid of the way it had felt.

Its legs scrabbled in the air. But slowly, as if it hadn't moved in centuries, locked away in its little tomb . . .

Cooper knelt down. Wincing, he ground the beetle under his thumb. The dry, papery stuff crumbled into the dust.

He pulled his hand away and stood up. In the light from the fire, the beetle's legs flexed. Like thorned twigs, drawing into the dark smear where the body had been, then straightening out, trying to crawl from the spot.

He ground it under his heel. Until there was only dust.

The fire had died down to embers. His skin tightened across his arms. He turned and walked toward the car, careful not to start running.

18

He saw the hitchhiker on the road up ahead. He'd been driving all night, pushing on long after his body had told him to stop. Staring into the darkness until his eye sockets felt as if they'd been filled with sand, gritty and sharp-edged; when another car's headlights had unexpectedly swept across his face, they had gone like needles to the back of his skull.

Past sunrise, he'd been able to get more gas, with no incident other than the pump jockey asking to be paid in advance. Must look like hell . . . He'd rubbed his unshaven jaw and caught sight of himself in the shiny strip around the car's windshield: red-eyed and shabby, like a sick dog.

The road heading north wound down from the hills. Into another valley, separate from the citrus orchards farther south. It looked like root crops, green foliage down close to the rows of earth. Or what was left of it, the season finished in this area as well, the plants already plowed under. The few people he saw, from up on the crest of the road, were probably just stragglers, the last to leave for the picking jobs that remained up in the central valley, cotton or whatever. Hunched-over figures, their cars at the sides of the fields, families searching for anything that might have been left to rot. When he'd turned his gaze from them, the hitchhiker had looked like a scarecrow dressed in rags that somebody had uprooted and posted at the side of the road. Cooper drove right past the figure, catching only a glimpse of a gaunt face and patient, waiting eyes. In the mirror, he saw the man slowly turn his head, to follow him through the car's dust.

Some poor bastard, worse off than himself. Or better, Cooper couldn't decide. The fellow might be starving to death—he'd looked it: a skeleton face, the skin remaining burnt dark from the sun—but at least he didn't have somebody on his ass, looking to beat him right into the ground when they caught him. He could just die in his own sweet time.

He drove on until the hitchhiker was a black stick figure against the morning sun. Then he stopped, pulling over to the side. Truck drivers picked up hitchers, he knew, just so they'd have somebody to talk to; that'd be the only way you could stay awake when you were on a long haul and there was no time for finding a cozy place and taking a nap. And you didn't want to fall asleep behind the wheel, wake up just as the truck went through the rail and over the cliff, slam into a tree trunk, and that'd be the last thing you'd see. He was right there on the ragged edge: can't stop and can't stay awake. Eventually you just wear out.

The fellow stood back there, the dust settling around him; Cooper studied him for a moment longer in the mirror. When they got that way, just standing there, not even walking anymore, just waiting for anything, you didn't have much to worry about with them. He swung the car around and headed back.

"Need a lift?" Cooper leaned across the seat to the side window. He'd already shoved the paper bag under, where it couldn't be seen—safe a place as any.

The hitchhiker gazed down the road, as if waiting for another car to come along. He turned and looked inside, his leather face expressionless; Cooper couldn't tell how old he was. One of those who'd aged fast, skin right down to the bone, and then stopped. After a moment, he reached for the door and got in. He stared out the windshield, waiting.

Gonna get a lot of conversation from this one. Cooper dropped the car into gear and pulled back onto the road.

"Where you heading?"

The hitchhiker shrugged. "Don't care." His voice sounded as if the dust had worked all the way through his skin and dried his throat to a desert.

"You looking to find work?" Cooper glanced over at him.

"I suppose."

The fellow had gotten so used to starving, maybe he'd found a way to eat it. Dust, maybe—swallow it until you were made out of it. Cooper looked at him from the corner of his eye. Dust clothes and dust skin underneath, he could be leaking dust right now, the way wind eroded a stone.

He looked like somebody Cooper had seen before. Or somebody just like him. You couldn't tell them apart, any more than you could tell one skeleton from another. All alike underneath. You could be one of them too, someday; that was what made them scary. It could be your eyes gazing patiently out of those hollow sockets. There were plenty of them: no car, no family, not even a pack to carry—that had all been stripped away, bit by bit. Cooper could have laid money into this fellow's hand, back at the camp; he'd tried to avoid looking right into their faces when he'd come out there with the payout book.

Another try. "You been working south of here?"

The hitchhiker nodded, slowly, his eyes half-closed.

"Down around the orchards?"

The voice grated through its dry layers. "Picked some oranges." The cracked lips scraped across each other. "It was all right."

Might as well give it up. Cooper rubbed his eyes as he concentrated on the road. If the fellow doesn't want to talk . . . Beat down so far, he probably didn't even remember where he'd been; all the same to him.

Besides, there wasn't any need for talking. The other's mere presence in the car nagged Cooper wide awake. Just catching a glimpse of the stripped-down, bony profile, gazing out at the road rolling under the car . . . The hitchhiker worried at his brain, like a stone in your shoe. Seen him somewhere. Maybe not at the camp. Back at the county lockup, in one of the other cells? Something to think about, instead of the other things, like where Bonnie was right now, that he didn't want rattling around in his head.

He kept on driving, glancing over every once in a while. The hitchhiker gazed straight ahead.

The fellow became more talkative later on.

They'd found a place to camp for the night. The wild hope—like waking up from a suffocation nightmare and finding you can breathe again—it had come into Cooper's head as the sun had started to set, turning the fields and the road all red, darkening slowly. After driving all day, nothing happening but more highway winding behind the car; nobody, in any of the little towns they went through, looking at them, pointing, running inside to the telephone, a siren wailing after them—none of that. And no sign of Bonnie, not yet. Maybe not ever. That was the hope that had inched its way into Cooper's thoughts. He couldn't figure it out. Things had stopped making sense, as much as they ever had, back at that old man's house. Maybe Bonnie was satisfied with Fay's death; maybe he'd gone down to the county lockup and taken a look—*Pool of blood . . . Can you beat that?*—and that had been enough for him.

Hard to believe. Except, as he'd always known, they were all crazy back there. But what about the money, letting that just go rolling down the highway out of sight? Not likely Bonnie would forget something like that.

Maybe—he couldn't stop himself from thinking it—maybe I got away. With the money and everything.

Maybe Bonnie was so stupid he didn't know what to do. How to come chasing after him, where to look. Even with them catching Fay, that whole thing dropped in his lap like a present, just so he'd know what direction they'd gone in.

Maybe I'm smarter than I thought. All he'd ever needed was just a little scrap of luck.

"What do you say we pull over for the night?" The road went over a narrow bridge; a dirt trail split off, winding down to the creek underneath. There was a sandy stretch along the water, marked by the ashes of campfires.

The hitchhiker shrugged.

"Yeah, I'm pretty bushed, too." The hitchhiker showed no reaction to the edge in Cooper's voice. "Long day." He couldn't get too irritated; underneath his fatigue, the small bit of hope kept singing.

The bridge made a good shelter, nearly high enough to stand up beneath. The previous tenants had left signs of their stay: empty cans, a torn blanket black with dirt, half-buried in a hollow scooped out where the bridge's cement underside angled into the earth. Tramps, Cooper figured, or just fellows like this one he'd picked up, getting from one place to another. As he stooped under the bridge, he kicked aside a pile of something thin and rustling, like old paper crumpled up. Corn husks, the remnants of a raid on some backyard garden nearby; farther on, he found the gnawed-on cobs strewn about. His stomach tightened from the reminders of food; his hunger had revived.

It would have to wait until morning. Dark enough already. Nobody would be able to spot the car from up on the road. He was tired to the point of being able to sleep even with his stomach gnawing away at itself. If he could get a night's rest, there were all sorts of things that would be possible. He rubbed his jaw, bristlier now. He'd have to get to another town, buy a razor along with some food—no problem, he could buy anything he wanted now—and get himself cleaned up. Otherwise, somebody would finger him for sheer disreputableness, driving a nice car like the Ford and looking all shabby. Might think I stole the thing. That made him smile.

The hitchhiker had squatted down by the edge of the water, gazing across the ripples and splashes on rocks, his flat, empty eyes reddened by the sun going down. Cooper watched him; the hitchhiker let his dirty, big-knuckled hands dangle in front of himself, wrists on his knees.

He could cut the fellow loose in the morning, tell him he didn't have a ride anymore. There wouldn't be any trouble; he could imagine how the empty eyes would just look back at him, no disappointment or any other feeling inside. He could drive away, and the fellow would just go up to the side of the road and stand there, waiting for the next car. The part that had expected the world to be fair, or even just less than laughing vicious, had been beaten out a long time back.

The hitchhiker came away from the stream later and over to the fire Cooper had built. Some tramp had left a cache of dry wood, scavenged from the tangled brush and trees farther along the bank. Cooper had dragged it out from under the bridge and got it going, pocketing the box of matches when the flames started to leap up. He'd nearly dozed off, arms folded across his chest, head nodding toward the soothing warmth, when he felt the other's presence next to him. Squatting down, in the same crouching hunker as before. The fire had burned down to a few red embers; Cooper could just make out the man's face, etched deeper in shadow and the dancing red glow. In his sleep, drifting away from this spot and coming back again, the sharp, thin-fleshed profile had looked drenched in blood, a dream blood that glowed like the last rim of the sun. That had scared him all the way awake. He laid some smaller twigs on the fire, then a thicker branch he'd snapped in two. The light came up yellow now; he could see the rest of the lean figure, the knobby loose hands dangling like sacks of bones, the wavering shadow reaching out into the darkness behind their backs.

"She was always talkin' shit to me."

Cooper heard the other's voice, the dry rasp mumbling through the barely parted lips. He prodded the fire with a stick, sending up a flurry of sparks. He glanced over at the hitchhiker. His mouth hardly moved at all when he spoke, the words sliding up from some hollow space inside. The centers of the man's eyes were shifting red to orange as he stared into the fire.

"All kinds of shit." Deep, brooding, the flat voice had a bitter thread running through it. "She'd say things to me she had no right to. Nobody does."

You wanted talking, this is what you get. Cooper shook his head. Some worn-out sonuvabitch, with all the problems in the world, starving to death, for Christ's sake—and what does he go on about? Some woman. The poor bastard.

The hitchhiker's eyes narrowed, his shoulders hunching lower. "She's my wife; she oughtn't say shit like that."

He looked like murder, his head down low like that, the reflection of the fire just two red lines under his eyelids. Cooper pulled away from him, slowly, drawing his own shoulders in tight. You didn't want to set somebody like this off, once they started talking so low and hard.

"Know what she said . . ." It wasn't a question, at least one that needed an answer from anyone else. The hitchhiker's hands tightened into fists, the cords on the backs drawing rigid. " 'Cause I was tryin' to do something. 'Stead of just lyin' down and takin' it, the way everybody else was. She couldn't see the good of that." The rasping voice had risen higher, louder, no longer a dust-filled whisper. "Couldn't see the good of anything 'cept scrimpin' and beggin' and lettin' 'em grind you down, just so they'd let you kiss their ass the next day. I told her I couldn't live like that, nobody could; and there was folks who were gonna do something about it. I was puttin' my lot in with them, I had to, I wasn't going to get kicked around and eat shit like that no more. That was when she'd start to holler and cuss me out, stuff she oughtn't ever said."

A chill the fire couldn't warm away came across Cooper's shoulders and down along his arms. He could just bear to look at the other from the corner of his eye, the ravaged profile in shadow and the dancing glare. If the face turned toward him, the way people did when they were talking out their buried thoughts, wanting you to understand how they had got that way, if the hitchhiker turned and looked at him, the face half black shade and half dying red light ... Cooper felt his mouth drying, unable to swallow around the stone in his throat. It looked so much like another face he remembered, a long time back, ages ago, ages that evaporated away because he couldn't forget.

The ragged voice shouting *I know who you are I know your fat gut* and the red on its face had been blood, dark in the glow from the lantern in the barn's corner ...

And he didn't want to see that face again. It was crazy thinking; he knew it, he shouted it inside his head, but he was still afraid. He couldn't get up from the fire and walk away; the hitchhiker's voice held him there.

Still staring into the fire. "She cussed me out, said things, terrible things, things to make me go crazy. You wanna know? You wanna know the shit she said to me?"

Without turning from the fire, the hitchhiker looked over at him, the narrowed eyes shifting. Cooper tried to open his mouth. *No. I don't want to know.* But he couldn't.

"She said she'd kill the children. She did. She said

that, she screamed it right at me, she just kept on screaming, and I couldn't make her shut up. Crazy damn bitch. If anything happened to me, if there was trouble 'cause of what I was doin', she'd strangle 'em like kittens, she said. She didn't wanna be left alone, she wanted me to be there to take care of her and all. But to say shit like that—say she'd kill them children—she had no right to. No right at all."

Another face this one all in the darkness a little hiding place made of cardboard with a ragged quilt inside and the face a woman's face her hands clutching two sweaty dollar bills she looked up at him and she said it she said it . . .

Then he was walking away from the fire, away from the figure crouching near it, still talking away in that rasping, bitter voice. Cooper didn't have a memory of getting up, of finally breaking away. His body had done that for him, moving on its own, while his thoughts had been frozen between the red face and the other, the same words spilling from both . . .

He stopped, looking at his shadow stretched out ahead of him, wavering from the fire. He closed his eyes, lowering his head so his breath brushed against his chest.

There were a million explanations for it, as many as you wanted. That was the advantage to being so fucking smart: you could think up explanations for everything that happened, make them into nothing. The sonuvabitch was back there at the camp. When I gave the woman the money. And he overheard the crazy things she said. It wouldn't have been hard; she'd been screeching like a banshee. Somebody out of sight could easily have heard everything she said, remembered it, made it part of his own memory, the way magpies and crazy people pick up the shiniest things and add them to their hoard.

Or maybe it was just a different man, a different woman. Maybe it was just the kind of crazy thing that a lot of women said, when things got so hard, when they were afraid of being left alone in some mean territory. The world was full of crazy people; it made them that way.

He could stand there and go on thinking all night. Smart fellow like you . . . You could think up all the clever explanations and make the things that scared you go away, until they didn't go away anymore. And then all you could do is stop thinking and scrabble across the dirt like every other dumb animal trembling in the dark.

Cooper looked back over his shoulder. The hitchhiker was still crouched next to the fire. I'll get rid of him in the morning. Spooky sonuvabitch. Or he could just leave, right when the sun came up—get in the car and take off, leave the bastard brooding over a pile of cold ashes. He couldn't do it now. The surge of fright through his blood had left him weak, exhaustion hollowing him out again. He didn't know if he could keep the car on the dark road, the way his hands had started to shake.

There was a blanket in the car; he remembered it from the times he'd driven it before. He walked over and got it out. As he straightened up, hand on the door, he caught sight of the corner of the paper bag, peeping out from under the seat.

The hitchhiker wasn't watching him. He reached down and pulled the bag out, the weight of the money solid and comforting in his hands. He rolled it up inside the blanket. It wouldn't do to just leave it sitting out there, where any lucky sonuvabitch might find it.

Under the bridge, he wrapped the blanket around himself, the bag clutched against his chest. The fire had dwindled down; he could barely see the hitchhiker silhouetted by the red embers. He closed his eyes and held the bag tighter.

She was in his arms again. With the waves moving against the pier, climbing slowly to the dark underside with its smell of brine and tangled seaweed, falling to the sigh of foam and luminous depth. The building turned, closing around them, the dead things watching and saying nothing.

She pressed her hand against his chest. It was so cold, ice against his pulse; he held her closer, letting the warmth of his blood seep into hers.

Her lips against his ear: a whisper, the words, the same ones as before . . . He didn't have to hear them to know; he'd always known. There was no forgetting.

And at the same time he knew it was a dream. He felt the sandy ground beneath him, the rough concrete of the bridge through the blanket wrapped around his shoulders. The hand, her hand—it wasn't there, drawing across his skin. Just a dream. If he kept his eyes closed, it would ebb away slowly, like the tide under the pier rolling back out to the ocean.

· But the hand was still there. That was strange; he couldn't figure that out. His thoughts were still muddled with sleep, the slow rolling of the dream time, as though he were underwater, gazing up at the dark shape of the pier, the small figures buried in it somewhere.

And the hand was cold against his skin, but it wasn't her hand. It wasn't soft, the small fingers gliding as though wrapped in silk. It felt hard and calloused, a man's hand. In the last dregs of sleep, he frowned and pushed at her, his hand batting at the air like a child's.

His hand landed against something wet, clinging stickily to his fingers. Underneath, it was hard, with small things like pebbles in a row.

The last tissue of sleep dissolved as his heart pounded in his throat. His eyes flashed open; in the darkness under the bridge he saw his hand, the wetness oozing dark between his fingers, pressed against the face above him.

The hitchhiker smiled at him. The troublemaker, with his lopsided grin torn through his flesh: the same face, the blood trickling over the back of Cooper's hand and twining into a thicker red cord down his wrist.

A cry broke from his throat as he struggled to free his other arm from the blanket. The other's hand had reached inside his shirt, caressing his chest, the fingers reaching down to the grooves of his ribs, drawing their broken nails along his skin. The grin, the teeth exposed behind the flap of ripped flesh, the place above the ear where the blows had caved in the bone . . . The moonlight sliding under the bridge showed them all, the face leaning down closer to his. A drop fell on the corner of his own mouth, something dark that didn't roll away. He tasted salt as his cry died in a gasp for breath.

His other hand came free, flailing loose from the blanket. His fingers clawed into the sand as he rolled onto his shoulder, turning his face away from the hitchhiker's. He felt the cold hand, its wrist tangled in his shirt, slide across his stomach, the wet smearing under its palm . . .

Then he was running, falling as the blanket's fold caught around his foot, scrabbling on his hands and knees, pulling himself upright by the cement edge of the bridge support. And running, his heart leaping in his chest.

He slammed up against the car, catching himself against the glass of the side widows. When he pulled his hands away, a red print remained, fingers spread wide. He found the handle and jerked the door open.

His brain only started working again when he was on the road. He found himself behind the wheel, staring through the windshield. Complete darkness. He hadn't switched on the headlights. He lifted his foot from the gas and let the car drift onto the gravel at the side; it came to a stop, rocking him back against the seat.

For a minute or more, he stared out the windshield at the dark road. He took his hands from the wheel and brought them down his face, fingers pressing into the flesh, his nails stopping at the ridge of his jaw, his thumbs over the pulse in his neck. As if trying to tell if he himself were still alive ... His hands felt cold, dead things that could move.

Don't think. If he tried to think, to come up with explanations, to make the red face in his memory go away, he might not be able to, and that would be worse than being scared. There would be no getting away from it then. He was safe here for a little while; he touched the door beside him, the tips of his fingers against the reassuring solidity of it. The car was a safe place, a bubble surrounded by the night. He could just wait it out here until the morning light came. Or he could start driving again, put more distance between himself and the red face back at the bridge. All he had to do would be to take in one breath after another, each one slower than the last, feeling his heart pace down to that rhythm. If he thought about each breath, tasted it in his open mouth, he could stop thinking about the other things, the things he didn't want to see again.

Just don't think. The engine was still running; all he had to do was drop the car into gear. And go. Things happened, they were happening all the time; you could be smart and try to explain them all away. Or smarter and not even think about them at all. You could just go, not even looking in the mirror to see what was behind you. Maybe that was what everybody did, what they'd learned to do, all the people you thought you were so much smarter than. Maybe they'd learned not to think.

He put his hands back up on the wheel. His exhaustion had burned away, though he couldn't have slept more than a couple of hours; it was still deep night outside the car. He could drive now and keep the car on the road. He looked at his hand as it reached for the gearshift and saw beyond it, down on the car's floor—nothing. The money. It was back at the bridge.

Forget it. Just go. He squeezed the gearshift in his fist, still staring down at the floor. His heart sped up at the thought of turning the car around, going back to the bridge, seeing the red face again ...

If it was there at all. Maybe the hitchhiker, the poor bastard he'd pinned his nightmare on, putting that face out of memory over his—maybe he'd found the money. He knew I had it. That was what the hitchhiker had been looking for when Cooper had fallen asleep. He was probably long gone by now, loping through the woods, laughing at his good luck.

That was what had happened; he was sure of it. That was the way things worked, he knew. The kind of luck you get in this world. You kill somebody, you don't get to keep the money. Somebody else gets it. It was better to believe that, to just go away empty-handed. If he believed it, he wouldn't have to go back.

Another minute passed. He held on to the gear-shift, his head bowed. Then he put the car into gear and swung it around.

At first he thought he'd been right: the hitchhiker was gone. Cooper got out of the car, parked in the same tiremarks that he'd left from before. Looking down to the stream, with the ashes of their fire a black smear on the sandy ground, then over to the bridge, he knew he was alone. You can tell, from the absence of any breathing sound, or the subtler feel upon the skin of your arms. Nothing moved, except the water splashing against rocks.

Gone. Cooper looked around, then over his shoulder to the car. He could get in and go now. Easy come, easy go. The sort of thing you could laugh about someday. All that money in his hands, and then . . . gone.

Still, that was better. Than that other thing. The red face.

As long as the fellow was gone. Christ, maybe he'd gone hightailing it himself, scared out of his wits. Way I jumped up and started shouting, poor bastard must've thought . . . I was crazy or something. He smiled, though his gut still felt hollow. The spooky sonuvabitch had just had the bad luck to walk into someone else's nightmare.

Walked into it . . . Maybe the fellow hadn't been looking for the money. Looking for something else, his dirty hand creeping into the blanket like that. The thought of it, laid on top of the fright he'd had, made Cooper feel sick. Some of these tramps, they've been out on the road so long . . . They'll never know what a woman is again; that's something from another world they've fallen out of. So they look for other things.

But that meant . . . The money. A spark lifted the hair on his neck. It might still be there. Maybe the fellow hadn't known it was there at all. It could be.

Dark under the bridge. Its shadow stretched in the moonlight toward him. He walked into it, slowly, lowering his head to see.

Then he saw it; he knew he wasn't alone. But not with anything alive. Even before his legs could carry him away, the body smarter, faster than his thoughts, he saw the dead thing sitting there, its legs spread before it, back against the cement flank of the bridge, underneath in the darkness. The face was the troublemaker's, red and torn. But long dead, the blood dried to black, a crust layered over its throat and chest, the ragged shirt stiff with it. The skin underneath had turned to gray, like dirty paper the bones could tear through.

Teeth grinning through two mouths. Its jaw had clamped tight, the lips drawn back. The flap of skin ripped away from its cheekbone dangled across its neck, the black-mottled teeth exposed above. The eyes, under the half-lowered lids, gazed at Cooper through clouded veils, waiting.

If it's dead, it can't hurt you. Your brain could tell you that, and you could believe it . . . and still be unable to move. He stood frozen in place, his heart battering against his ribs, his mouth drying to ashes.

Something brushed against his ankle; his shoulders jerked upward, startled. He looked down and saw the paper bag, torn open and empty, pushed by the wind. It turned, dragging against the sand, drifting to the edge of the water.

The money. It still had to be here, somewhere.

He saw it then, clutched in the dead thing's hands, a thick wad, crumpled together like dry leaves. The heels of the gray, knobby hands pressed against its gut, the money wadded between the curled fingers. *Mine.* Cooper could see the corners of the bills, twenties and fifties. The grin, with black leaking around the teeth, hovered above. As if telling him with delight, *It's mine now.* The clouded gaze watched to see what he'd do.

It's dead. Cooper tried to swallow, but couldn't. He ran his dry tongue over his lips, his breath a shallow gasp. *It's dead, it can't do anything to you, just take it, take it—*

He stepped forward, reaching down, his hand trembling. The picture came in his mind of the dead thing suddenly moving, snatching the clump of money to one side, like a child jealous of its toys. *Don't wanna share.* His fingers touched the fanned edge of the bills.

He had bent down so close to the dead thing that he could smell the odor of old flesh, decay seeping out from between its teeth. The two smiles had locked around something inside, holding it in, until the jaw would swing open and the black would vomit out, the rot would spill out and drown the living face drawn close to it . . .

The money. Cooper's hand closed around it, the thick wad gripped between his thumb and first two fingers, as much of it as he could get without touching the dead thing's skin. He tightened his grip and pulled.

It didn't move. The dead fingers were clamped rigid around it, the tendons shrunk tight. *Mine.* The grin above. *Try to take it.*

Cooper couldn't breathe; the dead smell had seeped down into his throat, choking him. He could feel himself swaying, the ground tilting underneath. He drew back from the dead thing, fighting to keep his balance.

Leave it. Just leave it. His hand still held on to the money, what he could grip of it. You don't need it, just go . . .

As if watching another, someone smarter, cleverer, he saw his thumb peel back the bills at the outside of the wad, then slip down onto the one beneath. His two fingers did the same on the other side. Then he pulled again, his grip straining his hand white, the cords rising across the back.

The money slid free. Most of it. His fist closed around the center of the bundle. His hand came flying up above shoulder height as the money finally came loose. He closed his eyes, his breath flooding back into his chest, feeling the wad clutched against his palm.

He took a step backward, straightening up, before he opened his eyes.

The dead thing still grinned at him. Its hands had clamped tight around the bills that had remained when the center bulk had slid away. A thin wad, crumpled inside the stiff fingers.

Cooper looked down at the wad in his own hand. It was enough; he didn't need the little bit left behind.

Go on. Grinning at him. You win. It's yours now. The black inside, oozing around the teeth. Enjoy it.

He backed away a few more steps. Then crammed the money into his pocket and ran for the car.

19

It was there with him, in the car.

It wasn't; he knew there was nothing, nothing on the seat beside him, nothing behind. Just the darkness that flowed in through the windshield, a wave solid as the movement of the ocean, impenetrable, the road curling off into a ribbon, then a thread, and then lost. Nothing, a scream inside his head, the one word over and over, as he gripped the wheel and leaned forward into the dark battering his face, the headlights no good now because the dark ate up their dull glimmer until there was nothing left. He rubbed his eyes with one hand, digging at the corners until sparks swarmed up behind the lids.

He could feel it there. The other thing in the car, waiting, wrapped in its dark time, face heavy with the still blood behind the skin. While he kept driving, staring at the faint, curling line of the road, the one word beating against the curve of his skull. Nothing. Nothing to be afraid of, nothing at all. All you had to do was drive, just drive and don't turn around or look in the mirror, because there's nothing there, nothing at all . . .

Even before he heard it, the soft whisper of it moving, he knew it was there. He wondered, in a dull haze, which one it was, which of the dead things.

Or if it was always just the same one, behind the different gray faces.

There was one face he didn't want to see. He prayed as he leaned over the wheel, the dark washing over him and filling his eyes. Not to see her . . .

It breathed. He heard it, a rasp as the air drew into it, then a sigh as it exhaled. But not alive. It breathed because the living did, and the thing inside it wanted to be alive somehow. The breath would still be cold, though, and sour with the rot setting into its gut. He could smell it, the odor of decay, sharp and nauseating. A trace of it curling inside his nostrils, then stronger, until it became a thick film along his tongue and down into his throat, choking him.

Don't look. He clenched his teeth, a tear squeezing from the corner of his eye as he strained to see the road. As long as you didn't look, even the quickest glance up to the mirror, you could tell yourself it wasn't there behind you, no matter what you could hear or the smell thick as smoke.

Now it breathed at his ear, and he wept as he drove. He could feel the cold brush of air against the hinge of his jaw. The rasping sound, the tongue swollen in its throat, became louder; it wasn't the car's engine or the road sliding under the tires. Louder than that: it was trying to speak, to force one word out. He bit his lip, keeping his own scream inside, a trickle of blood seeping over his bottom teeth.

Don't look . . .

In the back seat . . . it had lifted itself up from where it had been waiting, waiting all along. The same way the hitchhiker, the troublemaker, had been waiting out on the road. Once you were in there with them, in that narrow, dark world, there was no getting away from them. All they had to do was wait.

It lifted itself up, its gray hands grasping the top of the seat by his shoulders, the stiff fingers curling and digging into the upholstery. Then straining to shift the torso with its weight of unmoving blood inside, the mottled face with the tongue thrusting out, the jaw lolling open . . .

Don't look, don't look—for Jesus' sake, don't look—

The word, the mouth opening wider, an inch from the side of his face, then closer, rasping louder, the stink of rot filling his head until he couldn't see at all.

Don't—

He didn't scream when it touched him. A relief. His own breath, pent up in his chest, burst out with a soft cry as the cold hand circled around his throat. He let go of the wheel, falling backward as he clutched at the fingers pressing under his chin.

His back arched away from the seat. He turned his head and saw the dead thing's face, Vandervelde's face, mouth straining wide, lips pulled back from the yellow teeth. The word, red vomiting up from its gut . . . He closed his eyes and let it wash over him.

He lifted his hand and felt something warm at the corner of his brow. His trembling fingers smeared the wet stuff. He looked and saw his own blood, black in the darkness, staining his palm.

Alone in the car—a throb of pain behind his eyes, and the space around him became more real. His shoulder lay against the door, the seat tilted beneath him. He reached up and gripped the steering wheel—it was also wet, sticky—and pulled himself up. A tree branch, thick with leaves, pressed against the windshield.

He tumbled out onto the ground when he opened the door. On his hands and knees, he stared at the dirt; a drop of blood made a black dot in the moonlight. Turning and grabbing hold of the fender, he got his unsteady legs beneath him.

The Ford wasn't damaged too badly. One headlight smashed, and the other fender crumpled where it had plowed into the tree. He couldn't have been going fast when he'd hit it. Asleep, lost in those dreams. He peeled back the splintered bark from the metal, the sap oozing out and mingling with the dried blood on his hand. The car could have been rolling for a mile or more until it had drifted off the side of the road. And all the while he'd been listening to the old man, the dead thing, exhaling its cold breath, the word it kept trying to speak.

His spine contracted, the smell of rot still strong in his nostrils. He turned away from the car, stomach heaving, but nothing came up but white spit.

He wiped his mouth with his sleeve. The weight of the money dragged down the side of his jacket; he thrust in his hand and felt the wad of bills, and his knees buckled under the warmth released from his heart. He closed his fist tighter, squeezing until his arm ached. Got it—no matter what else happened, the nightmares or anything else. There was still the money.

The car wouldn't roll back from the tree. He gave up pushing at the radiator grille and looked closer at the crumpled fender. Now he saw that the wheel was caught between two twisted roots; he reached down and felt around the rim to where it had bent, the tire sagging from it.

Too dark to do anything about it. If there had been light enough, and if exhaustion weren't sapping the strength from his limbs . . . His brain worked sluggishly, the elation from finding the money in his pocket now draining away, down to the fear he could still taste in his mouth. He felt like curling up in the dirt beside the car and falling asleep, real sleep, not like before, sleep without dreams.

In the morning, when the light came, then he could do something about the car. Or he could just leave it. Maybe he'd gotten as far as he could with it, or as far as he needed to. It felt like he'd been driving for years. He rubbed his jaw, the stubble grating against his hand. No way of telling how far away he'd gotten from the Vandervelde place; he hadn't the dimmest idea of where he was. When you go hightailing it down the road like a turpentined cat, with every dead thing between here and the grave bearing down on your ass—he rolled his spit on his tongue, thick with the odor of decay—then maps were no use. He looked around: trees, a row of them past the one he'd hit, a farmer's windbreak along the road. A gurgle of water sounded from a ditch on the other side of them. He could have been anywhere. In the middle of the night, lost. He touched his forehead; the blood had dried to a crust.

The money, though. He patted his jacket pocket, feeling the wad against the point of his hip. He looked back at the car, at the dark inside it. Empty—he knew it was. But his legs trembled as he backed slowly away from it. Then he turned and ran.

If the house had looked as though there were anyone inside it, he wouldn't have gone in. But he could tell it was empty.

Not much more than a shack, out on the edge of the field. Some other poor bastard had been told to head down the highway, dragging his raggedy-ass family behind him, and nobody had gotten around to bulldozing the place yet. The wind had peeled shingles off the roof, exposing the beams underneath; the screens had rusted free from the window frames, hanging down like flaps of rough skin. Behind the broken glass, boards had been nailed up from the inside.

Someplace where he could rest—with walls and a roof between him and the dark.

The front steps creaked under his weight. At least it would be someplace where he'd be safe, out of sight. The board across the door had already been wrenched free, dangling to one side. He stepped across it, into the house.

A dim rectangle of moonlight fell across the floor and onto a wooden table. The signs of whoever had been there before him were still visible: a candle toppled onto its side and gone out in a puddle of hardened wax, and an empty bottle. The smell of cheap booze still hung in the air. He picked up the rickety chair from where it had been thrown, and set it by the table. Before he could sit down and lay his head on his folded arms, he heard the sound from the back room.

Someone breathing, so quietly that he thought it might have been the wind brushing against the roof. He stood still and listened. Awake now, the dreams ebbed back into the night.

In the doorway to the back room, he waited for his eyes to adjust. He could see the figure now, a woman in a bed of tattered blankets laid on the floor planks. Her face, drawn down to the edges of the bones beneath, stared up at the ceiling.

She didn't turn toward him as he crouched down beside her. Mouth open, she panted for breath. Her hair, touched with gray though she had been young only a little while before, was plastered with feverish sweat to her brow.

Fay would have been afraid of her, he knew. The way she had been afraid of the old man, there at the end. Afraid of the dying, but not the dead.

The woman coughed. A bright spot of red welled up at the corner of her mouth. He knew what that meant, the skin so pale it seemed to make its own light. His sister had looked like that in the little box on the kitchen table. Like a porcelain doll, translucent over white; for her, there hadn't been time for the bones to cut through.

Her hand, a paper claw, trembled across the floor beside the blankets. "Jack?" A hollow voice. She knew somebody was there with her.

Jack wasn't there. He didn't see any point in telling her. Jack—her husband, maybe—had drunk up the hooch that the last of their money had gone for, and had kicked over the chair and gone stumbling off into the night, letting the candle sputter out into darkness. Jack had gotten her this far, maybe even carrying her on his back while her breath sighed and panted, to some place where she'd at least have a roof over her head. And then Jack just couldn't take any more. Cooper could understand that. You reach a point and then you just can't. Lots of people afraid of the dying. And to be stuck in some run-down hovel, with your wife bubbling up her lungs onto a rag . . . You poor bastard. You just didn't understand yet.

He understood now. There was nothing to be afraid of. Ever again.

He sat down, back against the wall, and covered her hand with his. The woman closed her eyes; it was enough. With his other hand, he stroked her brow. It felt like fire under the white skin.

When her breath stopped and the little room was silent, he woke up. Still dark outside. He had no idea how long he'd slept. Through the doorway, he could see the flat rectangle of moonlight, tilted now against the wall.

The woman looked as if she were still sleeping. Peacefully, as though her breathing were so soft that it couldn't be heard at all. He looked down at her, watching. And waiting.

It didn't take long. He saw the eyelids tremble, and he knew she was there. The eyes opened—they were clear, the clouded film not yet formed—and gazed up at the ceiling. Then they turned slowly to him.

A whisper. "I just didn't . . . I didn't want to leave you."

For a moment he wondered if it was her. Perhaps the other woman was still there. But why would she say something like that? It must be her. He knew it. Fay. He had always known it.

He stroked her brow. The skin had turned cold, fever gone, the blood stilled underneath.

Her gaze locked on his, sank deep inside. To the center.

Everything he had known had come true.

He lay down beside her, folding the dirty quilt back so he could hold her in his arms. Her cheek rested against his, drawing away the warmth of his blood. Her hand, blue in the dim light, brushed against his chest.

The whisper again, so quiet he could barely hear it. But he knew. In the dark, he felt the ocean surge through the pier again, the coiling water pulling at the timbers. The building rocked, the boards creaking in place, the dead things in a row stretching farther back into the dark, each of them lowering its head in its long sleep, standing watch over the two curled together on the floor.

The whisper, close at his ear, the cold lips moving against his skin. The same words she had said then, back in that other dark.

"I didn't want you to be alone. Ever again."

He held the dead thing tighter in his arms. Its blank eyes gazed past his shoulder; its hand slid away from him, falling to the quilt.

Fool—the words had scared him when she had spoken them the first time. You fool. Now he knew.

He held her, letting the dark wrap closer around them.

The morning sun came through the boarded windows, slits of gray light.

Cooper looked down at the dead woman. The mouth parted, the eyes clouded gray, empty. The Jack she'd called for, or anybody else that came along, could take care of what remained. It didn't matter now. He turned away. The shack's door banged against the wall as he went down the wooden steps.

He found the car where he'd left it. Light enough now, he could see what he had to do. He could jack up the car to free the wheel from the roots. Then a good shove, his back against the tree trunk and his feet braced against the bumper, to topple the car off the jack and bouncing back onto the ground. That'd work, he supposed.

Working it out in his head, he didn't hear the steps behind him, or anything, until the voice said, with a smile, "Good to see you again."

He turned around and saw Bonnie standing there. Grinning, with his father's shotgun slung under his arm.

"I'm glad we waited around here." Bonnie poked at Cooper's stomach with the gun. "I kinda figured you'd turn up when it got light."

He said nothing. The other men, a dozen or so, stood behind Bonnie in a half-circle. They slowly distanced themselves, going around to either side of him. They were grinning as well. All except the trustee. He gazed at Cooper, eyes sad. He shook his head over the waste of all his good advice.

"I think you got something belongs to me." Bonnie reached out and patted Cooper's jacket, then reached in the pocket and pulled out the wad of money. He stuffed it inside his own jacket.

Bonnie broke open the shotgun. "You know"— Cooper watched Bonnie's hands loading it with a couple of shells—"we woulda come after you a lot sooner, but there were other things to take care of first. More important things." He swung the barrels into place and raised the gun, pointing it at Cooper. "A man dies like my dad, there's a lotta things to take care of. Business stuff. I couldn't be bothered with a little shit-ass like you—least, not right away." His smile grew wider. He looked more like old Vandervelde now, his face broader. "You could've gotten clean away. If you hadn't been driving around in circles all this time."

He felt like laughing as he looked at the two black mouths of the gun. In circles, it figured. The gun didn't frighten him.

Bonnie jerked the gun's muzzle up into the air. The first shell didn't fire. They were from the crate Cooper had dragged back to the house. The second one did, its boom echoing through the trees around them. Then Bonnie threw the gun onto the ground.

The other men came in close; one of them pulled him away from the car and pinned his arms behind his back.

Then they started.

20

They could have killed him. Easily—but they didn't.

He woke up with blood and dirt in his mouth. One eye wouldn't open; from the other he saw the ground pressed up against his face. Fuzzy at first, tinged with red. It took a while for it to focus. He lay there, waiting, feeling his hands close around fistfuls of the damp earth. Each breath made his head throb, his pulse going louder inside his ear. His ribs ached and turned into a sharp-pointed hook until he exhaled.

His swollen tongue drew back and he spit out a red wad. He turned his head—slowly, carefully—away from it. Now he could see the tire tracks drawn in the dirt and the overlapping footprints of the men. All gone. They'd left him here when they were done with him.

He knew why they hadn't gone ahead and killed him. Why they'd stopped just short. They wanted him to know. He wasn't important enough. Somebody who could cause them real trouble—then they'd go ahead and finish the job. He'd seen them do that. Easy enough for them. But he didn't even matter that much. That was what they wanted him to know.

He didn't care. It didn't matter to him now, either.

The throbbing in his head had ebbed down. He tried standing up, drawing his legs under him and pushing with his hands. His shirt was sticky wet; the dirt clung to it as he raised his chest.

One leg slewed out from under him, and he fell on his side. The impact knocked his breath out. He had to wait until his panting slowed before he could try again.

As long as he didn't try to lift his right foot, just let it drag, he could move. In the bright sunlight, he heard the sound of water somewhere nearby. Slowly, each step tightening a knot of fire in his knee, he headed toward it.

The bushes near the stream's bank were too thick for him to push his way through. He had to get down and crawl, letting the branches scrape across his face and neck. When he reached the edge, he stopped for a moment, the cold water pulling around his wrists. Then he dragged himself farther and laid down in it, rolling over on his back. The stream splashed against the side of his face, high enough that he could open his mouth and let it wash across his tongue. He swallowed, coughed, then drank deeper, gazing up at the empty sky.

When he turned his head, he saw the water running dark from him, red fading to clear again, beyond the reach of his hand.

He walked in the stream, the water lapping against his ankles. He knew what he was looking for. The sun weighed on his back, his shadow darkening the smooth stones rippling in front of him.

The bridge—he recognized it, though he had only seen it at night before. In the shadows underneath, something waited for him.

He walked across the sandy bank. The dead thing was still there, its back against the bridge's curved underside. A hiding place, where nobody would find it. The head bent low over something clutched together in its hands. The money—the thin sheaf of bills that he'd slid the rest free from. A long time ago.

The walking, pushing against the aches knotted in

his bones, had tired him to a stagger. He knelt down in front of the dead thing. When he pulled in his breath, the smell and taste of rot filled his throat. He raised his head and saw the flies on its face, clustered around the clouded eyes.

Nothing to be afraid of. Not now. If it had spoken, he would have leaned closer, to hear. To hear again.

The dead thing stayed silent. It had only one mouth now, the jaw hanging open. He didn't know its face; it looked like an old man now, gray stubble on the hollowed skin. The other mouth, the flesh of its cheek torn open to show the teeth—that was gone. A fly crawled over its lip, then inside.

He reached out and closed his hand around the money. The bills came away easily, the dead thing's fingers spreading open. They slid out of its grasp, and he closed his fist around them.

Against his chest, he opened his hand and spread the bills out. He looked down and counted. There were seven twenties and a couple of tens. That was what was left.

It didn't matter. He looked back up into the dead thing's face. The gray eyes looked at nothing.

He stood up and shoved the crumpled bills into his pocket. When he stepped out from the bridge's shadow, in the sun's glare he found the trail going back up to the road.

He heard the car pull up alongside him.

"Hey! Hey, fella!" A man's voice, loud and brash. "Need a lift?"

He stopped, gazing down along the road in front of him. Its dust had dried his lips to cracking. He didn't turn his head to look at the car; he hadn't been thumbing for a ride, just walking, putting one dragging foot ahead of the other.

"You look like you need something, that's for sure." The driver laughed. "That's a beaut you got there. How'd you get that?"

He reached up and touched his swollen eye. That

was what the driver meant, he knew. He still couldn't see out of it.

"Come on, get in." The car's door creaked open. "I'm a decent soul, a regular saint, just trying to give a helping hand to my fellow man. Come on."

He turned and saw the driver's face, smiling as he leaned across the seat, holding the door open. After a moment, he nodded, then climbed in.

"What's your name, fella?"

The driver had already told him his, but he didn't remember it. He shrugged, closing his good eye and letting his head loll on his neck with the car's shaking. An old car, beat up; the springs bottomed out with every bump in the road.

"Oh-kay, have it your way. They don't call you Lucky, I bet, not the way somebody's laid into you!" The driver laughed again.

He barely heard him. The other man could have been miles away.

"Now, a lot of fellows wouldn't have picked up somebody like you. They woulda seen ya there on the road and thought to themselves, There's a rough sort of a character." The driver's voice pattered on, heedless. "Looks like real trouble, they'd say. The way they figure it, only a fellow who's trouble gets into trouble. But the way *I* look at it . . ."

The voice paused importantly. Cooper opened his eye and looked out its corner at him.

"I figure, times like these, it's just too easy to get into trouble. Can happen to anybody. People get hungry, they get mean, could do all sorts of things. I don't hold it against them, just human nature." He lifted a hand from the wheel, pointing upward with his finger. "But you know what?"

Cooper sighed. He licked his dry lips. "What?" His voice sounded like a croak.

The driver nodded, his jaw set. "These times ain't gonna last. They can't last. We're gonna turn the corner on 'em real soon. It's turning around already, I know it is! Things ease up, people got a little cash to spend. It's gonna be a golden opportunity for somebody with a little grit, a little hustle. Now, you take the business I'm in . . ."

Cooper closed his eye again, letting the voice fade away, until he felt himself being prodded in the shoulder.

"Go ahead, just take a look at what's in the back seat. You just take a look."

The driver fell silent, waiting. Cooper pulled himself up in the seat, wincing, and turned his head.

The car's back seat was heaped with rags. Old clothes, musty with age and sweat worn into the cloth.

A rag man; he'd seen one, a long time ago, at the pickers' camp. You could make a little money, dealing in the last scraps that a family had to sell when there was nothing else left.

"Now, I can't say business has been great; as a matter of true fact, I've just been scraping by. But things are gonna change in this country. Old clothes and stuff, who needs 'em? People are gonna want new, believe you me, when they got the dough in their hands; they're gonna want to treat themselves to something nice. You're gonna want to be in retail, that's where the money's gonna be." The driver sucked in his breath, whistling through his teeth. "I got my eye on this little storefront, nice high-traffic area, you got people going by it all day long. And I could nail down the lease on it for a song, believe me, I could. The old boy who owns it doesn't know what he's sitting on, doesn't know what it's worth. But I sure do." The voice turned wistful. "Get some nice stock in there, haberdashery, women's frocks. They got buildings full of sewing machines up in Los Angeles, just waiting to get going. I could get stuff on commish, like that!" He snapped his fingers. "Little bit of money to nail down the property's all I'd need."

Money . . . Cooper wished the other man would just shut up, stop nattering in his ear. What was the point of talking, anyway? He dug into his pocket and brought out the bills folded into a square. "How's this?"

He watched as the driver, eyes wide in surprise, took the money and counted it one-handed as he drove. "Whoa! How in hell did you get this?" As if it were thousands of dollars.

He shrugged. It didn't matter. "That enough?"

"Well, it's a start. It sure gets the ball rolling!" He jerked the wheel, pulling the car back straight on the road. "You may not know it yet, but this is a lucky day, for you and me!" He slapped his fist against the wheel, the money fanned out in his grip. "I'll make you whatever deal you want, sixty-forty—hell, fifty-fifty!—and I promise you, you won't have to worry about a thing. We put our backs into it, there's no limit, I'm telling you. Come on, pal, shake on it!"

Cooper looked at the other man. The money had disappeared into his pocket somewhere. The hand reached across the seat toward him.

Cooper looked away from the smile and the feverish, glittering eyes. The hollow, empty voice went on, rustling like paper, like dry leaves with things moving underneath, creeping in dust.

It didn't matter. Outside the car, beyond the window at his side, the green land stretched to the mountains. Under the soil, the dead things would be moving, turning in their dark beds, the blind eyes looking for him. Opening their mouths to whisper, to say what he'd already heard, what he would hear again.

He closed his own eye, falling into the dark inside. It didn't matter. She had promised him, and that was enough. He'd never be alone again.

He laid his face against the cool glass, and listened.

About the Author

Born in Los Angeles, K. W. Jeter now divides his time between London and San Francisco. *Dr. Adder*, his first book, was described by Philip K. Dick as "a stunning novel that destroys once and for all your conception of the limitations of science fiction." Jeter has also written *The Glass Hammer*, which he describes as the thematic sequel to *Dr. Adder*, and *Infernal Devices*, a Victorian fantasy, both available in Signet editions. His next Signet novel will be *Farewell Horizontal*, the first novel of a projected trilogy.

K. W. Jeter is the descendant of French Huguenots who came to America in 1703. Not that it matters.

TERROR . . . TO THE LAST DROP